Seven Summer Weekends

JANE L. ROSEN

BERKLEY
New York

BERKLEY
An imprint of Penguin Random House LLC
penguinrandomhouse.com

Library of Congress Cataloging-in-Publication Data

Names: Rosen, Jane L., author.
Title: Seven summer weekends / Jane L. Rosen.
Description: First edition. | New York: Berkley, 2024.
Identifiers: LCCN 2023046671 (print) | LCCN 2023046672 (ebook) |
ISBN 9780593640913 (paperback) | ISBN 9780593640906 (hardback) |
ISBN 9780593640920 (ebook)
Subjects: LCGFT: Romance fiction. | Novels.
Classification: LCC PS3618.O83145 S48 2024 (print) |
LCC PS3618.O83145 (ebook) | DDC 813/.6—dc23/eng/20231011
LC record available at https://lccn.loc.gov/2023046671
LC ebook record available at https://lccn.loc.gov/2023046672

First Edition: June 2024

Printed in the United States of America
1st Printing

For Raechel, Melodie, and Talia

Lucky me, lucky me, lucky me

Oh Lana Turner we love you get up.

—Frank O'Hara

*Fire Island. Where there's nothing to do and not
enough time to do it.*

—Fred Lifshey

Seven Summer Weekends

Chapter One

When Addison Irwin reflects on the fateful day in June when her life was upended, it plays out in front of her eyes like the opening sequence of a nineties rom-com. Music and all.

In her mind, Vanessa Carlton belts the title track "A Thousand Miles" as Addison makes her way downtown "walking fast / faces pass," though she's work bound, not homebound. It is summer in Manhattan, and Addison is dressed in a crisp white blouse, tan linen capris, and ballet flats. She ascends from the subway station at Fifty-Third and Lex with the confidence of a thirty-four-year-old woman rumored to be first in line for promotion to art director at the Silas and Grant Advertising Agency.

This will most definitely be a day to remember, she was happily thinking to herself. She wondered where it would stand compared to receiving the Danhausen award for sculpture at art school graduation or attaining her highest-ranking title thus far: Color War General at Camp Mataponi.

Addison's rumored promotion would make her not only the youngest to hold the role of art director at the firm, but the first woman to do so. She'd been channeling the seventies advertising icon Shirley Polykoff, who was the inspiration for the fictional Peggy Olson on *Mad Men*, since she had first arrived. Unlike most women her age, whose motivation to move to the Big Apple stemmed from watching episodes of *Sex and the City*, Addison Irwin was a *Mad Men* girl. Though it should be noted that she ended up with a matching set of friends to Carrie Bradshaw's three besties—if not in personality, at least in hair color.

Today, all the years of late nights and canceled plans would finally pay off. Addison crossed her fingers that the company's illustrious CEO, Richard Grant, would make the big announcement— her big announcement—during the company-wide Zoom this morning. She picked up her pace.

Richard Grant, the grandson of the Grant in Silas and Grant and the heir to the seventy-year-old advertising agency, had been groomed to lead the company since birth. He was competent enough, and fairly democratic in his leadership style, but there was a disconnect that prevented anyone from truly liking him. He was tone-deaf to the point of embarrassment, and while his tendency to see things only from his own perspective made for hours of interoffice laughter and camaraderie, it annoyed Addison immensely. While Addison loved the fact that the firm had been in the same family since its start, she recoiled when Grant bragged about his accomplishments, personal and business, as if his success had nothing to do with his prince-like status and familial connections.

Addison caught her freckled reflection in a store window on Madison Avenue and twisted her wavy brown hair into a high pony. *You got this*, she thought to herself, pushing any remaining butterflies from her belly.

As she stepped out of the elevator and into the cold but chic reception area of Silas and Grant, all eyes turned to her, corroborating that the office buzz matched her gut instinct regarding her promotion. Today would indeed be the day. She brushed her hand past her mouth, hiding the small grin that had escaped.

Emma, her favorite junior staffer, approached, doing an awful job of hiding her excitement. She looked as if she might burst. Addison had recruited Emma two years earlier at a job fair at their shared alma mater—the School of the Art Institute of Chicago. She saw a lot of herself in Emma, especially her laser focus on career goals. Like Addison, Emma was that unusual combination of right-brained creativity and left-brained logic.

Addison tucked away the impostor syndrome–based anxiety that she'd been fighting all morning, winked, and returned Emma's smile.

As with any good rom-com, the music continued in the background as Addison closed her office door behind her and did a brief happy dance to the beat in her head. She sat down at her desk, applied a fresh coat of lipstick, took a deep, cleansing breath, and pulled up the Zoom link with minutes to spare. Soon the screen exploded with both familiar and unfamiliar faces from the London, LA, and New York offices.

She pinched her leg, hard, to keep herself from looking too happy.

CEO Richard Grant's moon-shaped face appeared, front and center, pushing the other zoomers to the peanut gallery. Though Addison was still careful to keep her composure—hands folded, smile pasted—she checked her image in the floating thumbnail window. She couldn't remember the last time she felt this self-conscious.

A few minutes in, after basic intros and niceties, Richard Grant promised a few exciting announcements, beginning with his own.

"I am thrilled to share that I will appear on the front cover of next month's *Adweek* as the number one philanthropist in the business. I was equally shocked and honored."

It was the perfect example of exactly what annoyed Addison about this guy. The "honored and thrilled" was fair. The "shocked"? So clueless.

Emma private messaged her—as they always did during Zooms—with the childish goal of making the other laugh on camera.

And by philanthropy, we mean ability to write a huge check.

Addison smiled—and while she wasn't about to desecrate her game face with a laugh, she couldn't resist a comeback. There had been a *New York* magazine cover story overanalyzing nepotism, declaring a nepo-baby boom and pushing the phrase *nepo baby* to the forefront. Emma, like most recent transplants to the city, was obsessed with *New York* magazine. Addison crafted her response.

Number one nepo baby is more like it!

She homed in on Emma, waiting for her reaction. Emma's hands flew to her face.

Got her! Addison thought.

But when her hands came down, Emma looked more pained

than amused. In fact, everywhere Addison looked, people's hands were flying to their faces, one by one by one, like a wave in the stands at a ball game.

Addison looked to the group chat at the top of her screen, where her name and words sat for all to see—including Richard Grant.

Addison Irwin: Number one nepo baby is more like it!

The world as she knew it came to a crashing halt, along with the nineties soundtrack.

The blood drained from her face, and her chest burned with a heat so strong that she wondered if she was having a heart attack. She controlled her trembling hands enough to delete her comment and switch to her away photo. The picture of her with bright eyes and a big toothy grin almost made it worse.

It was, indeed, a day to remember.

Chapter Two

Six days, a zillion missed calls, a dozen grilled cheese sandwiches cut on the diagonal, and seventy-three episodes of *The Nanny* later, Addison Irwin pulled her fired ass off her sofa and answered the insistent buzz of her apartment intercom.

"I didn't order anything, Anthony," she answered impatiently.

"Your friends are here to see you, Miss Irwin."

"Ugh. Tell them I'm not home."

"We can hear you," her three besties shouted back in unison.

"Go away," she barked in return.

Within seconds, they were banging on her door. It was clearly an intervention of sorts as the three women bounded in like the Catastrophe Avengers, armed with groceries and flowers and self-help books titled *Better Days Ahead* and *Now What?*

That last one really got to her. "Now what?" was not a question Addison had ever contemplated before.

Addison was a planner, and once she set goals in her head, she had tunnel vision until they were achieved. Nothing and no one would get in her way. Losing her promotion and then her job in such a public manner was not something Addison had ever envisioned. She did not know if and when her career, and her self-esteem, would rebound.

It certainly was a cautionary tale, and as such Addison was sure it had already been repeated up and down Madison Avenue and beyond. And if, by chance, someone in the ad world didn't catch the story of her career-ending faux pas, it landed on Page Six of the *New York Post*. With her photograph. A stellar career snuffed out by one dumb joke.

Lisa Banks, the first to enter, pulled Addison into a strong embrace.

Addison had met Lisa, a single, straight-haired, straitlaced psychologist and fellow Chicago native, while bonding over their accents years earlier at a Midtown bar. She was the blonde of the group and the most affectionate of her friends, as evidenced by the one-sided hug she currently had Addison enveloped in. When Lisa finally released her, she preached, "The universe is telling you what I've been saying for years!"

Lisa often lectured Addison about her all-consuming work ethic—warning her of the dangers of putting work first and life second. Addison was in no mood for *I told you so*s—though she gave her a knowing nod.

"Save the shrinking for another time," Kizzy Weinstein piped in, while habitually twirling her index finger through one of her deep-brown curls. Kizzy was a headhunter, married to her Manhattan prep school sweetheart. She added, "I know all the candidates for your replacement—they don't touch you."

"My team feels awful—especially Emma. They call every day."

"With questions, no doubt. You ran that place, let's see how long they last without you," added Prudence Parker, a redheaded attorney originally from Georgia, married to another easily sun-burnt ginger, with whom she had one adorable red-haired baby boy. You could practically see the gears in her head quietly turn-ing, in search of a litigious angle. Addison sighed. She had to admit that it was nice of her friends to come. It felt good to be cared for. She may have put her job above her love life over the years, but at least she had nurtured her friendships. She thought of her last breakup. The guy had claimed he came in fifth place after her job and three besties. He was right.

Her phone rang. It was a number from an unknown law firm that she had been ignoring all week. "Who's that?" Prudence asked, while glancing at Addison's mobile.

"Nelson, Nelson, and Leave Me the Hell Alone. They've called me at least six times this week—they're probably ambu-lance chasers for wrongful termination suits or whatnot."

"It would thrill me to get them off your back." Prudence held up the phone and stepped into lawyer mode. She never met a debate she didn't win.

"Knock yourself out," Addison encouraged.

Pru walked away with Addison's phone and returned ten minutes later, carrying the last remaining contents of Addison's fridge: a bottle of Bottega prosecco she'd been saving for her pro-motion and four glasses.

"Addison. Do you have an aunt Gloria?"

"Um, yes, my father's estranged sister, Aunt Gicky. We were never close."

"Well, we are meeting with her lawyers tomorrow morning at nine. Apparently, you were close enough for her to leave you her house on Fire Island!"

Week One

Chapter Three

Addison arrived at the Fire Island ferry terminal wearing a sundress, chunky heels, and a lost expression. The entire scene was unfamiliar to her. For starters, she was dressed for a summer soiree while everyone else looked like they were going to a clambake. She quickly realized that most of the contents of her four pieces of luggage, aside from bathing suits, tanks, and cutoffs, would remain unworn. She studied the crowd: families pushing strollers and carts overflowing with beach toys and baby gear; rowdy twentysomethings with cases of PBR and White Claw, and the obvious homeowners—holding little more than a paperback, a cup of clam chowder, and their dog's leash. There were a lot of dogs.

It was only the second week in July, but from the look of the homeowners—tanned, toned, and tranquil—you'd think it was already mid-August. As Addison surveyed the crowd, she flashed back to the lunchroom in middle school, at a loss as to where she would fit in. She chewed on the side of her thumbnail, a habit she had only recently taken up, wondered if the inner spark she had carried around since birth would ever return, and began chewing on the other thumb. So much of who she'd been as an adult had been tied to her job, and now, without it, she felt at sea.

As blissed out as those sun-kissed locals looked, becoming one was not currently a part of Addison's plan. She was excited to meet the real estate agent on the other side of the Great South Bay and ask her what she could get for her aunt's house. A quick Google search revealed that it was quite a lot.

While most millennial procrastinators entertain themselves by scrolling through memes of baby hippos and of raccoons stealing tacos, their New York City counterparts spend a lot of time scrolling through apartment listings way above their means. It was Addison's favorite form of distraction, and getting this inheritance of the Fire Island house would up her purchasing power significantly. Fulfilling her dream of buying an apartment could keep the dreaded "What next?" question at bay for at least a month or three. Though it may be difficult to pass a co-op board as an unemployed, uncoupled, sparkless woman. Maybe by the time she found a place, the scandal would blow over and someone in the advertising world would take a chance on her again, reigniting the low-burning flame in her belly. Kizzy was already headhunting for her, though she had warned Addison that there wasn't much action in the current job market—not much happened over the summer.

Addison waited in line for a ferry ticket. The woman who sold it to her was wearing a T-shirt with the words *Fire Island, Blissfully Unaware* embroidered across her chest. Addison imagined her own version: *New York City, Painfully Suspicious.* Maybe she could embrace the ferry worker's version for her stay—heed her friends' advice and reinvent herself a bit.

"All aboard, Bay Harbor," the captain barked, causing Addison's stomach to drop to her feet, nervous to step into the unknown. With four large bags, two hands, and a considerable line forming behind her, she contemplated her options, when a tall stranger offered, "Need a hand?"

She wondered if his words sprang from valor or impatience.

"I got it," she insisted.

"Are you an octopus?" he asked with a hint of indignation.

Impatience, she decided.

"I am not." She smiled in return, attempting to soften him. It worked; he reluctantly smiled back. She quickly sized him up: sarcastic tone, hard-to-earn smile. He seemed like the type of guy Addison usually steered clear of. She favored simplicity in a man. The you-get-what-you-see type.

I got this, she thought, but after a quick glance at the restless crowd behind her, she gave up and accepted. With two bags in hand, she followed the tall stranger to the roped-off luggage area on the boat and placed them down, knowing full well she would worry about her belongings the entire ride.

"Thanks again," she said, and smiled before heading up the stairs. He matched her expression, and she noted the cute dimple that formed at the corner of his mouth and the mischievous twinkle in his eye. She also noted his ringless finger. Maybe he wasn't so bad after all.

Her friends had encouraged her to dial down her unapproachable, no-nonsense vibe and embrace hot-girl-summer energy. They dubbed her adventure the Summer of Addison, which they insisted must include a summer fling. But Addison was always better at easing into things than jumping off a cliff. When the tall stranger took his grumpy energy to the front of the ferry, she purposefully headed to the back.

Addison slid onto one of the blue metal benches that lined the boat, stared out at the bay, and soon became hypnotized by the whitecaps and the cool breeze running through her hair. She even forgot her troubles, until about twenty minutes later when the island came into view, snapping her out of it. Her stomach churned with excitement, like a bottle of pop at that first turn of the cap. The feeling surprised her. It had been a while since she had embarked on an adventure or thrown herself into uncharted territory. She had stocked up vacation days and lived in the same rental for the past ten years. Never took the time to move. People, especially in her building, had come and gone—getting married, relocating to other cities, fleeing to the suburbs. But Addison had remained where she was.

She thought about her decisions over the years, her broken engagement a decade earlier, new jobs Kizzy had unsuccessfully encouraged her to apply for, the insane amount of time she had wasted at the expense of all else to rise to the top at Silas and Grant. That last bit was the thing that kept her up at night. She knew her life had been unbalanced while it was happening, but she never set out to rectify it. It always felt like a task for another day. Plus, if she had to admit it, she felt much safer throwing herself into work than a romantic relationship with an uncertain future. She had no interest in heartbreak, yet ironically, as it turned out, being fired had cracked her right in two.

Chapter Four

As the boat did a one-eighty in the small basin, Addison headed down the stairs to beat the crowd and claim her luggage. She saw only two pieces, which worried her, until she spotted the tall stranger standing by the door holding the others. The boat landed and, first to exit, she could see him place her bags on a bench on the dock.

"Thank you," she said, barely audibly and to no one.

She scanned the crowd, pondering which one was the real estate agent she was meant to meet. Smiling faces abounded, except for one. A woman on her phone wearing a conservative getup and Joan Didion sunglasses was shifting her weight impatiently from one leg to the other. *Bingo*, she thought. Clearly the only person who was there for business versus pleasure.

She was right.

According to Gicky's attorney, Nan Murphy had been a real estate agent on Fire Island since she was in her late twenties. Now, at sixty, she had outlasted them all. Apparently, she was the child of an affluent New York City real estate family who used all she overheard at family dinners to corner the market on this narrow spit of sand.

Addison wound her way through the chaotic crowd and approached her with a tentative "Nan?" The impatient woman suddenly morphed into agent mode. A big fake smile lit up her face, followed by a firm handshake and a "Nice to meet you."

Nan had a golf cart—which was good because Addison's heels would not survive the cobblestone walk. She helped Addison load it with her belongings. Their mode of transport felt weirdly elitist. Everyone else was fetching and loading up wagons—old-fashioned wooden versions with witty names carved on the back for the sentimental types or industrial-looking green plastic crate models for the more practical.

"There's a wagon over there, somewhere, with your aunt's name painted on it. You can come back for it whenever you please. Hopefully, she left the combination," Nan said as their golf cart scooted off ahead of the throng.

"Wow, the streets are so narrow," Addison observed.

"You call them narrow streets, we call them wide sidewalks. It's our version of glass half-full."

Ugh. The woman had her figured out already. So much for leaving practical, glass-half-empty Addison on the other side of the bay.

Addison guessed that people who chose to live on a tiny sliver of land where the threat of one big wave lingered constantly weren't overly preoccupied with practicality. Not to mention the fact that they put up with all that schlepping to houses you could get to only by boat.

The broker looked down at Addison's heels.

"First time?"

Addison blushed and smiled.

They heard the words "Hi, Nan" a dozen times between the ferry dock and the house. By the third or fourth, Addison felt compelled to ask, "Does everyone know you?"

"Everyone knows everyone," Nan said dryly.

She couldn't tell whether Nan thought that was a good thing or a bad thing.

Addison had spent the summers of her childhood in a close-knit community on a small lake in Michigan, but this felt next-level. For starters, she saw that Bay Harbor had only one market and a small liquor store. She would have to go to other towns to find restaurants, bars, ice cream shops, and possibly friends. According to Nan, it was a tight-knit group. Houses often stayed in families for many generations. Their children, who befriended other children, had children of their own, who befriended their children. It had been like this since the first beach cottage was erected in 1907, Nan explained, when Gilbert P. Smith had closed his fish factory and began selling off parcels of land.

Nan's lecture on island history felt like the perfect segue to inquire about selling Gicky's house, but Addison felt funny bringing it up straightaway. The feeling only got worse when they arrived at the house, where the agent immediately handed her a sealed letter from her aunt.

"You are lucky to have had an aunt who loved you so much," said Nan. "Gicky was only sick for a few months before she died, but she had explicit instructions. She was a legend in this town— and exceptionally vocal about keeping things the same. She hasn't touched this place since the eighties, but the house has great bones. Though if anyone were to buy it, they would probably knock it down and build some bloated monstrosity—as Gicky would call it."

Despite Nan's words, Addison guessed by the real estate agent's Hermès sandals and Celine sunglasses that Nan did not mind the lifestyle that flipping beach shacks and turning them into bloated monstrosities afforded her. On their way to the house, Addison had noticed the disparity between the original cottages and the new constructions that towered over them. It made sense that some residents would be troubled by the transition, especially her aunt Gicky. From the little she knew about her, she was as much a hippie as Addison's father was a conservative. It wasn't a surprise that those two hadn't seen eye to eye on things. Especially when it came to the Big Terrible Thing that divided them, whatever that was.

Addison realized she had a small window to inquire about selling before going against whatever was written in the letter— a small window not to look like a complete and total ingrate.

"The thing is, I'm not sure I can afford the upkeep of this house," she moaned, setting the stage.

She felt proud of herself for coming up with possibly the only "I'm not a total ingrate" excuse. The feeling was short-lived.

"Gicky had that all figured out," Nan explained. "The property comprises three structures. The main one-bedroom house, an artist's studio, and a guest cottage that Gicky rented by the weekend to pay for the expenses and more. Word is, she bought this place outright with the profits from a lucrative gallery run in the early eighties. It was right after Hurricane Gloria decimated the island, when houses sold for beans. The rental income covers taxes, town dues, and some upkeep. And if you wanted to turn her studio into another guesthouse, you could double that. Plus, if you're not like Gicky, who cared about alone time, you can rent it by the month or week."

The story of how her aunt had acquired the house did not surprise Addison. She had found an article from the *Times* circa 1985 among the clippings in her father's desk drawer about a gallery show Gicky had been in with Keith Haring and Jeff Koons. And while both these artists saw far greater success than Gicky had, she supported herself nicely with her art.

"You'll have no problem affording it. If you want to, that is. Come on, let me show you around."

The main house was quaint and cluttered, with a distinct hippie vibe.

"She was a self-confessed maximalist," Nan said, sugarcoating the fact that Aunt Gicky was a bit of a hoarder. Addison was the opposite, never caving to sentimentality. She kept nothing. If she were to think about why that was, she could probably blame it on her mother. Beverly Irwin placed materialism above most everything else, and while Addison liked nice things as well as the next girl, she never placed much emotional importance on them like her mother did. While Gicky seemed to collect things that brought back memories, her sister-in-law Beverly was more interested in collecting status markers, like designer bags and shoes.

"I don't envy whoever has to clean this place out," Addison stated, until she realized that would be her.

The agent read her expression and added, "Houses on Fire Island are sold with all of their contents—aside from personal stuff. It makes things much easier for the seller. Not so much for the buyer."

Addison took it all in. The house was enveloped in whimsy—doorframes covered in sea glass, walls turned into canvases, the bathroom ceiling flanked by angels in bikinis. While it wasn't the Sistine Chapel, it made the thought of tearing it down all the more egregious.

The tangerine-colored sofa with a dark wood frame had a kaleidoscopic crocheted throw draped over the back. A tremendous macrame owl with wooden-bead eyes covered the wall behind it.

The kitchen appliances looked nearly original to the mid-century house, as did the vinyl floor. A list was taped to the refrigerator—the words *Guesthouse To-Do's* written on top in a rainbow of colors. Everything was an art project. Addison homed in on an adjacent recipe that read *Gicky's Favorite Scones*, ironically held in place by a *Life's a Beach and Then You Die* magnet. The recipe looked easy enough to follow, Addison thought. Maybe she would take up baking. So far in her adult life, she had only mastered boiling water.

She opened the lid of a handmade cookie jar shaped like a Volkswagen Beetle. It was filled with dog treats.

"Did my aunt have a dog?"

"Not that I know of."

The bedroom was more minimalist than the rest of the house, except for a series of oil paintings of an exceptionally handsome man at different ages. Addison was immediately curious about the model, who appeared to be a consistent fixture in her aunt's seemingly autonomous life.

The hallway adjacent to the bedroom was dedicated to images of summers past. Sunsets, group shots, and a handful of pictures of Gicky hamming it up for the camera—Gicky on the ferry, Gicky at an art show, Gicky with a baby girl. Addison looked closer at that one. On further inspection, it wasn't just any baby girl—it was *her*. The photograph gave Addison a pang of regret. Her aunt clearly had memories of Addison, while Addison barely had any of her.

They stepped into the studio, where the smell of clay startled her before pinching at her heartstrings. Some people don't like the smell, but to Addison it was akin to a garden after the rain. Even better than that, it smelled like a memory, one of her last of her aunt Gicky.

Addison flashed back to one of her aunt's yearly visits—one of those early childhood recollections that leave an indelible mark on your brain—fuzzy pictures with unexplained feelings attached to them. Her aunt, ever the artist, had brought Addison and her younger sister a large lump of clay and a set of sculpting tools. Her sister, Ivy, didn't like how the clay felt on her hands and got under her nails, but Addison relished it. She and her aunt spent most of the weekend elbow deep in the earthy substance.

Addison popped open a vat of clay and rolled a piece between her fingers. Could bonding with a child thirty years ago over ceramics have led to this outrageous inheritance? It seemed implausible, besides being sad and somewhat cautionary. An entire life lived with no one to bequeath your greatest possession to. She thought again of the picture of the two of them in the hallway, and when she did, she remembered how her sister's daughter, Lucy, had captured her own heart the minute she was born. In fact, Lucy's existence and the love Addison felt for her were the only thing that made Addison question her ambivalence about having kids. Ivy often drove her mad, but Addison would literally throw herself into oncoming traffic for that niece of hers. And though Addison had never considered it before, Aunt Gicky must have loved her as much as Addison loved Lucy. In fact, if someone had asked Addison right then and there to write her will, she would probably leave this house and all of her earthly possessions to little Lucy. And if she and her sister couldn't get past some Big Terrible Thing, like the one that had divided her parents and her aunt, she would grieve losing contact with Lucy more than the rest of them combined.

She considered asking Nan more about Gicky, but then thought better of it. From the contrasting looks of the two women—the broker buttoned up to her neck, even in the heat of summer, and her aunt, judging by her photographs, happiest in bikinis and caftans at any age—she doubted the two had been close. Nan confirmed her suspicions when she admitted how quickly she had become the enemy of people who want to keep things the same in this town.

"There's no stopping progress," she said. "It was only a matter of time before outsiders found this place and started Hamptons-izing it. It is not my fault people want bigger and better, and someone was going to profit. May as well be me."

Addison didn't care to make a comment on the subject.

"One of your neighbors wants to buy the place, by the way—he swears Gicky promised to sell it to him for half the asking price. Says he has it in writing—though I've never seen it, and I'm sure you can confirm it wasn't in the will."

"It wasn't." The will was very specific. Everything aside from her artwork was left to Addison. The artwork was to be featured in a retrospective in the fall, curated by her longtime gallerist,

CC Ng, with the profits going to a children's art charity in Harlem where Gicky had often volunteered.

"Well, I'm warning you. Your neighbor has been champing at the bit for this place. He's been a bit off since his wife passed away a couple of years ago. I heard he stood in front of a bulldozer that was set to dig up the old cement sidewalk to replace it with pavers. Something about destroying sacred land where his wife's footsteps had walked."

"That's so sad."

"You say sad, I say crazy. Just don't let him or his even nuttier best friend bulldoze or sweet-talk you. Everyone around here pulls the sentimental card when it comes to real estate—you should remain immune to that. If you want to sell this place, I can get you two or three times what your neighbor will offer you."

"Got it! I will not be sweet-talked!"

"Great. Your aunt arranged things mostly on her own this summer, so don't be surprised if random people show up the next few weekends."

"Oh, lovely." Addison smiled sarcastically. The agent enjoyed it.

"I believe there are three open weekends. Let me know if you want to keep them available for renters or not."

"I was hoping to have my friends one weekend, and I'm sure my parents will want to visit." As the words left her lips, she knew the latter was most likely false. For her parents, missing a summer weekend at the lake was like breaking one of the Ten Commandments. The only thing that would get her mother to Fire Island would be a resolution to the Big Terrible Thing that had come between them and her aunt Gicky.

"How much does it go for?"

"Gicky charged three fifty a night, focusing on weekends, so her weeks were free to paint and sculpt."

Addison did the math in her head.

"That's lucrative, but I still think it may be best for me to sell."

"As I said, houses with this size property rarely become available. If you still want to sell in September, it will be easy." She looked around at the cluttered house and added, "There's a white elephant sale at the end of August. Weed through all of this stuff before then so we can stage it properly."

"Noted. Thank you."

"I will let you get settled. Here's my card. Text me with any questions."

She said "text" in a way that screamed, *Don't call me unless the house is on fire—and even then, don't call me.*

And she was gone.

Addison sat down on the afghan-laden couch and carefully opened the letter. The lingering smell of clay still had her under its spell, rendering her more nostalgic than usual.

Dear Addison,

I don't expect you to remember all the time we spent together when you were a little girl, but in your eyes, I saw a light, a curiosity that reminded me of myself. A twinkle that I had only ever seen in my own. And while I chose not to have children, as I aged, I sometimes regretted it. Regretted not having someone to leave my beloved home on my beloved island to. Regretted being here and gone without creating more sentiment than "that Gicky made a mean lime rickey," or "Gicky was a poet" (previous case in point). It may just seem like a house on a beach, but if you let yourself, you will soon find that it is so much more. It is, in fact, a road map for a happy life. A circle of the seasons that always leads you back home, to peace and tranquility, to the ocean. To the familiar, especially in this increasingly unfamiliar world. To your loved ones—your chosen family.

It would be my preference that you don't sell. I have spent the last few years of my life living full-time on this little island. Our street is one of the only ones left that looks as it did when I first fell in love with it. My wish is that it both stays the same and stays in my family—and you are my family. I see that you don't yet have one of your own. If you ever choose to become a mother, there is no better place to raise children.

While I hope that the young girl with the twinkle in her eyes is still there, there are no actual conditions for this inheritance. I have lived my adult life doing what's best for me and would never stipulate you do anything but. My freedom meant the world to me, and I respect yours as well. So, please consider spending the summer here and then, in September, do what you want with the place.

With love,
Aunt Gicky

The finality of Gicky's death sank in. Addison's stomach ached, whether from melancholy or hunger, she wasn't sure. She went with the easiest to fix.

Popping open her luggage, she pulled out a pair of cutoffs, a vintage Bruce Springsteen shirt from the River Tour, which she usually slept in, and her flip-flops. She looked in the mirror and admired her transformation before heading to the store—she looked like a local.

The Bay Harbor Market reminded Addison of the market back home on the lake in Michigan. It sported the same painted wooden shelves and narrow aisles. The kids behind the register—whoever was of the age that summer—were ringers for the kids doing the same back home. Addison herself had worked at the Lake House Market over many a summer before and after sleep-away camp.

Too hungry to do a big shop, she headed for the deli counter and waited in line for a sandwich.

The tall man from the boat approached, flashing his dimple.

"You again," he said with a smile.

Addison blushed and smiled in return.

"What's good?" she asked, motioning to the vast array of deli meats and cheeses in the case in front of her.

"It's more like *who's* good," he whispered. "Insider tip. Position yourself so that you always order from *that* guy." He pointed to the tallest of the three behind the counter.

"That seems tricky."

"It's not. When any of the other guys ask to help you, say, *I'm still thinking*, until Little Les over there asks. Watch and learn."

A skinny guy with huge ear gauges asked, "What can I get you?

"Still thinking, bud, thanks."

The ear-gauge guy moved on to the next customer before the tallest one approached.

"The usual?" he inquired.

"You like turkey?" her new friend asked Addison.

"I do."

"Avocado?"

"Yes."

"Make it two," he told the chosen one, "one for me and one for my friend, You Again."

Addison giggled. She wasn't a giggler. Soon, Little Les handed them each a perfect sandwich wrapped in white paper.

"See you around," said the tall stranger, who smiled before flashing his sandwich to the cashier without stopping to pay.

"Not if I see you first," she joked, before berating herself for the cliché response.

She grabbed a few more things and placed them all down at the register. The young girl behind it sized her up. Addison had no idea that the checkout staff here were the greatest purveyors of gossip in town.

"If you will be here for a while, you should set up an account. Will you?"

"Yes, OK," Addison answered cautiously. She was glad she had the summer lake experience to reference. Everything felt like a setup for one of those new-guy-in-small-town horror flicks.

The girl copied Addison's name on top of a simple, lined form.

"House number?" she asked.

"Oh, I'm not sure. It's my aunt's house, right across from the ball field," she said, not wanting to share her personal windfall with this rather aloof girl.

"Are you Gicky's niece?" she asked, with a whole different 'tude.

"Yes," Addison responded quietly, in great contrast to the girl's enthusiasm. The girl called out to her friend behind the other register.

"It's Gicky's niece!"

Everyone in earshot stopped, stared, and gave her the once-over. This was not an exaggeration. Horror story vibes seeped back into Addison's head, and she didn't know whether to laugh or cry. The silence broke with a flurry of introductions and condolences. She felt strange accepting the latter but did so graciously. She left feeling that her aunt was a local treasure. It was a nice feeling.

After lunch (which was unexpectedly delicious), she took a quick peek at the beach. It was overcast and empty. She returned home and began looking through her aunt's things. It was a weird experience: part snooping, part treasure hunt. She thumbed through photo albums brimming with pictures of Gicky in far-off places. Hard-to-decipher words were scribbled in cursive throughout the yellowed pages. A terrarium filled with sand from different beaches and another with hundreds of matchboxes—from Caesars Palace, Kusky's Bowling Alley, the Royal Bombay Yacht Club, the Brown Derby. She could have spent hours just reading the covers. Every artifact left her more curious about her aunt's life while reminding her how little she herself had lived.

Addison went to bed early that night, cracking the window a bit and listening to the distant sound of the ocean. The day had been endlessly long, and she fell off around nine. She remained asleep until early the next morning, when she woke to the sound of loud barking that seemed to come from inside the house. She peeked out the bedroom door to see a large shaggy black dog on the other side. She closed it just as quickly. To say she wasn't a dog lover was an understatement. She'd had a pretty big fear of dogs since being bitten as a kid. This merited a text to the agent, she thought. She sent one. No response. The dog quieted down, and Addison got down on the floor and peered under the door to see if it was still there. All she saw was a pile of fur. It appeared to be sleeping on the other side.

This was reason enough to climb back into bed and call her mom. Addison had been determined to handle this whole thing on her own, but was suddenly feeling like she had made a big mistake. Maybe she should have considered her mother's advice, which was, "Dead or alive—don't get involved with that woman!"

On the phone now, her mother repeated her unhelpful opinion, adding a few more choice words. Luckily, her tirade was interrupted by a text from the agent.

Agent Nan: Is the dog black and white—and shaggy?

Addison: Yes. Very.

Agent Nan: It's your neighbor's dog. I'll text him. You should nail shut the doggie door. I believe that dog visits regularly.

Within minutes, a man, the dog's owner, was standing in her living room. He knocked *while* entering. No introducing himself, no waiting for Addison to invite him in. He and his dog were obviously cut from the same inconsiderate cloth.

"Hello," the man shouted. "Getting my dog."

Addison looked down at her see-through white tank and skimpy undies and cracked open her bedroom door just enough for her voice to spill out.

"OK."

"Sorry about that. She's used to Gicky giving her a morning treat."

The dog barked again, seemingly in agreement.

"I'll grab one for her," the man said, again not waiting for an answer before opening up the Volkswagen Beetle cookie jar. At least now she had an explanation.

"Next time, just give her one of these, and she'll leave."

"I don't like dogs," she yelled back. "Please make sure there's not a next time."

"Well, you should have that dog door closed up if you're not a dog person," he said huffily, as if the door were an invitation. Though, now that she thought about it, being that Gicky didn't have a dog, maybe it was. Addison peeked out of the bedroom. They were gone.

"This place is filled with nutters," she said out loud.

Addison was most definitely not a nutter.

No sooner did the entitled dog owner leave than her phone dinged with another message from the agent. No *hello*, no *what happened with the dog*, just—

Confirming—July weekends are booked. August 7, 21, and 28 are available. Let me know if you want to list any of them.

"More nutters, I bet," Addison said out loud. As if on cue, there was a knock at her door.

Chapter Five

Margot Ginsberg grew up in the apartment directly below the Irwin family on the Grand Concourse in the Bronx. As an only child, she spent countless hours with her best friend, Gloria (Gicky), and, more often than not, Gicky's kid brother, Morty, too. When the weather was good, they would play sidewalk games in front of the building, under the watchful eyes of all the grandmothers (Margot's included). There was a lot of yelling in Yiddish and Italian, which the kids understood to mean the same thing—stop having fun. When the weather was bad, their play comprised sliding down banisters or messing with the buttons on the elevator. Bad weather shenanigans were often followed by a one-sided game of hide-and-seek with the super. And just when it all felt stifling, or at least redundant, Margot's grandmother took Margot and Gicky by the hand and indoctrinated them into an entirely new world.

She taught them how to cross the Grand Concourse.

Navigating the bustling multilane thoroughfare that was loosely modeled on the Champs-Élysées was a rite of passage that divided a Bronx kid's life into before and after. When the after began, so did their future. And though Gicky was often saddled with helping Morty with his homework and having dinner ready when her dad arrived home from work, the girls had plenty of fun. There was Napoli's pizza place, where they had their first taste of pork sausage. And the bowling alley where Gicky had her first, equally nonkosher, kiss with Bobby Benedetto. There was the corner deli where they bought their first pack of Lucky Strikes and the platform of the Jerome Avenue el train, where Gicky's dad caught them smoking. And neither Margot nor Gicky ever forgot seeing their first R-rated movie, *The Graduate*, at the Loew's on Boston Road, with its giant vertical marquee and plush red seats. It seemed nothing could get more decadent than the young Benjamin Braddock's affair with Mrs. Robinson, until one steamy August day in 1969, when a powder-blue Plymouth Road Runner pulled up in front of their building. The Who's "My Generation" was blasting from the radio.

Morty was still at sleepaway camp in the Catskills at the time, leaving Gicky to feel a sense of freedom she had never experienced. At eighteen, Margot and Gicky had already aged out of camp and were left to sweat out the summer in the concrete jungle. They were sitting on the stoop in front of their building, Gicky sipping a Fresca, Margot, a Dr Pepper, when Heshie Friedman, a kid they went to high school with, arrived in his dad's car. His best friend, Mo Price, called them over from the passenger seat.

"We have two extra tickets to a concert in the Catskills!" Mo yelled, waving them out the window for temptation.

It worked. The girls stood up to investigate. Margot snatched one from his lanky fingers and read it out loud: "Woodstock Music and Art Fair."

"That's right near camp!" Gicky blurted, as if that made considering their invitation less outrageous. Margot shot it down with a foreboding look, but it didn't work. Gicky jumped into the back seat of the car and never looked back. She wasn't even wearing shoes.

It was in that moment that everything changed.

By the time the powder-blue Plymouth drove out of sight, Margot was already regretting her decision not to go with them. And when Gicky came home, by all counts, much cooler than when she had left, Margot regretted it even more. Trying to close the chasm that had developed between them and sick of hearing sentences that began with "At Woodstock, we . . ." she had a little adventure of her own.

Margot lost her virginity to her on-again, off-again boyfriend, Stanley Sacks, in the back seat of his Ford Torino. One month later, she discovered she was pregnant. Two months later, Margot and Stanley were married in the rabbi's study. And by the time the baby was born, they had moved into a small split ranch in Valley Stream, Long Island.

Gicky took the railroad out to see Margot in her new home and painted her first-ever mural on the ceiling of the nursery as a gift for the new baby. She visited a couple of times after the baby was born, but Margot didn't remember her visiting after that. What she remembered was how the two women, who had stayed up all night on childhood sleepovers simply because they had too much to say, spent that last visit navigating awkward silences. While Gicky regurgitated the words of activists like Abbie Hoffman and Gloria Steinem, Margot was busy quoting the famed pediatrician Dr. Spock. She even had photographic evidence of the disconnect—a picture taken in the driveway of her house. Margot was dressed in a knee-length skirt and matching blouse, her hand resting on the baby carriage. Gicky wore bell-bottoms and a halter, and her hand was raised above her head in a peace sign. Margot carried the photo with her always.

The two old friends had drifted apart quickly after that, until one Sunday in the early aughts, when fate placed them across the aisle from each other at a matinee of *Wicked*. They locked eyes shortly before Idina Menzel and Kristin Chenoweth's final duet, "For Good." During the curtain call, they met in the middle and clung to each other. No words were necessary. The two divas onstage had said it well enough when they crooned, "Because I knew you / Because I knew you / I have been changed / For good."

Their reunion brought a staunch promise never to let so much time pass between them again. Even though they were around fifty then, there was plenty of time left to get reacquainted. At their core, they were still the same two girls playing ring-a-levio on a Bronx sidewalk. After that, Margot began visiting Gicky every summer, first with Stan, and when he passed away, for longer stints on her own.

Margot was with Gicky in her last days at hospice, feeding her ice chips and playing sixties music on her phone. They had already spoken ad nauseam about Gicky's estate. Leaving the house to Addison gave Gicky peace—making it the obvious choice in the end. And though Gicky never said it, Margot knew that in her heart, the thought of her brother's daughter living there went a long way to healing the rift between the siblings. Gicky wanted to add a stipulation that Margot be allowed to continue her weeklong summer visits, but Margot declined. This would be her last trip, she thought. It would be too hard to be there without Gicky.

Standing on Gicky's front stoop now, she pulled the picture of the two of them from her purse and spoke right to the image of her hippie friend as if she were there.

"I'll tell her all about you," she said, "just like I promised."

She looked at the photo one more time, put it back in her purse, and knocked on her best friend's front door.

Chapter Six

Addison threw on her robe, gave her hair a quick shake, and opened the front door to find a smiling woman who looked to be around her aunt's age.

"Addison?" she asked familiarly.

"Yes," Addison answered, with an air of caution.

"Wow, strong genes," the woman observed, staring deeply into her eyes. Addison couldn't help but blink.

"I'm Margot," the gray-haired woman said, pushing the door open with her hip and wheeling in her bag. "Gicky sent me." She sat down on the couch and took a deep, *that was a long walk from the ferry* type of breath.

Her air of familiarity was unnerving. Addison immediately leaned out, acting more like the proprietor of a bed-and-breakfast than an interested party. She grabbed the handle of the woman's wheelie bag and said, "It's nice to meet you, Margot. Let me show you to your room."

Margot stood and followed.

The guest cottage was clean and already stocked with everything on Gicky's list except for the fresh flowers and cold water. Addison would pick those up while the woman settled in and then spend the rest of the weekend, aside from the daily awkward breakfast ritual, avoiding her.

As with all of her best-laid plans lately, this one soon went awry.

"Yoo-hoo," Margot called out, with a light rap on the back screen door. "Can I come in?"

She looked quite adorable, in that old-lady way, in a black-and-white-polka-dot swim dress and an enormous sun hat. The hat must have been a recent purchase, because Margot's skin was tanned to a shade between saddle and *I've never heard of sunblock*. Addison pictured her covered in baby oil, sitting with a reflector somewhere, like Miami, or at one of those famous old beach clubs on the south shore of Long Island.

"Want to hit the sand?" she asked. "Take a dip in the ocean?"

Addison was more of a lake girl. The waves scared her. She had never been in deeper than her ankles.

"I have errands to run in town," she said, thinking fast. Since she had to board up that doggie door, she would go to the hardware store and get supplies. At least she hoped there was a hardware store.

"Nonsense," Margot said. "Your errands can wait. We have so much to talk about."

The horror movie scenario ran through her head again, sending a shiver up her spine.

You can take her, Addison thought while giving all five feet nothing of Margot the once-over.

"Do we?" she said with a cautious smile.

"Yes. I told you; your aunt Gicky sent me. You know, to

explain things. There is a lot more involved than what it says in the letter she left you."

Answers!

"I'll only be a minute!" Addison exclaimed before hightailing it to her bedroom to change for the beach.

Addison and Margot sat on the sand under an enormous umbrella. At first their chairs were side by side, but soon, after Margot began opening up about Addison's estranged aunt, Addison found herself more focused on Margot than on the picturesque ocean. She adjusted her chair accordingly and devoured each word and every expression.

Addison had learned early on that asking questions about her aunt Gicky was not welcome. Her father's eyes would tear up at the mention of her name, and her mother's would harden and recoil. Margot's eyes filled with delight as she spoke of her oldest friend.

She went on to explain how her nickname—Gicky—was supplied by Addison's father. For most of his childhood, Morton Irwin had depended on Gicky as more of a mommy than a sister. For little Morty, *Gloria* plus *mommy* came out as *Gicky*—and the nickname stuck. Addison's grandmother, whom her father rarely spoke of, was in an institution for most of their childhoods. Margot described her as a sweet, kind soul who never recovered from the circumstances that had brought her to America from her small Russian town. It did not surprise Addison that she'd never heard this story. Mental health issues of any kind were not discussed in the Irwin family.

"I can only imagine what she went through, though my gut says it was unimaginable," Margot bemoaned.

Addison teared up for the grandmother she never knew. It surprised her. Margot noticed Addison's reaction and softened things.

"I don't want you to think it was all bad. It was anything but—especially for your dad. Gicky adored him. She taught him everything she knew—how to retrieve pink Spalding high balls from the sewer and sell them back to the kids playing stickball for a quarter, which Morty would hold on to till he heard the ice cream man. She taught him how to play all the sidewalk games, ring-a-levio and kick the can, and how to read—even though the teachers at school insisted that Morty had learning issues. Which, mind you, was not how they described it in the sixties. By the end of sixth grade, Morty was at the top of his class."

"I can't believe my father never told me any of this!" Addison interrupted, breaking Margot's stride.

"Your father, I hate to say it, was quick to put all that behind him and never speak of it again. I never understood it, and neither did your aunt. I can tell you that your dad was overly concerned with blending in, while Gicky was always more interested in standing out. And yes, it was tough growing up with an absentee mother and a father who was always working, but there was still a lot of love in the house. In the end, if you are fed and clothed, which your grandfather made sure of, feeling unconditionally loved goes a long way toward a happy childhood. I don't want to bad-mouth your mom, but I think the rift had a lot to do with her. The Grand Concourse was a long way from the tony Chicago suburb where she grew up, and your mother rarely let anyone forget it."

Addison knew what Margot was saying was the truth. Her mother was a snob and quite controlling. It was one of the main reasons Addison hotfooted it out of Chicago as soon as she became an employable adult.

"I think when Gicky got away from it all, when Morty left home and she no longer had to care for him, she desperately craved freedom," Margot said. "There was only enough money for one child to go to college, and it was common back then for the boy to get the education. Plus, when it would have been time for her to go to art school, which is what she wanted, Gicky was at home taking care of your dad. She was so excited when you went to art school. She kept tabs on you through some cousins, and she occasionally checked out your social media. Gicky lived to travel, to paint and sculpt. She was always in motion. But she would come back here every summer. This island—it was her anchor."

"I'm not an artist like Gicky," Addison admitted. "I'm more of a sellout. I do graphic design for an ad agency. Well, I did. I'm between jobs."

Addison paused, thinking about the Big Terrible Thing.

"Did she resent my dad for it all?"

"No. She jumped for joy when he got into the University of Chicago. She couldn't have been prouder."

"Do you know what the Big Terrible Thing was?"

"You mean the final nail in the coffin? That's how Gicky referred to it."

Addison braced herself for the reveal.

"I do not. She didn't want to talk about it in specifics. We lost touch during that time, but I know she felt that losing your dad was the greatest failure of her life. And while she didn't care for your mother, she was quick to say that your dad was responsible for his own actions, no matter how tight Beverly's leash was."

Addison knew it to be true, but she was also familiar with the freedom of getting far away from family and relishing in that anonymity, as her dad had obviously done by staying in Chicago. She knew it pained her father to be estranged from his sister. She also knew how important it was to him to keep the peace at home. There comes a time, as an adult, when you take off the rose-colored glasses—or the crap-covered ones—and see your parents for who they are. People. With flaws. Like all other people. Addison was in that phase, though she felt embarrassed that her dad didn't appreciate the sister who had given up so much for him. But the truth was, she could cite many an example of times when she herself hadn't stood up to her mother. Beverly was a force better not to be reckoned with.

They talked and talked until the twelve o'clock siren—one alarmingly long bell that seemed to echo from every firehouse on the island to test the emergency system.

"What's that?" Addison asked.

"Gicky used to call it the chuckwagon bell. It goes off every day at noon. Time to ride to the market for lunch!"

Addison began packing up, but Margot stopped her.

"No one will take this stuff except the high tide, and that's not expected for hours. Leave it. We can come back after lunch." Addison leaned in and took her lead.

Margot was very familiar with Bay Harbor. Apparently, Bay Harbor was very familiar with Margot too.

"Margot Ginsberg!" an older man called out to them from

the top of the beach stairs as they approached. Margot's face lit up in recognition.

"Shep! As I live and breathe!"

"Surprised to see me still living and breathing?" he retorted.

The two hugged like old friends before Margot introduced Addison.

"Have you met Gicky's niece? Addison Irwin?"

"I have not had the pleasure." Shep wiped his hand on his shorts and reached out for a shake. Addison obliged.

"Gicky left me a painting, so she said. Keep an eye out for something with my name on it, please."

"Me too!" Margot added, laughing, "And I thought I was special!"

She put her hand on Shep's arm. "We will have a good look for them before I go."

Shep looked satisfied, then perturbed.

"So, Addie, let's come right out and ask. What are your plans for your aunt's house?"

Aaaah. *Introducing the crazy widowed neighbor,* Addison thought, before reminding herself that he wanted to steal her house. *I will not be bulldozed,* she promised herself.

"It's Addison, not Addie," she corrected him, adding a smile so as not to come off too rude. "And I have no plans. I only just got here."

"Well, the entire block is worried you're going to knock the place down and build a monstrosity. I don't know if you've noticed, but we are possibly the only monstrosity-free street in this whole town. We asked the real estate agent about it, but she was quite tight-lipped. That young lady is only interested in one thing."

Young lady. Addison laughed inside, while Shep rubbed his thumb and forefinger together—the universal sign for money.

Margot sensed it was time to change the subject.

"Are you free for dinner tonight, Shep?"

He was. The two clearly had a lot of catching up to do.

"You can join us," Margot said to Addison afterward, adding, "Gicky told me Shep has been crazy lonely since his wife died."

Addison thought to joke, *I don't know about lonely, but I got an earful on the crazy from the real estate agent,* but then thought again. There was no need to be mean. She cited a prior commitment instead. She was happy to have a break. The complex family history was a lot to take in, and she knew the afternoon would be filled with more of the same.

And she was right. Later, back on the beach with their lunch, Addison learned how Gicky occasionally struggled with depression herself. She had been old enough to remember her mother rocking and crying on the bathroom floor and being taken out of the house in a straitjacket. Scenes that Addison's dad had escaped by being too young to recall or by Gicky protecting him.

"The thought of having a toddler hanging on her leg again, or, God forbid, passing down her mother's depression gene, stopped her from ever considering having children of her own. Until she reached her forties and began worrying about her old age and keeping her beloved house in the family."

That part frightened Addison. She'd be thirty-five on her next birthday. Surely, she had time left for a family, if she decided she wanted one. A month before, she wanted nothing more than that promotion at work, and now her future felt like a blank slate—a scary blank slate.

"Family was everything to Gicky—and then it was nothing.

That sense of loyalty defined who she was for so long. I guess it never left her. She loved this island too, though, and leaving this place to your father would have been an insult to it. He may not have even visited before selling."

Addison knew that wasn't true. She knew that his estrangement from his sister upset him terribly. She remembered witnessing him crying in the den when she was young. She had climbed up on his lap and put her hands on his cheeks, asking him, "What's wrong, Daddy?" And even though she was just a little girl, he had answered her honestly. "I miss my family," he'd said. His parents had both passed away by then. "And I don't know how to make things better with my sister." He'd wiped his eyes and changed his tune from remorseful to forceful, adding, "Promise me you will never let anything come between you and Ivy." And even though she was quite young, she always remembered that promise. Sometimes, when her sister was particularly awful, that promise was all she had to keep her from crossing the line.

Addison took pity on her dad. She herself was often guilty of compromising just to keep the peace at home. In her gut, she knew that was most likely the lion's share of his reasoning here. At least that was the excuse she had used when he took the easy road in life—which meant siding with their mother. It wasn't a good excuse, but it was what they all needed to do to survive. And she had to admit, leaving your baggage behind was quite tempting.

"I'm not trying to pressure you," Margot added kindly. "You should do what you need to do regarding this place."

Addison reached into her bag to apply more sunblock. She usually forgot to reapply, but Margot's leathery skin worked like an ad for the stuff.

"I understand about my dad, but why did Gicky leave the house to me alone, and not to me and my sister?'

"Ivy, right?"

"Yes."

"She said that Ivy had settled down and that you seemed to be anchorless."

"Anchorless." Addison repeated it quietly, like a word she needed to keep in her pocket to think more about later.

Chapter Seven

The next morning, Addison woke to the smell of eggs and sausage. The neighborhood dog was resting her head in Margot's lap while she read an old *People* magazine with the headline JUDE LAW: SEXIEST MAN ALIVE. From the amount of hair on Jude's head, it seemed to be from the early aughts. Addison had glanced through the mountain-like stash in the guest room closet, a diverse pile of reading material left by visitors over the years, from *Popular Mechanics* to *Variety*. An interesting array of faded names and addresses were affixed to their corners.

"Wasn't I the one who was supposed to make *you* breakfast?" Addison pointed out sheepishly. "I was going to attempt Gicky's famous scones."

"That's OK. I'm not exactly a paying customer." Margot smiled. "Everything's on the stove. Help yourself. I don't want to move this happy girl."

Addison couldn't believe the dog was back. She had to board up that door.

She sat down on the couch with a cup of coffee and a plate of scrambled eggs. They were simple but delicious.

"Thyme?" she asked, trying to figure out what she was tasting.

"Yup, there's a little herb garden on the side of the back shed."

"Who knew?"

"Me." Margot smiled and put the magazine down. Addison reached over and tapped on it.

"So, did my aunt Gicky always have a hoarding problem?"

"You see a pile of old magazines where Gicky saw a potential collage. One year when I visited, she was decoupaging old surfboards. I'm all thumbs, but she let me assist—a little." Margot turned to look at her.

"What's on your schedule for today?" she asked. It made Addison laugh. She had nothing on her schedule for the foreseeable future. She was, in fact, anchorless.

"What do you have in mind?"

"A long bike ride would be nice. Have you broken out the bikes from the back shed yet?"

She hadn't even gone in the back shed yet—she had considered it, but it gave her those horror film vibes again. Somehow, with five-feet-nothing Margot by her side, she felt braver.

Addison slid the shed door open, bracing herself for a sleeping raccoon. Instead, she was happy to see a trove of regular shed stuff transformed, in typical Gicky fashion, into treasures. If Nora Ephron's mother had famously said, "Everything is copy," then Addison Irwin's aunt would have declared, "Everything is an art project." The watering cans were painted as a menagerie of trunked animals. The leaf blower was decorated to look like an aardvark, and a rainbow of rakes and brooms stood in the corner. The centerpiece, Gicky's bicycle, looked like a mermaid's chariot, with froth-crested waves painted on the frame and a wreath of shells adorning the front basket.

"Aaah. Annette Kellerman!" Margot exclaimed.

Addison spun around, expecting to see another one of Gicky's contemporaries behind her.

"The bike," Margot laughed. "Gicky named it Annette Kellerman. She loved this bike. Let's take it for a spin—I'll take the plain one."

By "plain" she meant a bright red bicycle covered in orange flames with the words *Hot Tamale* painted across its carriage.

Through a smile, Addison swallowed a lump in her throat— more regret that she hadn't known her aunt. She could blame it on her parents as much as she wanted to, but she was old enough to have reached out herself. Although the same could be said of Gicky. She thought to ask Margot about it, but really didn't feel like going down the regret path. She went with, "Who is Annette Kellerman?" instead.

"Annette Kellerman was a lesser-known feminist icon."

"Of course she was." Addison smiled. "She sounds like someone you knew from the Bronx."

"Nope, she was from Australia, I believe. She was a famous synchronized swimmer who invented the women's bathing suit. Before that, women wore pantaloons to swim. Imagine?"

Addison pictured herself drowning in pantaloons.

The two set out on their bike ride, Addison riding Annette Kellerman and Margot the Hot Tamale. They stopped at the market to pick up turkey sandwiches—the good ones—before heading east on their journey. Once there, Addison found herself looking around every corner for You Again. When she recognized her disappointment, it surprised her.

Margot, it turned out, had embarked on this particular adventure a half dozen times with Gicky. It began with talking themselves into the gated community of Point O'Woods, an insular village where the land is owned by an association, with century-old houses passed down from generation to generation. Most were built in the New England style, with weatherworn gray shingles beautifully maintained by their preppy-looking inhabitants. The community reminded her of a J.Crew ad she'd once worked on. They rode by the clubhouse, tennis courts, and church. Addison took it all in and concluded that this would be the best location for the horror film in her head—she could get Jordan Peele to write it.

At the far end of POW, they locked their bikes and continued their adventure by exploring a board-walked nature preserve called the Sunken Forest. They stopped to eat their sandwiches at the picnic benches in the next enclave, Sailors Haven, which was not much more than a marina, before backtracking and heading home in time for Margot to catch the early evening boat.

They nearly forgot to look for Margot's gift from Gicky and searched like mad in the fifteen minutes before they had to leave for the ferry.

Margot found it in the back of the guest room closet—wrapped in brown paper with the words *For Margot* written across it in script.

Even though she was basically out of time, Margot carefully untied the bakery string that held the brown paper wrapping in place to see what her friend had made her.

It was a painting of her and Gicky at around age twelve, seated on the living room floor of the old apartment on the Grand Concourse. Margot was holding an autograph book with the page open to Gicky's salutation. She leaned in to read what it said, smiling and crying simultaneously.

Make new friends. But keep the old; those are silver, these are gold.

She wiped her tears and wrapped it back up.

"Let's go," she said, adding, "Keep an eye out for Shep's painting. His wasn't in there."

By the time they arrived at the ferry, a line had already formed down the block to board it. Addison helped Margot with her things, and they embraced for longer than either of them expected. Her affection for her aunt's best friend had grown substantially over the weekend.

"I hope you'll come back next summer," Addison gushed, adding more reasonably, "if I don't sell the place."

"If you don't, I would love to," Margot responded, happy the time with Addison had been valuable for them both.

The line began to move, and before moving with it, Margot patted Addison's cheek lovingly.

Addison said a final goodbye and then took a few steps back to take it all in. The atmosphere at the dock reminded her of her childhood summers at the lake. Although there were no ferryboats there, Sunday nights meant an early dinner before her dad drove back to the city for the week. His goodbye would leave her mother softer for the hour after he left—slightly vulnerable and a bit melancholy. Now, as an adult, she realized it was love. Addison had never felt that longing for someone. When she was engaged to her college boyfriend, they were always together. And even when they broke it off—when *she* broke it off—she waited to feel that ache that her mother had clearly felt when her husband had only left for the week. But she never did. Nor did she feel free and unburdened, as she thought she would. She felt little of anything, and that's when she began wondering if she had ever been in love with him to begin with. Years later, she still wondered.

She watched a woman say goodbye to her husband and kids, who were clearly staying out for the week. The youngest held on to her mom's leg as if she were going off to war.

"Don't be so dramatic, Harper. I'll see you in four days," the mom promised, wavering between guilt and amusement. Her husband held his wife's face in his hands and placed a somewhat comical smooch on her lips. The woman released her laughter, and a feeling Addison could only describe as envy sank in. She turned her head, embarrassed that she had taken in their private moment. When she did, she noticed You Again standing on the dock.

Ooh!

It had been a while since Addison had felt the heart-stopping *ooh, he's cute* feeling, and she had forgotten how good it felt. Ever since she had met him on the boat, she found herself looking for him at every turn.

She controlled the width of her smile and reached her hand up to wave hello. As she did, a woman exited the ferry and met him in a warm embrace that he returned tenfold. Addison quickly retracted her wave and turned her now crimson-cheeked face away from them.

The sun was setting as Addison walked home from the ferry, and though there was no denying that she was bummed to see that the cute guy had a girl, she was now relieved. To begin with, he was way too much to be her type. She valued modest over cocky. Add in the fact that he had clearly been flirting with her when he had a girlfriend, and she felt spared.

The streets were quiet, and the competing smells of Sunday night barbecues made her stomach rumble. The deer were already gathered on the grass-covered ball field for their evening buffet. After only a few days, Addison had grown accustomed to cohabiting with the herd, who were clearly quite used to cohabiting with the locals. Both were unfazed by the other's existence.

Once back at the house, she stripped Margot's bed, threw in a wash, took out the garbage in advance of Monday's pickup, had nothing more than a big bowl of cereal for dinner, and crawled into bed with a book.

I couldn't do this with a husband and kids, she thought with a smile.

Affirmation of her "anchorless" existence.

Still, she tossed and turned all night.

Week Two

Chapter Eight

For the sixteen hours that Paresh Singh was in the air, he dreamed of Gicky.

Short spurts of sleep, short spurts of dreams. He began at the beginning, some sixty years earlier, with a young woman standing barefoot in the kitchen of the house in Delhi, trying to work the percolator. *Can I help you?* he had asked, in Hindi, startling her and causing her to drop the carafe of water in her hands. It shattered on the cold clay floor, and she bent to gather the broken pieces. When she stood up again, there were tears in her eyes. He gently wiped an errant droplet on her freckled cheek with the back of his hand. It wasn't a conscious decision to do so—to touch the face of the American woman standing in the kitchen of the house where he worked—but it was as if his hand were no longer controlled by his brain, but by his heart.

Now, on the airplane, in between babies' cries and bites of inferior airline dosas, Paresh dreamed of the first time Gicky painted him on the roof of the sprawling haveli he helped manage. The job, which had been sold to him by his father as an internship with India's greatest modern architect, was in truth a gig as a glorified groundskeeper. It was fine by him. He was happiest among nature—until he met Gicky, that is. After that he was happiest with her. He remembered how she coaxed him, a shy young man at the time, to pose for her. How after just a few strokes on her canvas, they were in each other's arms, making love in the morning light to a chorus of birds singing and peacocks meowing, as they do.

He remembered the year they tried to make a go of it back in the States. How cold it was in New York City. The chill had stayed with him for months after they had given up and parted ways, temporarily at first, but if neither were lying to themself, more permanently. And how it truly became permanent when his father had a heart attack and Paresh was called on to return to the family real estate business. After that it was just stolen weekends, a layover in Mumbai, a week here or there in Goa, and, more consistently as they got older, a couple of weeks in July on Fire Island.

By the time the pilot announced their descent into JFK airport, Paresh had completed their journey together in his mind. He remembered her last words to him, a call in the middle of the night from her hospice bed.

"Your love has meant more to me than anything else in my life. I have a favor to ask of you."

"Anything," he had responded.

Paresh rode the ferry to Fire Island, he imagined, for the last time. His heart sank when he looked to the shore, noting the absence of his love, who had always been waiting for him there, as if he had never left. He wondered where he would be if he had never left all of those years ago. If he had defied his father's wishes and acclimated to a city, and a world, he didn't quite understand how to navigate. Would he have returned home, now, at his age, to his beloved India, or would his life have remained here? He rarely left his present thoughts as he had during this journey, and the sinking feeling he had in his gut reminded him why that was. He recited a mantra that had been kidnapped by Hallmark cards and wooden painted signs, reminding himself: *Be present.*

Paresh arrived at the house very early Saturday morning and stood quietly at the front door until he heard stirring inside. Only then did he knock. A young woman answered it and took his breath away with her wavy brown hair and olive freckled skin. It could have been Gicky forty years before.

Chapter Nine

an I help you?" Addison asked with a serious expression.

The man put his palms together and bowed his head. She found herself returning the motion.

"Hello. I'm Paresh," he said. "Gicky sent me."

Why? she thought, and then figured the man standing in front of her was the most likely source of the answer, and said it out loud. "Why?"

"I'm not sure," he replied. "I guess we will find out together."

Addison didn't know whether to laugh or cry.

After settling him into his room, she headed to the studio. Her original intention had been to straighten and organize before Gicky's gallerist visited to collect her work. The date was a few weeks away, but there was a lot to do. But the moment she sat down on her aunt's bench and took a brush in her hand, everything changed. The feeling brought her back to college, where the pull of her fine arts classes always won over courses in graphic design or print media.

She really wanted to sculpt, but felt that painting was the first step toward that for her. Something about seeing and translating with a brush seemed to come before working in three dimensions. She had excelled in her fine arts classes in college—even though her parents limited her to two per semester, agreeing to support her as a graphic artist with a lucrative future as opposed to a starving artist with none. Their words exactly. After everything she learned from Margot, she was beginning to wonder how much her similar passions to her aunt Gicky had fueled that conversation with her parents.

Besides all that, she hoped her absence would encourage her new guest to entertain himself without her. She was wrong.

Paresh walked in drinking tea from one of Gicky's mugs, ironically swiped from the Taj Lake Palace in Udaipur. Or maybe it wasn't ironic, maybe it was purposeful. Maybe the two had stolen a long weekend together at what Addison imagined to be a lavish and romantic old Indian palace turned hotel.

She studied Paresh's features until he caught her doing so. She felt like she had seen him before, though she knew that wasn't really possible.

"You are a painter as well, I see."

She noted how his accent made ordinary words sound beautiful. She wondered what her midwestern drawl sounded like to him, though she knew it had definitely faded over the years. She sometimes caught herself sounding like a New Yorker, especially when ordering coffee or water.

She had clipped an old picture of Gicky to the top corner of her canvas. It was a shot of her from behind, staring out at the ocean in a very Andrew Wyeth *Christina's World* kind of way.

That's not why she chose it though. It had been a long time since she had painted, let alone painted faces, and she was too insecure to attempt one yet.

"I paint, but I wouldn't call myself a painter," Addison answered.

"Semantics." He smiled. She smiled too. It felt good to be called an artist, even if she didn't quite believe it. "I'm an architect," he offered, before changing the subject. "You look just as she did at your age," he noted, with an obvious hint of melancholy.

He pulled a photo out of his wallet. It was one of those small square-bordered images with the date printed on the corner: *July 1972.* Gicky looked to be younger than Addison was now, but they were both at that age where it was hard to tell for sure. Everyone had always said that Addison looked like her dad, so it wasn't a surprise that she would resemble his sister—though she had never noticed it before. In all fairness, her mother had removed all photos from their house after the Big Terrible Thing, and there were few images of Gicky online when Addison had googled her over the years. Putting in her name mostly brought her to auction houses and sites like 1stDibs. But there was no doubt that Morty Irwin and his two daughters resembled their father's Yemenite ancestors far more than their mother's Russian side.

Paresh stood behind her, staring at the photo.

"It's nice for you to paint beautiful Gicky. I was often her muse."

And suddenly Addison realized where she had recognized him from. He resembled the portrait of a young man that hung in her bedroom.

Curiosity piqued, she no longer wished to avoid him for the weekend. In fact, she wanted a shot at painting him. Gicky could wait.

"Can I paint you?" she asked tentatively.

He smiled, pulling up a cane-backed chair, and sat in it, catty-corner. She had her answer.

Paresh sat quietly for a good long while as the morning light danced across his face. At first Addison was intimidated thinking back to what she remembered of her aunt's decade-long series of portraits of him, but then she made it her own. Leaning into her fear of painting faces, she went for a more abstract approach.

After a bit, the silence became painful.

"You can talk," she said. "And no need to sit perfectly still."

"Gicky insisted on silence and stillness," he said. "It wasn't a problem, as I'm quite fond of both."

"Not me. Silence makes me nervous."

"I guess you don't meditate, then."

"Not a chance. I tried once. It was torture."

He laughed, a laugh that lit up his face. She wished she could capture it.

"Gicky claimed meditation elevated her art to a higher level. Your aunt said a true artist hears with their eyes. Do you feel that way?"

"I hate to disappoint you, but I am not a true artist. I'm a sell-out. At least I was till I lost my job a few weeks ago."

"At the advertising firm?"

Addison put down the brush and approached Paresh.

"Can I ask you a question?" She didn't wait for an answer. "If Gicky kept such close track of me, even shared where I worked with her friends, why didn't she ever reach out?"

"It's hard to say. I know the rejection from your father left her wary of opening her heart. Plus, she feared giving him ammunition against her. She worried that contacting you behind his back would have angered him more. She always hoped he would come around." Paresh looked into her eyes, and she found it hard to turn away.

"But please consider this—she is reaching out now."

"Isn't it too late?"

"Not at all. Sit with me."

He opened up the closet, pulled out a threadbare rug and two cushions, and placed them on the floor in the corner of the sunlit room. He sat with his back against one wall and motioned for Addison to do the same on the other.

"I told you. I don't meditate."

"Indulge me."

She sat, copying his posture, back straight, shoulders relaxed, eyes closed.

"Focus on your breath. Notice the sensation of the air as it enters and exits your nose. Place your left hand on your belly, and lose yourself in the rise and the fall—the rise and the fall."

Out of respect more than conviction, she dove in. She knew from prior experience it was only a matter of seconds before her thoughts would stray to any of the million little things that kept her up at night. She had never possessed a quiet mind—and Paresh seemed to read it. Maybe it was just Meditation 101, but as soon as she began to drift, he said, "Be present, Addison. Don't fight your thoughts and distractions. Acknowledge them without judgment, and then gently bring your attention back to your breath."

She did, but a short time later, she was thinking about how

her once best friend, Phoebe Thomas, stole her cupcake in the fourth grade. She couldn't even keep her thoughts in the decade, let alone the moment. She focused on wrestling the random memories and distractions, hoping to return them to whatever corner of her brain they had escaped from. The experience reminded her of a childhood toy. An unsuspecting can of mixed nuts that, when opened, released a coil-covered snake that sprang out, offering a surprisingly satisfying prank. She had quickly excelled at wrangling the snake back into the can.

Her grandfather had brought her that toy on a visit from Florida. Her thoughts floated to her mother's father, whom she had adored like no other, and who had become a far greater disappointment than Phoebe Thomas.

Focus on your breath, she heard Paresh say, unsure whether he had actually spoken again, or if she had remembered his words from minutes before. Either way, she complied, pushing aside the upsetting thoughts of her grandpa and placing her left hand on her belly and silently chanting, *In, out, in, out.*

She managed to breathe like that for a minute or two, but it didn't last.

She adjusted her gaze to meet his eyes. No words were necessary.

"Sometimes listening to a story helps. Can I tell you a story?"

"Please do," she said as she crossed her legs and lowered her gaze, giving it a real try.

With his quiet voice rising and falling within the syllables of a word in almost a hypnotic way, he told the tale of the weaver and the princess.

"Once, there was a talented weaver who created beautiful and intricate patterns on his loom. He was known throughout the land for his artistry and skill. One day, the weaver was commissioned by the king to create a special tapestry for his daughter, the princess.

"The weaver accepted the challenge and worked on the tapestry. However, he found he couldn't create anything that satisfied him. He worked for many days and nights, but the tapestry remained incomplete.

"Feeling frustrated and defeated, the weaver took a walk in the woods. There, he met a sage who asked him what was troubling him. The weaver explained his situation, and the sage said, 'Love is the thread of creativity. Without love, your work will remain incomplete.'

"The weaver realized he had been so focused on the technical aspects of his work that he had forgotten the love that he had for his craft. He returned to his loom and wove a new tapestry with love in his heart, pouring his passion into the task. He thought of his adoring mother and his beautiful wife. Of his young daughter who clung to his hand when walking through town. He thought of his grandmother who had raised him. The patterns he created were dense with the energy of his love, and his work came to life. When the princess saw the completed tapestry, she was amazed at its beauty and wept with joy.

"The weaver realized that the sage was right, love truly was the thread of creativity. In order to create beauty, you need to have a warm heart."

The story sank in and left her with a palpable feeling of loneliness that she didn't quite understand. It felt hard to breathe. Addison blinked her eyes, surprised to feel tears coming on. One escaped, and Paresh noticed it.

"I'm sorry," he said. But Addison knew he wasn't truly sorry.

Had Gicky sent him there to crack open her heart? She wiped her eyes and stood up. She felt naked and vulnerable in a way that made her very uncomfortable. She badly wanted it to stop.

"I'm going to head to the market to pick up lunch before the afternoon rush."

"Isn't the afternoon rush the best part?"

"Not for me."

At the market, she decided to err on the side of caution, and filled her basket with ingredients for a salad, operating on the assumption that Paresh was a vegetarian.

On the bike ride home, Addison thought of Paresh's words— *in order to create beauty, you need to have a warm heart*. With her grandfather still top of mind, she thought of the day her heart turned cold. Though *cold* may be too harsh—more like *temperate*. Her heart was temperate. Welcoming of warmth, but wary of heat. Never willing to risk what it would take to get carried away by someone else's love.

Addison had adored her maternal grandfather with all of her heart. His warm smile, his hearty belly laugh, the way she and her sister took turns dancing on his feet. His hugs when he greeted her, wrapping his arms around her little frame in a layer of love and strength that Addison carried with her long after his visits ended. At twelve, when he passed, she promised herself she would carry the feeling of his hugs with her always. But always didn't last more than a day.

The cousins were bored at the shiva and decided to play a silent game of hide-and-go-seek. With dozens of people coming in and out of their grandparents' house, no one would know they were missing except for the kid who was seeking (at that point, her cousin Astrid). Addison slipped into her grandparents' room.

She lifted the lid on her grandpa's mahogany humidor and breathed in the scent of Cuban cigars that had always engulfed him. She slipped one out, waved it under her nose, and placed it in the pocket of her dress for safekeeping before taking her favorite hiding spot under her grandparents'—now only her grandmother's—bed.

Within minutes, she heard the door crack open and squeezed her eyes tight, waiting for Astrid to call her out. But the stockinged feet that approached the bed were not Astrid's. They were her grandmother's. Her grandmother lay down above her, her slight frame barely indenting the mattress over Addison's head. Addison thought of wiggling out and climbing up on the bed to comfort her. Surely it was more important than winning hide-and-go-seek, but her grandmother began to cry and, feeling as if she were invading her privacy, Addison chickened out. Soon her mother entered and sat on the bed, causing a slightly bigger indentation. Addison inched away from it.

"Hey, Mom," her mother said to her own mother.

The bed moved, and Addison imagined her mother rubbing her grandmother's back, as she had thought of doing a few minutes earlier.

"We all miss him," she said sweetly.

She could feel her grandmother roll over—presumably to face her mom.

"Beverly," she said, "when I die, I want you to make me a promise."

"You're not dying, Mother," she said, in her all-too-familiar sarcastic tone.

"Just make me a promise."

"OK," her mother agreed, "anything you want."

"I want you to bury me with my back facing your father."

"Mom. That was a long time ago."

"Your father was unfaithful to me from the day I married him till the day he died. Promise me you will bury me with my back to him, the way I was forced to sleep through most of my marriage. I will never rest in peace if you don't promise me this."

Her grandmother let out a painful wail, and Addison felt it pierce her young heart.

It never fully recovered. She had rolled under that bed a child and had rolled out a cynic.

"New rider on your right!" a guy yelled now as his wobbly child approached on a two-wheeler.

Addison, deep in thought, overcompensated and veered left, swerving off the sidewalk and toppling off her bike. Radishes and cucumbers rolled in all directions.

"Sorry," the dad yelled, still running behind his wayward son.

Addison collected her produce, sat down on the grass, and cried. She wasn't really sure why she was crying, but there was no controlling it. She cried for the aunt she never really knew and the grandpa that broke her heart. She cried for the career that she had put everything into that hadn't returned the favor. She cried because she knew she hadn't properly nurtured the thread of love in her heart. And of course, as fate would dictate, at the exact moment she sat crying in the dirt, up walked the man from the ferry.

"Hey. You Again!" he called out from a few feet away.

Addison quickly pulled on her sunglasses, but it was too late. You would have to be blind not to see the rawness in her eyes. For some reason, she found herself explaining her state of mind to the tall stranger   You Again.

"I've been cracked wide-open," she said, now all out sobbing.

He sat down on the sidewalk next to her. "Can I put my arm around you?"

"What would your girlfriend think of that?"

"I don't have a girlfriend."

"Did you and the woman you picked up at the ferry break up?"

"Oh, her? She's gay, and also my sister."

Addison laughed, and tapped her shoulder as if it were an invitation. She could really use a hug, and a half hug would be better than none. He threw his arm around her shoulder and squeezed. She sank in a little, and his touch eased her suffering until a few seconds later, when awkwardness set in.

"I feel better. Thanks."

He jumped up, clearly feeling awkward too, and reached out his hand to help her. She took it, and they both held on a little longer than necessary. Upon realizing that, embarrassment registered on all four of their cheeks.

At least, that is how Addison interpreted it. This guy was pretty obviously flirting. Or so she thought. She always found herself wondering if she would be able to differentiate mutual attraction from one-sided attraction.

He picked up her bike and held it upright while she collected her salad ingredients from the sidewalk.

"Uh-oh," he said, pointing to a deer munching on her iceberg lettuce.

Addison laughed. "I guess I'm heading back to the market."

"I'm heading that way too. Maybe you should try walking for a bit."

She agreed, even allowing him to walk her bike. There was something so comfortable about this guy.

"So, who broke you? If you don't mind me asking. Wait. Let me guess—your mother?"

"No, I haven't given her that kind of control in years."

"Was it a guy?"

"Yes, but not that type of guy."

"Your boss?"

"No. I'm bossless right now, which may partially account for my little breakdown. I called my boss a nepo baby in front of the entire company—accidentally—on Zoom."

"Oh man. I think I read about something like that in the *Post*?"

"Yes, it made the *Post*, next to an article about erectile dysfunction. As if it weren't bad enough, the penis in the photo seemed to be pointing at me. I'd always thought it would be fun to be on Page Six."

"It rarely is," he said, adding, "Let me guess one more. Was it your shrink?"

"No. An architect."

"Of life?"

She laughed. "No. Of buildings, I presume. He taught me to quiet my mind, and I guess in the end I didn't like what I heard."

"Ohhh. That's happened to me. I took to my bed for a week once after taking ashwagandha with some swami at a sweathouse in Joshua Tree."

She laughed at the way he said *took to my bed*, as if he were a southern belle—or her mother.

"Really?" Addison asked.

"Yes—the guy kept repeating one sentence over and over again."

Addison waited for him to spill—but he didn't.

"What was it?" she asked with more than a hint of impatience.

"I don't like getting it stuck in my head."

"Oh my God. Just—whisper it."

He took his hand and gently pushed her hair away from her ear. She could feel his warm breath on her neck, and the intimacy stirred her until his words set in.

"You don't know what you don't know."

She jumped back.

"Oh my, what does that mean?"

"I don't know."

They both laughed. Hard. Like old friends in on an inside joke.

They arrived at the market, where he gallantly placed her bike in the stand and joined her in the produce section. He grabbed a head of lettuce and tossed it to her.

"You Again! Think fast!"

She caught it, and he seemed weirdly impressed.

"Since we keep bumping into each other—maybe it's time we exchanged names?" she suggested, with an awkward laugh.

"I don't know, I was kind of enjoying this little 'You Again' flirtation we have going on," he laughed back.

Aaaaah. She knew he was flirting. The confirmation felt good though.

"Is that what this is?" she teased, with a coy smile.

"It's been a while, but I believe so. There's a big block party this Sunday night on the bay. Want to meet me there on purpose and maybe flirt some more?"

"Sounds good." She smiled, reined in the pheromones a bit, and headed out.

At home, Addison found a note from Paresh. Well, it wasn't much of a note; it was more a word.

Wandering.

At first, she was relieved. Whatever path he had taken on his walk, she was glad it wasn't the path to her enlightenment. But, as the day went on and the sun began to set, she found herself pining for his return. Eventually, she gave up on any attempt at mindfulness and embraced mindlessness instead. She made a bowl of pasta with butter, crawled into bed with her laptop, and watched *Love Is Blind*. It was just the decadent thing to do that she had never had time for when she was working.

In the morning Paresh was standing over the sink, looking out the kitchen window, drinking tea. Even in his seventies, she could see the beautiful young man in the painting by her bed.

She wondered where he had been but wasn't sure she wanted to know.

"Late night?" she asked, fully aware of the absurdity of her question.

"I sat on the beach for hours. It was a buck moon."

"What's a buck moon?"

"A full moon named for the new antlers that appear on the male deer in July."

She stretched out her jaw and pressed her index and middle fingers into the spot where the mandible and the maxilla meet. She must have been grinding her teeth all night. What used to be a once-in-a-while thing seemed to be a regular occurrence since losing her job. He noticed and approached.

"Can I?" he asked, holding four fingers in the air as if he were about to make air quotes.

She nodded, though had no idea why she was agreeing. She

only knew that she had woken like this every day for nearly a month. He sensed her hesitation.

"Trust me," he said.

She winced. Trust was a hard thing for Addison.

He held her face in his hands and circled his fingers deeper and deeper into the spot where her jawbones connected. And the tension began to release—at first slowly, but then quite suddenly, until it felt as if there were only one layer left. One impermeable layer. He looked into her eyes.

"This is more than a lost job. What are you holding on to?"

She shook her head. She didn't know. Her eyes welled up again, the third time in as many days. She was not usually a crier.

"I don't know," she said.

"Well, maybe it is time you found out."

The rest of the morning was a repeat of the day before. He modeled, she painted. He asked her rather ordinary questions about her life, and she surprised herself with her candid answers. She was hoping to get at the trust issue that, if she were to admit it, definitely played into every decision and indecision in her life.

Trying unsuccessfully to capture the soulful quality of his eyes, she painted them and painted over them half a dozen times before giving up entirely.

"Should we try meditating again?" he asked.

She agreed, and they sat on the floor, where the rug and pillows remained from the day before.

"So, you and Gicky? Was it love?"

"I like to think of it as a love story. Though some may call it tragic. I have a big family in Delhi, and while I had my freedom for a while and got to embrace nature and my spirituality—and

Gicky—my independence was short-lived. I was called back to run the family business.

"Gicky was fiercely independent. Living in India, being tied down to one place, was not something she could stomach for too long. I never really loved another as I did your aunt. We were so young when we met. I was working at a farmhouse outside of Delhi. The owner was a famous architect who had met Gicky at a show in Greenwich Village and brought her to India to paint a mural on one of his buildings. It was an avant-garde idea at the time. It was supposed to take a month or so, but she ended up staying the year. Mostly because of me. We fell in love after one week."

"That quick?"

"You say it like you don't think it's possible. I'm here to tell you it is."

She nodded in agreement, though she didn't at all agree.

He stood, and stretched his back before sitting down again.

"How about you? Have you ever been?" he asked.

"To India, no. But it's on my list."

"That's nice, but I meant in love. Have you ever been in love?"

"Oh. I was engaged once—to my college boyfriend. Well, we didn't go to the same college. I studied graphic design and visual communication at the School of the Art Institute of Chicago, and he was a finance major at UChicago. We met our sophomore year at this dive bar everyone went to called McGee's. It was a funny mix of the artsy types from my school with the brainiacs from his. We bonded over beer pong—do you know what that is?"

"I don't."

"I could show you. It was a long time ago, but I was pretty

good at it, though I doubt Gicky has any red Solo cups in the house. Can't imagine she was much into single-use plastic."

Paresh looked at her rather blankly, and she became über-aware that she hadn't answered his question and was instead spewing utter nonsense. She paused, contemplating the thing she had never really admitted, even to herself. She stopped beating around the bush and babbling to this serious man who could obviously see right through it.

"No. I don't think I have ever really been in love. I mean, I love my family and my friends, and I was mad for Trixie, my childhood cat, but looking back at my relationship with Philip— my ex-fiancé—I really liked him, and thought, at the time, that he loved me enough for the both of us. And that felt really good, and really safe, until the day the wedding invitations were mailed, and it suddenly didn't. I ran—I ran all the way to New York."

"If you have to wonder, you were not. I think it was a blessing that you lost your job. I think you lean toward the status quo when you're meant for so much more." He quickly changed the subject, preventing her from arguing with him.

"Gicky said that she left something for me, a painting, I think. Have you seen it?"

She went back to the storage closet where Margot had found hers. Paresh's gift was leaning against the wall. A frame, covered in brown construction paper, tied up in string. He took it and slid it under his arm. She was bursting to ask him to open it but felt it would be invading his privacy. She imagined it as a painting of them in the compound in Delhi where they met, a Garden of Eden.

Addison hugged Paresh goodbye at the ferry.

"Thank you. I'm so honored to have learned meditation from

you—you were much better than the YouTuber who I learned it from the first time. You must have had an excellent teacher."

Addison pictured him learning from a great sage at an Indian ashram.

"I learned on YouTube too!" He laughed.

"Really?"

"No. Your aunt taught me. I was never interested in any of it until I met her."

The ferryboat pulled into the marina, and suddenly their goodbye felt too rushed.

Paresh reached out for another hug.

"Thank you for a lovely visit," he said with more than a hint of melancholy. She stared into his eyes, memorizing them so she could paint them one day. She promised she would keep trying to meditate. He told her to keep an open heart, which she ridiculously followed up with a promise to teach him how to play beer pong the next time he visited. They both knew there would be no next time.

Tears fell down her face as the boat fell away.

"Open, enlightened, and present," she whispered out loud, "kind of sucks."

Chapter Ten

Addison spent a good hour getting ready for the Bay Beach block party, trying her best to look beachy casual rather than like she had tried her best. It worked. She looked beautiful in a silky lavender slip dress that she had never worn before and strappy sandals. You Again had definitely stirred something in her, and she daydreamed of their next flirtation more than she cared to admit. She snapped a selfie and sent it to the group chat.

Hot date tonight? Lisa asked.

Wear nice undies, Pru urged.

Stop! I'm just going to a party! she responded, before switching to her slinky floral thong, just in case.

The Bay Beach, a community gathering spot with a playground, basketball court, and cradle for swimming, sat at the end of her block, but as Addison reached it, she wished it were a bit farther. It was a gorgeous night—the kind that made her think she should truly consider putting down roots there. The island seemed to provide such balance to living and working in the city.

While not the kind of person to need a plus-one, she did feel awkward walking into a party where everyone knew one another—and she knew no one. Nan, the real estate agent, waved to her as she entered. *Well, almost no one*, she thought. She waved back at her and smiled as she scanned the crowd for You Again.

They saw each other at the same time from across the playground. She caught him doing a double take, his eyes turning from the blonde that had his attention to her. He held that gaze for a few seconds more than customary. It wasn't as obvious as Jack watching his soulmate Rose descend the stairs of the *Titanic*, but it was undeniably reminiscent of a Hollywood first look, and it filled Addison with confidence. Her breath got caught in her throat as she watched him approach.

The bar was behind her, and he motioned to it and asked, "What's your poison?" in lieu of a greeting. Even though he looked close to her age, he had a funny way with words that reminded her of the older men who wrote copy at the agency. She resisted asking him how old he was, which was hard because she was curious. Maybe she should learn his name first.

"Just about anything," she responded, anticipating the liquid courage her first few sips would supply.

They walked over to the makeshift bar and poured themselves a drink from what looked like a pitcher of mojitos. Her first sip was a bit tart, but it hit the spot. She took another, to fill the awkward silence. She was eager to lift the veil of secrecy. The You Again bit had run its course. Normally she would have totally vetted someone before letting loose as she had, spilling her guts to a guy she had just met. Her friends teased that she was the kind of girl who could find out everything about anyone in under an hour, yet here she was, falling for a complete stranger. She was eager to learn more about him, especially since she couldn't remember the last time someone's touch had made her stomach turn somersaults. She was about to put an end to the mystery with a proper introduction, when she noticed Shep, the old guy from her block, coming toward her. She spun around, quite obviously, to avoid him.

"What's up?" asked You Again.

"Nothing, nothing. This old guy from my block is coming this way. The real estate agent said he lost his mind after his wife died and I should avoid him at all costs. That he's a little . . ." She tilted her head and twirled her finger beside her ear, demonstrating the international sign for cuckoo.

She thought this would get a laugh, but his expression was anything but amused. The old man showed up from behind and slapped the now agitated younger man on the back. Addison refocused her attention on her new favorite habit and gnawed on the side of her nail.

"What ya drinking?" Shep asked, while peeking into their cups. "Oooh. That fruity stuff gives me gas."

"Pleasure to see you again, Addie," he added, wiping off his hands on his shorts and reaching out for a shake. The wipe really freaked her out. She couldn't stop thinking about what might have precipitated it.

"It's Addison," she quietly corrected, "and the pleasure is all mine." She followed their shake by casually wiping off her own hand on her dress.

"You two know each other?" You Again asked.

"We've met," Addison responded, adding with a smirk, "He is the lovely neighbor who wants to steal my house, I believe."

It was the first time she had said *my house*, and as the words left her lips, she felt like a fraud.

"I don't want your house—that would be your neighbor Ben here," Shep insisted.

She took it in, reflected on Nan's warning about bulldozing and sweet-talking, and felt irrationally betrayed. Maybe it wasn't irrational. What a phony! Was the You Again flirtation all a manipulation? Her chest burned, and she could feel the heat traveling to her cheeks.

"You're Gicky's niece? You never told me that," Ben barked, as if he had been wronged. Her cheeks burned brighter.

"Wait, *you're* the guy who wants to steal my house?"

"Not steal," Shep butted in. "Gicky sort of kind of promised him first dibs. Did you bring the clamshell contract with you?" Shep asked Ben with a laugh.

"A clamshell contract?" Addison protested. "She left a will, you know, a legal document that coordinates the distribution of your assets."

"We know what a will is, Addie," Ben mumbled.

"It's Addison."

"Sorry," he said, "I only know you as You Again." He smiled, thinking himself funny. It was obvious that she didn't.

"How convenient for you," she snapped in reply.

"What's that supposed to mean?"

Her hands began to shake, a common occurrence for Addison when anticipating a showdown. She was now feeling certain that this You Again thing was a scam to butter her up. He must have known who she was the entire time. She felt like such a fool, and there was little she liked less than feeling foolish. The notion fueled her response, justified or not.

"I heard about you from my real estate agent. Very swift with this whole 'let's not exchange names,' You Again thing. Well done, trying to get on my good side before introducing yourself. But guess what?"

You Again was completely taken aback. Shep stepped up. "What?"

"It didn't work."

As Addison turned to flee the scene, Ben grabbed her arm.

"Hey, wait, I swear I didn't know it was you, really. I didn't know." He let go of her arm and held out his hand for a proper introduction.

"Let's try again. Hi. I'm Ben. Nice to meet you."

She didn't return the greeting. She decided right then and there that she wanted out. She would take the money and put it toward her dream apartment in the city.

"I hope you don't mind if I don't say, 'Nice to meet you too.'" And with that, she turned her back to them and marched directly to Nan.

The effects of Addison's unfortunate interaction were still visible on her face, as the satisfaction she felt from her dramatic exit had quickly morphed into sadness. Things had soured so quickly. Even the standoffish agent took notice.

"Hey, you OK?" Nan asked. "I saw you talking to Ben and Shep. Remember what I said—don't let those two get under your skin. They can be quite charismatic, in an off kind of way."

"They got under my skin all right, like ringworm."

Nan laughed. "Want to mingle with me? I'm happy to introduce you to a few good people."

"No thanks. I've decided to sell." When she heard the words come out of her mouth, she quickly backpedaled. "Well, I'm leaning that way. So there's really no point. Maybe we can sit down sometime soon and discuss it."

"Absolutely. I'm available all week."

Week Three

Chapter Eleven

Addison tossed and turned all night, her firing playing over and over again in her mind, along with the unfortunate interaction with her neighbor that night at the block party. When she couldn't take it anymore, she turned on the light, opened her laptop, and pulled up Zillow. After checking off all of her preferences in the real estate app, images of ideal apartments filled the page. She hearted half a dozen of them and fell asleep dreaming of parquet floors and river views. While falling asleep mulling her urban options was pleasant, she had to admit that waking up at the beach was pretty delicious. She de-escalated, to simpler decisions—should she brew a pot of coffee or ride to the market for an iced version and a fresh-baked corn muffin? She was wary of leaving the house, not wanting to bump into Ben now that she knew he lived next door. It had been a while since she had allowed an untrustworthy man to fool her with his charm. But she really wanted a muffin, so defiance won. If she saw him, she would just ignore him.

With that in mind, she threw on cutoffs with the tee she slept in and hopped on her bike, barefoot and braless, like a real Fire Islander. She felt light—possibly even airy—and noted that her brief experience of practicing meditation was perhaps the source of her newfound buoyancy. The feeling, however, was short-lived.

"What the fu—" she began, but was quickly cut off by a flurry of curses from You Again right outside her house. Holding on to the dwindling lightness that was Paresh's gift to her, she quickly renamed him—Not You Again. She smiled at her own wit—but that too was short-lived. It was clear that some kind of animal had gotten into her garbage cans.

Not You Again's pails were sitting off to the side without a speck of garbage around them. The name *Silver* was sharpied on their sides.

Not You Again—real name Ben Silver, apparently—was furiously picking up her trash from the sidewalk while his dog, Sally, looked on anxiously. Of course Sally was his dog! Probably a part of the play—maybe there was a bug in Sally's collar.

As much as she wanted to run back inside, she addressed the situation.

"I'm sorry. I clicked closed the covers, I'm sure of it," Addison asserted.

"You didn't use the bungee cords correctly! It's so freaking . . . irresponsible!"

She helped pick up the trash, but was not about to cower to his tantrum.

"Take a moment," she said patronizingly.

He held an empty box of tampons in the air and matched her sarcasm.

"'Take a moment'? What are you, an Apple Watch?"

It was funny. Addison pressed her lips together, suppressing a smile.

Ben looked up at the tampon box in his hand, then back to Addison. His face turned a bright shade of red.

He looked back up at the box and tossed it in the can. "I don't want to be picking up your shit."

"Then don't. I got this."

"Obviously you haven't. You know, you may not care about this block, but we all do—very much." He motioned to the surrounding houses. His anger clearly went beyond Addison's not properly securing the garbage.

"Is that your dog?" she asked.

"Yes. Sally."

"So you think I should be able to control the raccoons and the deer, but you can't even control Sally?"

Sally sighed and lay down on the sidewalk, clearly insulted by Addison's tone, if not her words.

Shep observed the hoopla from his window and thankfully arrived, interrupting the heated argument. He attempted to bring down the temperature with a joke. It seemed to be his go-to tactic.

"What does a deer with no eyes call themselves?" he asked Addison.

"No idea," she said with zero enthusiasm.

"Exactly," Shep laughed. Addison did too. She couldn't help herself. Ben did not.

"C'mon, son." Shep put his hand on Ben's shoulder. "It's a rookie mistake. I'll teach Addie how to use the bungee cords."

"It's Addison," she mumbled uselessly under her breath.

Ben turned and walked away with little more than a grunt.

"Don't mind him. He's not a morning person," Shep advised.

"That's a generous way to put it."

He had come prepared and handed her a black plastic lawn bag.

"He takes some getting used to—your aunt adored him, you know. She hoped you two would be friends."

"Friends? You know, he never even introduced himself to me," she complained as she shook the bag open, trying to exonerate herself for any rudeness on her part.

"He wouldn't even know how—he hasn't been himself for a long while."

She didn't care to ask him to elaborate. Whatever this guy was going through, it was inexcusable to first play her, then berate her. Shep here was the one who had lost his wife, and even though he couldn't keep her name straight, he was at least being nice to her.

They finished cleaning up, and Shep showed Addison how to secure the cans with bungee cords—assuring her this would never happen again if she did it correctly. The sky turned dark, and a hankering for a cup of warm tea replaced her yearning for iced coffee. She washed up, put the kettle on, and brought her now favorite mug—the one from the Taj Lake Palace in Udaipur—out to the studio to work on her painting of Paresh. Once she was there, the meditation corner beckoned.

She sat down with her back against the wall and took a few sips of her tea before deciding to give it a go on her own. That man, Ben, had really taken away the zen that Paresh had left her with, and she was determined to get it back.

Putting the tea down, she swung one leg over the other like a yogi and practiced meditating. And while her mind ran to the things she needed to do for the renters (remake the beds, bake scones), how they were faring at work without her (she had received more than a few texts asking for her help, and Emma reported in almost daily) and replaying the incident(s) with her neighbor (jerk), she managed to reel it in each time and spent a few minutes emptying her cluttered mind. She was left with a single thought.

Addison stood, went inside, and called the real estate agent.

"I want to sell."

When she hung up from the lengthy discussion, she was determined to make a dent in cleaning out the house. One step back into the studio, though, and she put it off.

Gicky had left what looked to be a thirty-by-forty-inch blank canvas on the easel, a photo of a beach scene taped to the top. The scale of the project made Addison wonder about her aunt's state of mind before her death. It was a big canvas. Had it been sitting empty for months, or had Gicky set it up recently? If Addison had been living with Gicky's diagnosis—leukemia, the bad kind— she would have set up something half the size. She bet that her aunt would have described the sidewalks as wide rather than saying the streets were narrow. It amazed her that life had not squashed Gicky's natural optimism, and Addison made a silent pledge to be more like her, or at least to try.

Despite the overcast day, the light in the studio was fantastic. Addison thought about abandoning the painting of Paresh and taking a stab at the beach scene, but the vat of clay in the corner had been calling out to her ever since she arrived. Sculpting had always been Addison's true passion. She even came home one winter break from college with an entire "I am a sculptor" speech memorized. It didn't go over well. Her parents refused to pay for the rest of school unless she majored in something employable.

Her mother, especially, could not bear her daughter being in the same field as her "wretched" sister-in-law. When Addison won the most prestigious award in the department for sculpting, her mother hardly acknowledged it. Addison had felt so guilty about winning it. She knew her peers were pining for the illustrious honor to jump-start their careers as artists, while for her it became a symbol of what could have been.

Paresh had spoken of Gicky describing sculpting as a form of meditation—how while her hands were busy, her mind could *remain quiet*. Addison placed a block of clay on Gicky's turntable and kneaded it with her hands until it became malleable. She felt a connection while working the mud-like material between her fingers, relishing the texture and weight of the clay in her hands in a way that was almost intimate.

In her first attempt at forming an object (since college, that is), Addison created a small bud vase. When she was satisfied with its shape, she meticulously carved ridges on it with a scalpel-like instrument she found sitting in a jar on Gicky's table, as slowly as a surgeon performing surgery. She had been collecting cockle shells on beach walks, and they inspired the ridged pattern she imprinted in the clay. The cockles brought up a precious memory of collecting shells with her grandfather on the shores of Lake Michigan. He had taught her that each line across the width of the shell represented one growing season—not unlike the rings of a tree. So, a mollusk in a shell with two bands across it would have died somewhere between its second and third birthday. Addison had purposefully never googled this. She didn't want to be disappointed in him again, if it turned out not to be true. One betrayal was enough.

Addison became lost in it, lost in the clay, lost in herself. She wondered if she would ever be found.

It was nearly dinnertime when she realized she hadn't even eaten lunch.

The crappy weather held on the next day, and Addison continued to sculpt. Again and again, she became completely absorbed, losing track of time and the world around her. She felt a connection with the clay as she brought it to life that she had not felt in a long while about anything. Even creating her most successful campaigns, with their endless hours of planning and perfecting, did not compare to working with this lump of clay, giving it shape and texture and detail. How had she ever let this all slip from her hands?

Chapter Twelve

Katie and Jessie jumped on board the Long Island Rail Road leaving Pennsylvania Station for Bay Shore with seconds to spare. The train, headed for the southwestern end of Long Island, was packed with twenty- and thirtysomethings fleeing the city for the summer weekend. The women were lucky to find two seats together.

It's a cruel secret, never mentioned by the real estate agents of NYC, that once you can finally afford to move out of your parents' house and into an apartment, with its first month's rent and last month's rent and broker fees, and your half of a Craigslist couch, you have to start saving for a summer share.

When the temperature hits ninety, many postcollege, gainfully employed young New Yorkers do their best to hit the road—or the rails, as the case may be here. Jessie and Katie were of that breed. They had saved all year for a quarter summer share in the Hamptons. So far, they had only been once and had an OK weekend. They had spent a ton of time wondering where to go and how to get there. They were excited to try Fire Island, known for its simpler choices and casual vibe.

Katie and Jessie were childhood best friends who now shared a Bookstagram account on social media. They called themselves the Spice Girls and only featured books with spicy sex scenes. At this point, they had over fifty thousand followers, making their account one of the most popular bookish destinations on Instagram. Sometimes they posted book covers, and sometimes reviews, but mostly whole paragraphs taken from novels, both old and new, with steamy sex scenes.

The two twenty-five-year-old women had booked their weekend on Fire Island after a chance encounter with a fragile-looking gray-haired lady waiting in line in front of them at a book signing at the Union Square Barnes & Noble, months before. Aside from *On Fire Island*, the title that came with the ticket to meet their favorite author, the two women each carried a bag filled with Benjamin Morse's backlist—hoping for autographs on all. That's how they got to talking with the gray-haired lady—she had originally been in line behind them.

"You should go ahead of us," Jessie had insisted, adding, "We are gonna take a while." She opened up her tote bag to flash her collection with pride. The woman obliged.

"We're hoping he will sign them all," Katie interjected before motioning to the line that was snaked in and out of the aisles on the third floor of the massive bookstore.

"I'm sure he will—he's a sweet boy," she said with more than a smidge of familiarity. They were so obviously starstruck; it amused the old woman.

"He's my neighbor at the beach," she admitted before reaching into her purse and pulling out a card and handing it to them. It read: *Gicky Irwin. Artist.*

"I rent a room by the weekend—and have a few still available for this coming summer, if you're interested. He can sign anything you want then!"

"Oh my God," Katie had squealed. Jessie, the more restrained of the two, took the card and smiled. "We definitely will."

And they did.

"Tickets, please!" the conductor now bellowed, before announcing the stops along his route like he was calling out the winners at Belmont.

"Lynbrook, Rockville Centre, Baldwin, Freeport, Merrick, Bellmore, Wantagh, Seaford, Massapequa, Massapequa Park, Amityville, Copiague, Lindenhurst, Babylon, for points east, transfer at Babylon."

They were points east, by one stop. Bay Shore.

"Let's do today's post from the train," Jessie suggested, pulling up their shared Instagram account on her phone. Yesterday's post: One line from *Lady Chatterley's Lover*—a book that had its author, D. H. Lawrence, entrenched in a decade-long censorship trial—received 7,632 likes. On their signature Pepto-pink background with white lettering, it read:

"Rippling, rippling, rippling, like a flapping overlapping of soft flames, soft as feathers, running to points of brilliance, exquisite, exquisite and melting her all molten inside." —D. H. Lawrence (1928)

For this weekend, their entire stay on Fire Island, they were featuring only Benjamin Morse books. Katie pulled the complete collection from her bag. She arranged them and rearranged them on the burgundy leather seat until she was satisfied with the picture. She held it out to Jessie—who agreed that it was perfect, and they went back and forth collaborating on the caption.

They decided on:

BOOKING out to Fire Island to find Benjamin Morse! Followed by a plethora of crossed-finger emojis.

Jessie hit Post, and they agreed not to look at the results for the rest of the ride.

Neither had been to Fire Island before, and both loved the beach, but the promise of hobnobbing with Benjamin Morse aroused them more than the thought of Oliver Mellors nibbling on Lady Chatterley's thigh.

They arrived at the ferry with a rolling bag of books and looked for the gray-haired woman they had met at the signing on the other side. When they didn't find her, they stopped into the market, where they were given the bad news and directions to the house.

They were already at 2,300 likes.

Chapter Thirteen

On her third day entrenched in the clay, Addison heard a knock on the door and jumped a good ten feet in the air before opening it. It was sunny again. Her eyes adjusted to the light outside the studio and then to the two women, who looked to be in their mid-twenties, standing in front of her.

The first paying weekend guests, Jessie something and Katie something else, and she'd forgotten to pick them up at the ferry. She wiped her hands on her cutoffs and apologized.

"I'm sorry. So sorry. How did you ever find the place?"

"People pointed us in the right direction, and, you know." The blonder of the two reached into her bag and pulled out a well-worn copy of a book called *On Fire Island*. Addison recognized it from her aunt's bookshelves. She had planned on reading it, but hadn't picked it up yet.

"We kind of took your place for its location," the woman said.

She winked, leaving Addison to wonder if the blonde had something in her eye, aside from their obvious twentysomething hopefulness. She fought the urge to grab both by the shoulders and shake it out of them.

"Let me show you to your room," she said instead.

She was eager to impress them after the faux pas of not meeting them at the boat.

She pointed out the fresh towels and travel-size toiletries she had stocked the bathroom with after Paresh left. She had chosen the shampoo, conditioner, and body wash bottles lifted from the Capella Shanghai from a small trunk full of tiny toiletries. It seemed that her aunt had documented her lifetime of travel by swiping the contents of maids' carts and hotel bathrooms the world over. Every day Addison spent among her things fueled more resentment toward her parents for keeping this electric, eclectic relative away from her.

She returned a few minutes later with a vase of cut flowers and a pitcher of water. A bunch more books sat on the bed—all by the same author. Her eyes darted from one to the other, not wanting to appear nosy but too curious not to look.

"We're hoping to get them autographed. I'm sure you've read them all," Katie said, running her finger across the chain of the gold necklace that said her name in the same font as Carrie Bradshaw's. It made Addison laugh that twentysomethings were still moving to New York City, hoping to emulate a decades-old television show.

"I haven't," she answered, surprised that her guests were so literary.

"I'm new around here. I recently inherited this place from my aunt. Just finding my way, really."

Why am I telling her all of this?

"We are so sorry about your aunt; they told us at the market."

Of course they did. Smallest town ever.

"Here." Katie handed her a book. "This one's my favorite, and the shortest of the bunch—if you want to borrow it. I'm dying that he's given up writing novels—I'm hoping to find him—you know, for his autograph."

The other woman, Jessie, came out of the bathroom in a bikini.

"Do I look fat?" she asked her friend.

"You never look fat," Katie replied.

"Well, I feel fat."

"Well, you don't look fat."

"You know, I think I'd rather look fat than feel fat."

"Same."

Addison laughed, and they both turned to look at her, as if they'd forgotten she was there.

She suddenly felt uncomfortable, picturing their review on Airbnb: *Nice space except the creepy owner didn't stay out of it.*

She accepted the book and the beach-going inspiration and soon headed there as well, positioning herself far enough away from her weekend guests not to encroach on their privacy or bump into the dreaded neighbor, whom she spotted down the way. She was thankful her friends were visiting the following weekend. Loneliness had been setting in, and she was tired of feeling like an outsider. As if sensing that, her only friendly neighbor, Sally the dog, walked from her owner's blanket to her own and presented her paw. She took it. Her duplicitous neighbor soon followed, holding two bottles of Amstel Light between his fingers like a barback.

"Peace offering?" he asked, passing her one of the bottles. "I'm really sorry about the other day," he continued. "I overre-acted."

"I'll say." She took the beer, more out of politeness than inter-est. She didn't really like beer, and it was hardly cocktail hour. It seemed to go well with her book though, which was a lot sexier than she had expected.

"Enjoying the book?" he asked.

She held it up like a prop.

"My renters lent it to me. They are looking for the author to sign it."

"I'm sure they are. You liking it?" he asked, again, more forcefully this time.

"It's all right, so far."

"Are you always so brutally honest?"

"I'm leading by example."

"I swear, I didn't know you were Gicky's niece."

Addison raised her eyebrows.

"The book gets better," he said, changing the subject.

She was surprised he had read it, and she hated how he was standing and she was sitting. She had to block her eyes from the sun and squint up at him. She wanted him to leave.

"Well, beginning with cunnilingus was a bold move," she offered, hoping to scare him off.

The word *cunnilingus* uncharacteristically rolled off her tongue like, well, cunnilingus. She quickly took a sip of the Am-stel to hide how truly uncomfortable this encounter was making her. It was cold and refreshing. Did she like beer now?

"It always is," he retorted.

Now she was blushing.

"I'll leave you to it," he said as Sally put her face in Addison's lap. She clearly had no intention of leaving. Addison scratched the first dog that didn't scare her behind the ears to seal the deal. She didn't like dogs now, just this dog.

"Return her on your way home," he laughed. "She's obviously smitten, missing female companionship, I guess."

His comment was primed for a comeback, and after the way he'd spoken to her the other morning, she couldn't resist.

"Really? I'm surprised the women aren't flocking to you—with all those earnest flirting moves of yours, I would think you would have landed a keeper by now," she snarked.

He looked taken back, and now that the joke had landed, she felt bad for insulting him.

What was it about this guy that brought out the worst in her?

"Enjoy the book"—he winked—"especially page one thirty-seven."

Jeez, does he have it memorized?

"Thanks for the beer," she said instead.

He briefly flashed his dimple and walked off.

Her Spidey sense told her that the entire interaction was BS. She could hear the old guy, Shep, warning him about making an enemy of the woman with her trigger finger on the landscape of their block. Total BS for sure.

She skipped to page 137, read a few lines, and quickly put the book down.

This Benjamin Morse must be very good in bed, she thought.

She picked up her phone and opened her group chat to distract herself from what had awoken between her legs.

LET'S DISCUSS NEXT WEEKEND!

She attached the link to the ferry schedule.

WHO'S ARRIVING WHEN?

The answers—filled with excitement and emojis—excited her as well. She couldn't wait to show her friends everything—to laugh with them, hopefully not cry again, and mostly to not be alone.

Chapter Fourteen

Jessie and Katie rapped on Addison's back door around eight o'clock, Saturday night, looking for ice.

"Hey, girl!" they said, upon entering. "Wanna pregame with us?"

They couldn't have been more than ten years younger than Addison, but it somehow seemed much more. She contemplated sinking to their level, or rising to it, depending on what she wanted out of the evening. When Jessie whipped out a lime from her pocket, and Katie a bottle of Casamigos from behind her back, she gave in. She had already tried meditating away her angst. Maybe drinking it away would work better.

Following the cocktails, they invited Addison to party with them in town. She weighed the invitation against the draw of a particularly stubborn avocado that had just ripened and would surely be inedible by tomorrow. Both the offer and the avocado went equally well with the tequila. She couldn't quite place when she began prioritizing what she would feel like the next day over the endless possibilities of a random night out—but the shift had most definitely occurred.

Summer of Addison! she reminded herself. Her life had been a bit lacking in the fun department lately, and these two were definitely on the prowl for it. Even if their idea of a celebrity crush seemed to be a horny author.

"I'm in," she said, half meaning it.

"Yaaaay!" they said in unison, giving Addison pause. They asked her to take them to the hottest places, and she admitted she did not know where those were. It was a good thing she was venturing out before her friends arrived. They would expect her to know where to go too.

The three women dropped in on a few bars, one with a heavy metal band playing and another that advertised a nightly foam party at midnight. Addison wasn't sure what a foam party was and had no desire to find out. They settled on a place called the Salty Pelican, which seemed to have a rowdy but not too crazy crowd. The Pelican seemed fun, with a bunch of people in the back gathered around the dartboard.

"This looks like the place in *On Fire Island*, doesn't it?" Jessie said, before turning to Addison for confirmation. Her face was blank.

"I don't understand how you haven't read it."

"She told us—she's new here," Katie said in her defense, before turning to Addison with an explanation. "*On Fire Island* is kind of like a memoir. It's told by the author's dead wife over one summer here. The author is a widower—he really lost his wife. That part's true."

"That's so sad, poor thing," Addison said.

"You should put the other one aside and start it tomorrow. You won't believe it," Jessie added.

Addison shook her head in agreement. Katie ordered them

three vodka sodas with lime, and loaded nachos, while Jessie headed for the bathroom. She returned looking like the cat that ate the canary.

"What did you do?" Katie asked.

"You'll see soon enough," Jessie said, smirking.

With that, Addison saw her neighbor walking toward them.

"Ugh. Hide me," she warned her new "friends." "My neighbor Ben is coming over here. He's awful. Total tool," she added, in what she thought was their language.

Katie looked that way and covered her face with her hands.

"Oh my God, Jessie, you didn't."

"Yes, I did. You haven't stopped saying what you would do if you ever got ahold of Benjamin Morse in person. Well, here he comes. I sent him a drink—from you!"

Katie turned ten shades of crimson, bent her head under the table, and ran a wand of gloss over her lips. Addison's lips, on the other hand, remained agape.

"I thought that guy's name was Ben Silver? Is Benjamin Morse a pen name?"

"I don't think so—but you can ask," Jessie suggested.

A million contradictory emotions careened through her brain like a game of emotional pinball.

Anger, betrayal, sympathy, empathy, confusion, and embarrassment.

Embarrassment won. She was mortified by just about everything she remembered saying to this poor widowed guy on the beach: *I'm surprised the women aren't flocking to you. . . . I would think you would have landed a keeper by now.* That thought was replaced by an image of Ben, not Shep, as she had previously imagined, blocking the bulldozer from destroying her street like some kind of lovelorn tree hugger from Greenpeace.

Ben was Benjamin Morse. The banter about the book now made sense too. Had she insulted his writing as well?

Ben Morse. Flirt. Neighbor. Author. Widower.

Kill me, she thought as she watched her neighbor walk their way.

Ben Morse seemed like he couldn't care less about any of their unfortunate interactions. He smiled, motioned for her to shove over, and slid beside her in the tight booth as if they were actual friends. She could feel his leg grazing hers and practically hugged the wall to avoid it.

"I thought your last name was Silver," she quietly blurted, adding, "Your garbage cans say Silver!"

"So do my beach chairs. If it ain't broke!"

Addison looked confused. He clarified, "I bought my house from Shep Silver a dozen years ago—along with those cans. They're sturdy and snap closed. You should invest in a couple."

"First time on Fire Island?" he asked her two houseguests, clearly eager to steer away from the garbage can incident.

"It is!" Katie gushed. "We took a quarter share in Westhampton this summer, but have never been out here, so thought we would compare the two."

"Here summer is a noun. Out there it's a verb."

Addison laughed at Ben's highbrow joke, but her houseguests looked confused by it.

"We spend the summer on Fire Island," he explained. "They summer in the Hamptons."

Jessie and Katie laughed now too. It was just the kind of witty observation that made him a bestselling author.

Katie brazenly put her hands on top of Ben's and got right down to business. "I'm so sorry about your wife." She may have had a tear in her eye. He pressed his lips together as if holding back laughter at her dramatics, which made Addison do the same.

The drinks showed up, and Katie released her embrace to make room for them.

"I've read every one of your books and, well, let's just say, I may be your biggest fan," she added.

"I don't know about that. There is a woman in Wichita who named her baby after me, and it's a girl. Benjamina Morse McClusky." Katie and Jessie both winced while Addison raised a glass.

"To Benjamina!"

Only Ben laughed and downed his drink. Addison kept up. Why, she didn't know.

Things turned lighter after that. Katie and Jessie asked Ben a million questions, like they were interviewing him at a book talk at the Strand. It was surprisingly illuminating, though nothing Addison couldn't google; it took every ounce of self-control she could muster not to pull her phone from her pocket right then and there to fact-check, although the answer to her most burning question—*Why didn't you tell me who you were?*—would not be found on the internet. Still, she learned plenty from the girls' inquisition. Benign things like his writing routine, sportswriting versus novel writing (apparently, he had his own column in *Sports Illustrated*), and a long list of questions regarding his public statement that he would never write another novel. They were fangirling all over him, and he was eating it up. Is this how he got women? Playing off their sympathy for his losing his wife and then hoping he could live up to the sex scenes in his novels? She remembered their earlier conversation on the beach.

Especially page one thirty-seven! Ugh.

She was back to disliking him again. His witty Hamptons–Fire Island comparison had momentarily tipped the scales in his favor. She loved a guy who could make her laugh—though she couldn't remember the last time she had encountered one.

"Did you ever see Josie again?" Jessie asked, causing Katie to scoot in real close so as not to miss a word. She turned her head back to Addison, for a quick recap.

"Josie is a woman he met the summer after his wife died who made him feel like he may be able to love again."

Addison also focused on Ben for answers, and he addressed her, as opposed to the Spice Girls. It was odd, as if he recognized that Addison would be interested in his explanation for more than folly. Until she realized he was right—she was interested in his explanation for more than folly.

"Her name wasn't really Josie. I changed it, and a bunch of her details, for obvious reasons."

"That was smart," Katie said, taking back his attention. "Remember what happened with 'Hey There Delilah'!"

Addison and Ben locked eyes, and they met on the same wavelength—laughter—a bit more at them than with them. There was no denying that Addison was enjoying their company. Ben seemed to be as well, though she wondered if it was just because his ego was being stroked. When their laughter subsided, he continued.

"We went on a date, but it was way too awkward with all the happily ever after pressure of the book."

"Makes sense," Katie commiserated, taking the moment to touch his hand again in sympathy. Though clearly amused, Ben seemed to relish the attention. Addison couldn't help but worry about her houseguest, who was intent on getting her books signed. Her gut told her Ben wouldn't take advantage of her, but she didn't really know him. She thought back to what Shep had said about Ben, that he hadn't been himself for a while.

Will the real Ben Morse please stand up?

She looked him over while the girls continued fawning. There was no denying her attraction to him. He was handsome in an imperfect sort of way. Definitely strong and fit. And he was tall. Being five nine herself, Addison loved a tall man. His answer about "Josie" didn't address whether he felt able to love again. That would be nice to know. She wondered if he even knew himself.

At the end of the night, Ben Morse offered Katie, whose "feet were killing her," a ride home on the back of his bike, while Jessie and Addison walked. It left Addison concerned and—though she hated to admit it—a tad jealous.

"I hope she'll be OK," Addison murmured.

"She's a big girl—no need to worry about her," Jessie assured.

Truth was, she was worried. She didn't want this guy to disappoint her again—well, not this guy, but the "You Again" guy whose eyes she met with again tonight. She didn't want more proof that that guy was full of shit.

Chapter Fifteen

Katie walked into the kitchen the next morning, sniffing the burnt air. Addison was trying her best to follow Gicky's famous scone recipe that was taped to the fridge. At least three reviews on Airbnb had praised them. She was on her second batch of the day. The first lived in the garbage pail, their outsides burned to a crisp, their insides with the distinct texture of sandpaper.

Addison thought to greet her with *How was your night?* but decided against it. She really didn't want to know. She had grabbed Ben Morse's last book, *On Fire Island*, from Gicky's shelf, a hardcover with a picture of him and Sally on the beach as his author photo. She had been determined to read a few chapters, but fell asleep soon after, and did not know if or when Katie had returned. Alcohol and reading don't really mix.

She was shaping the dough into a disc before cutting it into wedges, as the recipe stated, when Katie walked in. She nodded with her head toward the kitchen table for Katie to retrieve her book. It turned out that there were signed copies of everything Ben Morse had ever written on her aunt's bookshelves.

"Do you want your book back? I know you were hoping for an autograph."

"I got one!" Katie happily proclaimed, inching up her T-shirt to reveal Ben Morse's signature scrolled in Sharpie over her left hip.

"I'm getting it tattooed back in the city."

The taste of vomit rose in Addison's throat. She swallowed.

"Nice," she said, diverting her eyes. "You may be his biggest fan, after all."

Addison thought of Kathy Bates locking James Caan in her cabin in *Misery*. Again with the horror stories! She was glad these two would be on their way soon and wished she would never have to see Ben Morse again either. She stopped her mind from wandering to what precipitated his signing above Katie's hip. What a perv.

"When are you headed out? Do you know what ferry you're catching?"

"Soon! Jessie has a Venus Viva appointment."

Addison was too embarrassed to ask what that could be.

"Do you want me to walk you to the boat with my wagon?"

"No thanks, we have our wheelie bags. We had a great time." She added, "And sorry again about your aunt. She seemed like a really nice lady."

"Wait, you met my aunt?"

"Yes! At one of Ben's book signings. Looking back, I think she was already sick. She invited us here."

All she could say was, "Hmmm," while briefly air hugging Katie goodbye. She was so looking forward to her friends' visit.

To make her feelings official, she texted Kizzy, Lisa, and Pru in the group chat the minute the women left.

COUNTING THE DAYS!

A succession of hearts washed the rancid thoughts of her neighbor having sex with her young houseguest from her brain. Until her next interaction with him in front of the deli counter at the Bay Harbor Market.

Addison waited in line, clutching her list. She had decided to shop for her dinner and the next day's meals all at once instead of riding to the market whenever she felt hungry, as seemed to be the local practice.

Ben showed up behind her and looked over her shoulder.

"Figures, you have a list."

She folded it up, as if he were looking to cheat off her on an eighth-grade Spanish test.

"What's that supposed to mean?"

"It's just not done here. Like walking to town instead of riding. You don't bring a list to the market—you look around, see what the guy in front of you is getting, what jumps out at you."

"Next," the ear gauge guy called out. Addison was hoping to get the good-sandwich guy, but for what she was ordering, she assumed it didn't matter. She opened up her list and again covered it with her hand.

"Half pound of artichokes and a piece of tuna, please."

"For how many?"

"Just one."

"Same for me, boss," Ben called over her shoulder. Addison shot him a look.

"What?" he said. "Why should he put the tuna away, only to take it out again?"

Addison rolled her eyes while they waited for their fish to be cut and weighed. Ben's presence seeped under her skin before making it crawl. She turned and asked him, quietly, "If you weren't intending on lying to me, then why didn't you tell me who you were?"

"You were reading my book. We spoke about it. My picture is on the back flap. I assumed you knew."

"Well, I didn't finish it yet. And you introduced yourself as Ben. Not Benjamin Morse."

"You're right. 'Cause Ben is such an odd nickname for someone named Benjamin. My sincere apologies."

"So you assume everyone knows you?"

Two people walked by. "Hi, Ben," said one. "Hey," said the other.

He threw up his hands in a *case in point* way.

Addison rolled her eyes again. His excuse seemed like more BS, like he was trying anything until something stuck. She didn't trust this guy one bit.

The ear gauge guy handed them each their bags, and Addison purposefully chose the register that Ben had not. Even so, they walked out the door at the same time and jumped on their bikes, leaving them in the awkward position of riding home together. When Ben eventually turned left up the bay block, Addison went straight. Still, they both reached their corner at the same time as a bunch of guys had gathered on the ball field.

"Good timing," Shep called out. "Did you forget we had a game?"

"I did. I'll put my groceries away and grab my mitt."

"Hey, Addie!" Shep yelled. "We are short on guys, wanna play?"

"She doesn't want to play," Ben laughed snidely.

Shep looked over at Addison, who took Ben's laugh as a challenge.

"Do you play?" Shep asked.

"I played in high school."

"Suit up. Let's see what you got."

"Don't put her on my team," Ben mumbled, loud enough for Addison to hear.

"I wasn't planning on it," Shep said, followed by, "I told you to be nice to her. Can you at least try?"

Addison purposefully held back during batting practice, wanting to see the look on Ben's face when it counted. When she was officially up, she angled her feet to the base, got under the ball, and hit it right over Ben's head into the outfield. The feeling of the ball hitting her bat, that moment of connection when you know it's gonna be good, and the thrill of running the bases all filled Addison with a strength and confidence she hadn't felt since that seminal moment at the office when the rug was pulled out from under her.

When she arrived on second base, he let her have it.

"There's no way you haven't played since high school."

"I may have played in the Central Park advertising league— I didn't want to overpromise."

"You just did. These guys are gonna be all over you now— young blood."

"Well, you would know about young blood."

"What's that supposed to mean?" he called out behind her as she ran to third base.

Ben spent a lot of time pacing and kicking the dirt until two innings later, when Addison was at bat again. Another double. As her foot landed on second base mere seconds before the ball, Ben repeated his last question.

"What's that supposed to mean?"

"Katie, my houseguest—young blood?"

"Please, it wasn't a big deal. Don't be such a prude."

Not wanting to spend another second around him, Addison took off for third base just as the next batter hit the ball. Unfortunately, it was caught on the fly, and she awkwardly played monkey in the middle between second and third, while Ben and the third baseman tossed the ball back and forth over her head. Ben eventually chased her down, tagging her with the ball a little too aggressively.

"You're out!" he yelled as she fell to the ground.

"Sorry," he reached his hand out to her to help her up. She ignored it, got up herself, and stormed off the field.

While she had clearly had enough of the IRL Ben Morse, she spent the rest of the afternoon entrenched in his last novel. She laughed, she cried, she relished in the community of the story and wondered how close to the truth it really was. It felt very close, and Addison was left questioning everything she thought about Benjamin Morse all over again. She had to remind herself that it was billed as fiction. She couldn't wait to rehash the experience with her friends and thought about sending them all a link to the book in advance—required reading.

Friday couldn't come soon enough.

Regardless of any of it, Addison went to sleep that night heartbroken for the sweet man in the book who had lost his wife and unborn child.

In the morning she felt inspired to take her sculpting to the next level. She had yet to attempt anything more intricate than a vase or a bowl.

She went out to the studio, where a full-length mirror shoved behind some boxes caught her eye. She happily recalled her sculpting classes in college. At first, she had felt awkward and uncomfortable with a naked man or woman sitting in the middle of a circle, especially a man. She was eighteen when she had started college and had never seen a fully naked man before. It took some getting used to. When she did, she happily found herself transposing their bodies expertly into clay, penises and all.

"Mastering the human form is imperative to mastering any medium," her professor would preach.

She leaned the full-length mirror against the wall in front of her and stripped off her clothes, taking in her image in detail, the length of her arms, the line of her jaw. She placed a block of clay on the turntable and set up an armature that Gicky had created from plumbing equipment and hanger wire, before slowly mapping out her intentions. Next, she remembered how, with practice, she had trained her eyes to replicate the shapes she was seeing with her fingers. Though rusty, the skill that had taken her years in college to master came back.

She felt happy in a way she hadn't experienced since being fired. Or maybe way before that. *Be in the moment, no judgment*, she thought, like the signs she used to scoff at in HomeGoods. She wondered if she was growing or shrinking.

Week Four

Chapter Sixteen

Kizzy Weinstein was endlessly looking forward to the weekend away with her girlfriends, but first had to navigate the "blessed event" that was her husband's thirty-second birthday. She strolled up Lexington Avenue and into the famous French patisserie that she had been purchasing madeleines and macarons from since she was a little girl, with the full expectation that the employees would greet her as if they had never seen her before.

"Bon après-midi," she said, in her best high school French, with no response from the mademoiselle behind the counter.

"An extra-large mille-feuille, s'il vous plaît, with *Happy Birthday, Rome* written on top."

Kizzy had ordered that same dessert, Rome's favorite, from that same bakery since they were married. Before that, his mother would order it for him. And for most of his life (a little over half) Kizzy had been there to delight in the thousand layers of puffed pastry and cream with the white chocolate card that read *Happy Birthday, Rome* perched on top.

Kizzy and Rome had dated since freshman year of high school, when he transferred to the posh private school she had attended since kindergarten. They stayed together through college, she at Brown, he, close enough for many a fun weekend together, at Tufts. They married after Rome had finished grad school, and soon purchased a two-bedroom on Seventy-Ninth and Park. It was only a few blocks in either direction from where they had each grown up. Kizzy hoped this would be the year that they replaced the guest room sofa with a crib. They were finally both set in their careers and, at thirty-two, the timing was perfect.

The woman barely acknowledged her before disappearing into the back of the bakery.

Aaah. The French, Kizzy thought as she looked down at the decadent array of pastries and cakes. She had been coming to this patisserie with its checkerboard floor and glass-topped mahogany display counter since she had to stand on her tippy-toes to see over it. As usual, the smell upon entering the shop brought her right back to those Sunday mornings with her dad, their repertoire always the same.

"Can I have a chocolate croissant today?" she would ask.

To which he would take his time contemplating his answer, as he always left the house with strict instructions of no sweets before lunch.

"OK. But don't tell your mother," he would say, as if it were a one-time-only event.

The memory made her smile.

A man came out from the back with a boxed cake.

"That was fast," Kizzy commented.

"I'm a little bit confused, mademoiselle. I thought when you called, you asked for it to be delivered?"

Kizzy felt her cheeks burn. She hated when Rome's mother took over. She would always call days in advance with things like this while Kizzy was a last-minute, stop-in-on-your-way-home type. Kizzy stood firm that both methods brought the same results. Case in point.

"Sorry. My mother-in-law strikes again."

"Ah, the dastardly belle-mère. I have one too."

It may have been the sweetest interaction she'd ever had at the Café Payard, until she looked down at the words scribbled on a yellow slip taped to the box.

Deliver to the Mark Hotel Suite 625 by 3:00.

Her whole body trembled as she walked the three avenues and three blocks to the Mark. Every step felt as if someone were hanging on to her ankles, pulling her back in the opposite direction. She did not give in to it, but instead, glided purposefully through the doors of the swanky European hotel and headed straight for the elevator. That feeling of stepping into a place, acting like you belong, usually brought her a wave of confidence that landed with a proud smile. Not today.

Please don't let this be happening again, she prayed absurdly as she watched the floors go by.

Two, three, four, five, six. Ding! *Life as you know it is now over.*

It had been two years and countless therapy sessions since Kizzy had discovered a room service receipt from the Mark Hotel in Rome's suit pocket. She hadn't been snooping; it had never even occurred to her to snoop. She'd been standing in the doorway of their apartment waiting for the dry cleaner to come for a pickup when she reached into his pants pocket and pulled out a room service bill for Suite 625 at the Mark—specifically buttermilk pancakes, eggs Benedict, and two banana-berry smoothies. The walls had spun around her, and her legs had swayed from side to side as if she were at the epicenter of an earthquake. Her husband was having an affair.

When confronted, Rome admitted it and swore he would never see the woman again. He promised that he got caught up, even obsessed with the fact that he had only ever been with one woman—Kizzy—for his entire life. He assured her he had absolutely gotten it out of his system. And though, in her wildest dreams, Kizzy would never imagine she could be the woman who forgave an indiscretion such as that, she did indeed forgive her husband. But things hadn't been the same since.

Once she knew that her marriage existed on a fault line, the stability it had given her was lost.

She knocked on the door of Suite 625, shouted, "Delivery," in someone else's voice, and held the cake box up in front of the peephole.

The door swung open to reveal the same robe-clad blonde that Rome had been sleeping with two years before—a woman he had known at Tufts. As she called back to him, "Close your eyes, birthday boy!" Kizzy wondered if this had been going on straight through or had recently started up again. She had detected a change in Rome lately. He seemed distant. She had even asked him about it. He cited stress at work, and she believed him. Believing was so much easier than falling back into the dark hole of doubt. She steadied her hands, determined not to make a fool of herself.

The blonde turned back around. Her face quickly contorted at the sight of her lover's wife standing there in front of her, taking her in. "Tell Rome he has one week to move his things out of our apartment," Kizzy managed.

She kept the mille-feuille.

Chapter Seventeen

Addison was quite excited for her friends to come. She missed them and was eager to take part in a group analysis of the contrarian next door. Even though they were not due to arrive until Friday, Addison had everything set. She would put Kizzy and Pru in the guesthouse and let Lisa bunk alone on the pullout couch in the studio. Even then, Addison imagined, they would still hear her snoring.

Until then, she would busy herself with the clay. *Busy herself* was actually an understatement. She would relish in it.

Addison had remembered from college how to work the kiln in Gicky's studio, but before doing so, she watched a refresher video, just to be safe. She didn't want to set the entire island on fire—though that would certainly make it easier to decide about the house. The next day, when she'd pulled the fired pieces from the kiln, she marveled at the explosive patterns of yellow and green. She knew exactly what she would use them for: she would place flowers in the vases and arrange them beside her guests' beds. The day before, she had combed the beach for oyster shells and decoupaged them with a floral paper she found in the kitchen. She painted their edges in gold leaf and wrote each of her friends' names on them to set on their pillows. It was a nice touch that, if she weren't selling the place, would make a great guest tradition—deflecting any scone disappointment. Addison loved making art again and vowed not to let it slip from her life a second time.

She fell asleep reading on the couch that night and was startled at around ten by her phone buzzing incessantly. She had unknowingly missed a bunch of texts from Kizzy. The last one being:

Pick me up at the 10:30 ferry.

It was ten thirty-five. She was late, but Kizzy was two days early.

She read back on the chain of texts.

Can I come to where you are?

I left Rome.

He's with that woman again.

I'm on my way to you.

PLEASE ANSWER

Addison threw on sweats and biked to the boat. When she got there, Kizzy was sitting on a bench curled up into as small a ball as possible, holding nothing but a purse and a cake box. Addison walked Kizzy and the bike home in silence, set her up in the guesthouse, and rubbed her back until she fell asleep. And while Addison checked on her often, delivering and collecting barely touched cups of tea and toast with butter or jam, Kizzy slept for two days, during which Rome texted Addison a dozen times looking for her.

On the third day, the one on which all three friends had been scheduled to arrive, Addison woke to find Kizzy standing in the kitchen in a hot-pink bikini (Addison's) fixing herself a cup of coffee. Sally, the dog, sat at her feet. Her hips were swinging from side to side to her new anthem, blasting from her phone.

"You traded in a Ferrari for a Twingo."

And just like that, she went from post-breakup Carrie Bradshaw to post-breakup Shakira. Kizzy lowered the song and turned to Addison.

"What's with the dog?"

"She's my tramp widower neighbor's, but I somehow have joint custody."

Kizzy laughed.

"You hate dogs."

"I don't hate dogs, I'm just sorta terrified of them—but this one feels human—she has people eyes."

"I noticed that."

"My suit looks good on you." Addison smiled.

"Thanks. I found it drying in the outdoor shower. Is there a place I could pick up a few things to wear? I kind of ran away after confronting Rome and his lover in their suite at the Mark." She handed Addison a cup of coffee with honey and almond milk, just the way she liked it. It was hard for Addison to believe that anyone would give up this person who was so beautiful, inside and out. She began to say it—

"Kizzy, I'm so, so—"

"Don't," Kizzy interrupted her. "Seventeen years of my life. I can't. I just can't waste one more minute on him."

After breakfast, Addison broke into Gicky's collection of caftans, each more fabulous than the last. The two women sashayed to the beach, Sally happily in tow. They both watched as Kizzy swam in the ocean.

"I hope you can save her, Sally," Addison told her new furry friend. "'Cause I'm useless."

Though it was quite obvious that Kizzy would save herself.

Soon, hunger kicked in for Kizzy, and the two rode into town for lobster rolls, fries, and Bloody Marys, followed by some shopping. The retail therapy definitely put a smile on Kizzy's face. She walked out of the last shop wearing one of those sweatshirts that read *Fire Island, Blissfully Unaware*.

"I wish I could stay here forever," she said, motioning to the catchphrase on the sweatshirt.

"You don't scare me. I would love it if you stayed forever."

"I have to get back to work."

"Do you though? You said it's dead in the summer."

"I'll at least stay the week. That's the deadline I gave Rome. What time do the shrink and the lawyer arrive? I can use them both, unfortunately."

"They'll be on the six o'clock boat. Should we go out tonight or stay in?"

"Let's cook tonight, so we can fill them in, in peace, and hit one of these places"—she motioned to the left and the right like a flight attendant pointing out the exit rows—"tomorrow night. Good?"

"Perfect."

They stopped at the market and bought fresh clams, linguini, a big loaf of Italian bread, and the ingredients for a salad, which they made before picking up their friends at the boat.

"Brace yourself for a scene," Addison warned as they descended on the Friday night ferry. Kizzy got lost in the middle of a very conventional family—a mom, two kids, and even a dog waiting for, she presumed, the dad. Pain washed over her face, and her eyes welled up, which, while sad, let Addison know she wasn't just burying the whole thing. That was what Addison would have done.

"I'm never going to have that, Addison."

"You don't know that."

"I'm starting over at thirty-two."

"So? I'm older."

"But you don't want that." She motioned to the family. The kids were now jumping up and down, yelling, "Daddy's home!" It tugged at Addison's heart too. She didn't *not* want it—she had just wanted to be a success in her career first. It was too upsetting to talk about, so she didn't.

"You'll have whatever you want, Kezia. I'm sure of it," she said instead.

Addison used Kezia's given name only when she was very serious. Derived from the Hebrew Cassius, meaning "cinnamon," it had been chosen by her parents upon looking at their newborn beautiful baby girl with her cinnamon-colored skin. Kizzy loved both her Hebrew proper name and the nickname she shared with a famous character from *Roots*. It felt like the perfect blend of her ancestors.

"How can you be so sure?" Kizzy asked, leaning in for a much-needed hug.

"Because you're a Ferrari, not a Twingo. You'll come in first. You'll win."

And while Kizzy did not know what it was she would be

winning, both the hug and Addison's words seemed to make her feel better.

"They're here," Addison announced. "Shake it off—or don't. Whatever you want."

Kizzy waved her hands in the air and shook out her whole being, greeting their friends with laughter instead of tears.

On the walk back to the house, Prudence and Lisa put into words everything Addison had felt when first arriving on the island but had been too embarrassed to share with the off-putting agent. The people pulling wagons, the catchy names on the houses, like Washing Towels and Glory Days, and the deer walking around like they owned the place. It all blew them away.

The same enthusiasm bubbled over when it came to her house. Their eyes darted from the knickknacks to the travel posters of the Montreux Jazz Festival and the New York World's Fair to the vintage appliances in the kitchen.

"This whole place is like a life-size time capsule," Lisa commented. "I love it!"

And they hadn't even seen the studio yet. Addison was saving that for after dinner. She had a surprise for them.

Addison made the clam sauce while the others sat around the kitchen table listening to Kizzy's lament. Yes, she was troubled by the state of her life and the end of her marriage, but she wasn't all gloom and doom about it.

"The truth is," she explained, "I'm a little relieved."

Six eyes stared at her, anticipating an explanation. She obliged.

"I went to a funeral with my mom a few months ago, a distant cousin of hers. The husband was bereft, crying at the grave, the whole thing. They were married for over fifty years, but apparently, when they were younger, the wife had had an affair with their butcher."

"It's always the butcher," Addison interrupted. Kizzy agreed, and in her best Jewish accent added, "Give a woman the right cut of brisket . . ."

"It's the baker for me," Lisa said, tapping on her "sweet tooth."

Pru smirked. "You know I love a good candle."

They all laughed, hard, like you do with your best friends, when laughter begets laughter.

"So, we get in the car to go home, and my mother says she couldn't believe how destroyed the husband had been after she had cheated on him. And I'm thinking it must have been last week, but it was thirty years before."

"People cheat all the time. What's your point?" Pru asked.

"I feel like I have a second chance not to be that man, standing at his lifelong love's grave with people pitying him—not because his wife died, but because she was unfaithful. Fifty years of sickness and health, children, grandchildren, weddings, funerals, vacations—none of that's what is remembered. It really depressed me when I thought about the fact that my marriage would be remembered like that too, and that so much space would be given to Rome's bad behavior."

"I can't believe your mother pointed that out. A little tone-deaf, no?"

"I never told my parents what happened with Rome the first time. I knew they would never forgive him, and you know how close we are to them both."

"Have you told them now?"

"No, but I'll have to. I came straight here. The only person I told was the train conductor. Apparently, they only accept cash on the Long Island Rail Road. All I had was a credit card and a sob story."

"There's an app for that, you know."

"Well, pity worked fine."

They all paused to think of their friend Kizzy breaking the poor conductor.

"Enough about me!" She smiled while topping off everyone's glasses. "This is meant to be a fun weekend. Let's talk about Addison's neighbor and how soon till they hook up."

Addison shouted, "No way," in protest.

Lisa countered, "Of course not, 'cause anyone who challenges you is automatically off-limits."

"That is not true."

"You are the only person I know who is searching for *meh*."

"That's ridiculous. I'm not searching for *meh*."

"Really? Do you want us to scroll back on the group chat to present evidence?" Pru said, stepping into lawyer mode. "Mitch from HR, that bartender you dated from the Pony Bar, Mike Stemple. You always go for the wet noodles."

"What about that other guy from the gym—Pete?" Addison asked defiantly.

"Why do you think we called him Pasta Pete? Wet noodle!"

"Not Philip, Philip wasn't a wet noodle," Addison proclaimed, defending herself.

"That's correct. Ergo, the broken engagement followed by the mad escape to the East Coast."

Oh my God. Had she left Philip because she was too scared that he would break her heart? No. She remembered it perfectly. She was too young—she felt trapped.

"It's time to shuffle the playlist, man," Pru insisted.

Addison laughed and conceded, "You may have a point—but this is a different scenario. I actually think I may hate this guy. He took advantage of my houseguest."

"Let me get this straight. You liked the guy that you met on the ferry, but at the same time you hated the guy whose dog keeps showing up in your living room."

"Not hated, disliked."

"OK. Then you liked the guy who lost his wife in the book, but disliked your neighbor who you think tricked you and then berated you over the bungee cord fiasco?"

"Hated."

"And now?"

Pru cut in. "Let's see a picture of this guy."

Addison pulled a few of his books from the shelves and passed them out. They all turned to various iterations of his author photo, followed by a deep dive into their phones. There was no shortage of images and reading material about Benjamin Morse. Pru was the first to pick her head up from the scroll.

"At least he's not boring."

"Stop!" said Addison.

"Remember that last guy who came for dinner with us. He said nothing for like five hours," Pru said, supplying evidence.

Lisa stood up for Addison.

"OK, enough, you two. Addison. Do not go for this guy. He clearly has a host of issues."

"I wasn't planning on it. I can't stand him."

"You couldn't stand that guy from the gym who never wiped off the treadmill, but you dated him for two months," Pru observed slyly.

"God. I really thought Kizzy's issues would take the spotlight off of me. Can we change the subject from my questionable sexual escapades?"

"You could probably use some questionable sexual escapades," Kizzy added under her breath. Addison wasn't having it.

"What I could use is a job. Let's figure that out, please."

Lucky for Addison, the last clam in the pan popped open, and they all sat down to break bread. Dinner was delicious, and after they had cleaned up, Addison brought them to the studio for the big surprise. She had set up four canvases in a circle and filled a table with some of the most eclectic objects she could find in the house. It was right out of Painting and Drawing 101. They all dove in, painting and laughing and drinking wine and eating Rome's birthday cake from the box until three in the morning, when they finally crashed.

Addison and Lisa (and Sally) awoke in the morning to a note on the fridge from Pru and Kizzy.

Gone for a bike ride. If you want to meet us, call.

They headed for the beach instead, where Lisa took the time to quietly slip in some friendly analysis.

"Why do you think you pick the wrong men?" she asked Addison.

"I'm not sure—but I have a feeling you have a theory."

"I do. I think it's a form of self-preservation."

Lisa really was a brilliant analyst—but Addison was in no mood for it. She thought back to her own developing theory—how, at the tender age of twelve, when kids are beginning to think about boys or girls in that coupling way, Addison had her heart broken by the finest man she thought she knew. Naturally, she pivoted.

"I am in a work crisis, not a relationship crisis."

Addison wasn't being entirely truthful. She didn't really understand how she had become anchorless, but ever since she'd heard that was how Gicky imagined her, she hadn't stopped thinking about it.

She shifted gears again, explaining, "Remember playing Chutes and Ladders as a kid? I feel like I made it three-quarters of the way up the board, then landed on that one shitty slide that takes you all the way back to the beginning."

"You will get another job. You're exceptional at what you do," Lisa consoled her, before going right back to her own theory.

"Have you ever been cheated on?"

Addison thought back through her relationships, way back, and landed on the very first.

"Does it count if it was in the eighth grade?"

"It may count more. Wasn't that around the time your grandfather died?"

"A year later. I'm surprised you remember that story. I've been thinking about it a lot lately. You may be the only person I ever shared it with."

"Well, that could be a part of the problem. Nothing stays bottled up forever. Tell me about the boy who cheated."

"Come on. Are we really doing this?"

"We may as well. Summer of Addison, remember?"

"I never agreed to that."

"Just tell me."

"Fine. It was eighth grade, and everybody was constantly asking each other, 'Who do you like?'"

"God, I remember that," Lisa said. "Suzy Carmichael texted me that question in biology, and I said Chris Tevlin—who I didn't even like, but I had to answer something. Then she told him."

"Bitch," they both said at the same time, before laughing.

Her response made Addison wonder whether Lisa was the type of therapist who sat silently nodding, admitting zero personal information, or the type who shared with her patients like they were a couple of chatting friends. Addison had never been to therapy. Thinking back, aside from the broken engagement, things had always gone as planned, and she never felt she had to. Now she wondered if that was really the case.

"Eighth grade was hell," she said, with a wince.

"Complete hell. So, what happened to you?" Dr. Lisa asked, again.

"Let me set the scene. I'm fourteen, haven't got my period yet, flat as a board. I had been dating Jeffrey Pearlman, the cutest boy in school, for six whole months."

"That's a long time for middle school."

"Right? I thought so too. Hell, it still is! So, we are all at Jonathon Strauss's house playing spin the bottle, and it's my turn. I carefully spin it—more like place it—toward Jeffrey. We kiss, and everyone yells eighth-grade things like 'Whoa, baby,' and 'Get a room.' We were good at kissing, probably much better than the other kids, you know, 'cause we had been practicing for six months, and there was literally nothing else to do. I mean, maybe I was at the point in development where it felt like there were marbles under each nipple. Remember that?"

"Not till you reminded me—but yes. Now I do. They really hurt, remember that?"

Addison nodded and grimaced.

"So, as per the rules of spin the bottle, it was his turn next. He spun without manipulation, which was the first stab in my heart, and it landed right in between me and Sofie Bonelli. Let me give you a visual. Sofie Bonelli was already five foot six and at least a 34C. She was adopted, and people were convinced she was really sixteen. Forget looking like her little sister. I looked like I could have been her kid.

"So Jeffrey leaned in, and I closed my eyes and puckered up for a repeat performance. When I opened them, he and Sofie were all out making out, as if we were playing seven minutes in heaven—not spin the bottle—and the entire circle of kids just sat there with their chins on the floor. The next day he broke up with me and the two of them became a couple."

"That is really messed-up," Lisa acknowledged. Addison greatly appreciated the magnitude of her empathy.

"Though you must know now that it was all about the boobs."

"I knew it then too, but from that day on, I was convinced that the dreamier the guy, the more likely he was to break my heart."

"And you resigned yourself to dating beneath you ever since?"

"Not consciously, but maybe."

"Realizing why you do something is the first step to changing a pattern."

Lisa rarely used modern therapy–speak. She was old school, reluctant to throw around emotional buzzwords like *gaslighting* and *trauma bonding* or labeling every Todd, Drake, and Hunter a narcissist. Lisa spoke plain English, and Addison appreciated it. She bet her patients did too.

Addison pulled out her copy of *On Fire Island* and handed it to her.

"Read this. I wouldn't mind your professional opinion."

"I thought we weren't obsessing over this guy."

"I'm not. I stand firmly on dislike in real life. But the guy in the book—he's a good one."

"So's Huckleberry Finn." She shook the volume like a maraca. "It's fiction."

"Read it first. Then comment."

Chapter Eighteen

Sun-kissed and relaxed, the four friends walked to town for dinner around eight. They ate at a little fish place at the east end, then headed to the bar that Addison had scoped out with Katie and Jessie. This time, she was greeted with open arms. Open ballplayer arms, to be exact.

"Addie the Slugger!" Shep Silver waved them over from across the bar. "Come. Drink with the pros."

"Addie?" Kizzy asked. "Slugger?" Lisa followed.

They weaved their way to the other side of the bar, where a big group of ballplayers congregated around the dartboard. The women nudged each other down the line till they each registered that Ben Morse was there too, playing darts.

"He's even taller than I thought," Pru whispered.

They all knew that was top of Addison's requirements in a man.

"Yet still an asshole," Addison responded.

The men made some room for the four ladies at the bar, and Shep ordered them all shots, Ben included, and proposed a toast.

"To our new homeowner with a killer swing!"

A leggy blonde grabbed Ben's shot from his hand and downed it with a mischievous smile.

Addison tried not to stare, but found it hard to focus on anyone or anything else. She whispered to her posse.

"Why do women find that man attractive? Please explain it to me."

"He's got that unattainable air about him. Women like the chase," Kizzy replied.

"Coat that in pain and loss, and he's not just a challenge, but a challenge with a cause," Lisa preached.

"Plus, you've read his books—I'm surprised you have to ask," Pru added.

Ben collected the darts from the board. "Who's next?" he asked. Catching Addison's eye, he joked, "Want to pretend you don't know how to play darts too?"

Addison gave him the death glare, turned, and headed for the bathroom.

"Wow, your friend really hates me," he vented to Kizzy.

"She's mad about you taking advantage of her houseguest."

"Taking advantage? She begged me."

"Wow. I'm starting to hate you too. She begged you to have sex with her?"

"What? I didn't have sex with her."

Kizzy looked skeptical.

"I just signed her hip—well, not really her hip—more like her stomach."

Kizzy laughed.

"You believe me, right?"

"Yes, I believe you. But I'm not sure it's good practice to go around branding women's hips."

"It was above her hip! But to be honest, I kind of regretted it the morning after."

The blonde approached, flipped her locks, and said, "I'll play—but you may have to teach me."

Ben gave in to said blonde, making her laugh as he showed her the proper form. When Addison returned from the restroom, she couldn't stop her eyes from gravitating to the two of them, wondering if the name of the shot, Sex on the Beach, was foreshadowing for their night's adventure. She wanted to grab the woman and warn her, though there was probably no point. She was likely hoping for a page 137 kind of night. Heat rose to Addison's face. Why did she care what this guy did? Her friends were right about her MO. Gicky was right about her being unanchored. She had to get her shit together, figure out what she wanted from life. She knew one thing for sure—she didn't want the equivalent of leaving her house to some niece she barely knew. She ordered another drink to numb her thoughts.

As Addison and her crew were leaving the bar, pathetically earlier than Shep, who was near fifty years their senior, the old man grabbed Addison's arm.

"Over-under game tomorrow?"

"What's that?"

"Old tradition, very fun. Big barbecue at my place afterward. Bring your friends. They won't play—but they can watch."

"I'll be there," she said, meaning it. It *would* be fun. She had loved being on the field and playing ball. It made her feel confident, strong, and like a kid again. There were so many things about Fire Island that brought about that feeling. The bike riding, the lack of a dress code, and, mostly, the being blissfully unaware thing. Though embracing that mantra seemed like inviting a big reckoning, if, when September rolled around, Addison was still jobless. *Unemployment is not conducive to carefreeness. Or is it?*

On the way home, Kizzy filled them all in on her enlightening conversation with Ben regarding the newly tattooed houseguest. And though she told Kizzy she didn't believe it, Addison felt a wave of relief, the magnitude of which she found alarming. She knew she was treading that thin line between love and hate, like a fickle teenager. She needed to stop wasting her time thinking about this emotionally unavailable guy. Wasting time was something she no longer felt comfortable doing.

Still, Addison fell asleep that night thinking of Ben. Not Ben at the bar playing darts with that blonde woman, but the other Ben. The one who helped her with her bags on the boat and talked her through her little breakdown on the sidewalk. She tried to push that Ben out of her mind, but the thoughts were too pleasant to dismiss.

She woke with a start to the distinct sound of a "truck" rumbling down her block. Garbage day! While her bungee cord game had definitely improved, she had taken to putting out the trash in the morning as an extra precaution. As she wheeled out the cans, she could see Ben at the top of the beach stairs talking to a blonde woman—seemingly last night's blonde woman.

And she hated him all over again. Though this time, she wasn't sure why.

She picked up her pace, but not enough to avoid him.

"You playing today?" Ben called out from the sidewalk as he passed. He said it in a benign way, which made it impossible to tell whether he wanted her to or not.

"Maybe," she said, matching his tone and clapping her hands

for Sally to come to her. Ben grabbed Sally's collar and guided her toward his own house.

"Tramp," Addison mumbled under her breath at her bewildering neighbor, before retreating into the house. An hour later, she was on the field stretching her quads. Her three hungover friends were in the bleachers nursing iced coffees.

The annual Over/Under game was created to honor two local heroes and legendary Bay Harbor ballplayers who were killed on 9/11. Now, so many years later, the Overs were mostly made up of the people who held memories of the two extraordinary men, while the Unders knew them only by their legacies. They were lined up by age, and Addison found her spot on the left side of the cutoff—an actual line drawn in the clay between third and home. Ben was the first person standing at the youngest end of the Overs. It had to have been a recent move from Under to Over for him. He looked up and down the line intensely, confirming her suspicion. They locked eyes for a moment, and she smirked knowingly. It had to bother him to be an Over. Whichever guy was in charge, Eddie, she believed, walked from one end of the line to the other, counting the players on the Unders, while Shep counted the Overs. At this point Shep played only one inning, more out of respect and nostalgia than anything else—but he was definitely the unofficial captain of the Overs. Shep and Eddie met in the middle.

"I've got thirty-two," Shep reported.

"Thirty-seven," Eddie countered before moving the last three guys on his line to the Overs, leaving Addison to be the oldest Under. She breathed a sigh of relief before catching Ben's eye again. Now it was his turn to smirk knowingly. He watched Matty, his across-the-street neighbor, a college kid who had recently returned from a month in Barcelona, make his way to the field. Everyone was thrilled to see him except Addison. It hadn't even entered her mind that she could be an Over, a thought more depressing than her aging ovaries. A mixture of bro hugs and big cheers from the Unders ensued, followed by the kid taking his rightful place on the Unders team, followed by Addison being slid to the other side of the line. Ben's smirk was now an all-out laugh.

She could think of nothing better than to stick her tongue out at him.

Shep called out the order. It was Addie third and Ben fourth. In the first inning, Addison got on base with a two out count, and Ben struck out, which pissed him off for sure. But in the last inning, everything changed.

The Overs were down by one. It was two outs when Addison got up at bat. Kizzy, Lisa, and Pru held their breath along with everyone else rooting for them. Addison hit a powerful line drive, boom, and ran the bases as fast as her long legs allowed—which was fast. She made it to second. Still two outs, Ben followed with a home run. The crowd rose to their feet as Addison rounded third and headed home, followed by Ben. When he reached home plate, Addison raised her hand for a fist bump, but Ben scooped her in his arms and spun her around instead. He was strong, and the scoop and subsequent spins made her feel, for lack of a better word, petite, possibly for the first time in her life.

You could almost see their joy turn to embarrassment. Ben stopped and stood Addison safely on the ground, gently placing his hands on her shoulders to steady her.

"I'm sorry," he said. "I got carried away. I can't remember the last time the Overs won."

"It's OK," she laughed, adding proudly, "We did it!"

She hugged him, partially to make him feel better for running her around the field like a trophy, and partially because she already missed being in his arms.

And that was it. That was the moment where she crossed that thin line between love and hate. Her friends looked out on the field and shook their heads in unison.

"So much for her not hooking up with her douchey neighbor," Lisa whispered in Kizzy's ear.

"I don't know. I mean, from what I've seen so far, she's not his type. I think the gentleman prefers blondes."

Lisa pulled out her phone and googled Ben Morse's late wife. Their *New York Times* wedding announcement came up, and Lisa passed the picture of his petite brown-haired bride down the line for all to contemplate.

"Hmm. He's not into doppelbängers, I guess," Pru quipped, causing them all to fall into hysterics.

Addison ran up the bleachers, her feet barely touching the ground.

"What's so funny?"

They blew off the question and changed the subject.

"So happy you won!"

"Should we hit the beach?"

"Yes. And we're invited to a big barbecue at Shep's tonight to celebrate. Want to go?" she asked.

"Lisa and I are catching the five o'clock ferry," Pru informed her.

"Kizzy? Does that mean you're staying?"

"Yes—I think I'll stay the week."

"But then she needs to go home and get a divorce. I want this whole thing behind her by the end of September," Pru said. "Without kids to worry about, it's truly possible."

Pru was all business, but it was obvious that the hard truth pained Kizzy. She wished she had a kid or two to worry about. Seventeen years with Rome should have given her at least that. Addison read her expression.

"Don't think about all that now, Kezia. Just enjoy the week."

"True, your troubles will still be there in seven days. You may as well put them aside for a few and enjoy yourself," Lisa counseled.

"Besides, for all I know, I may be right behind her."

Pru said this casually, very casually. Her tone almost gave them more pause than her words. Then she backpedaled.

"Only kidding. Let's get to the beach."

On the beach, Pru sat next to Kizzy, who took the opportunity to make sure her friend, the only one of the four with a husband and child, was OK. She pulled her nose out of the 1984 *Rolling Stone* she had found in the house, the first of twenty-three issues featuring Madonna on the cover, and asked her straight up, "Everything OK at home, Pru?"

Pru peered over her *Time* Best of '90 issue, a forced smile rising over an image of Bart Simpson. "All good," she said unconvincingly. A few minutes later, the truth slowly came out. It's not uncommon for a coupled person to question their own relationship when a friend goes through a breakup. Clearly Pru was deep in introspection about her marriage.

"You really didn't know, Kizzy? There were no signs?"

"Of course there were signs. What's up, Pru?"

Pru put down her magazine and spilled it.

"It's not him, it's me."

Lisa, who had always thought of Pru's marriage as exemplary, especially compared to the many couples she counseled, couldn't help herself from butting in.

"Pru, are you having an affair?"

"No! Absolutely not. It's a little thing—I feel silly even bringing it up."

"Just tell us," Kizzy said.

She leaned forward in her chair, and they all followed suit, even though the nearest person to them was a beach block away.

"Tom is a brooder, while, as you all know, I'm more explosive. So, when he's angry at me for anything from forgetting to pick up the dry cleaning to me saying something mean or insensitive, he gets quiet and doesn't want to talk about it till he's ready. I need to talk about things right away or I escalate—quickly. We've tried to work on it over the years—you know, meeting in the middle somewhere—but we never really figured it out, and now it's our pattern when we fight. He broods, I explode."

"Couples fight," Lisa said, rubbing Pru's back as she did so. "To some degree, it's healthy."

"Well, I stopped fighting. Just me. He broods, and I don't give a crap. Three hours later, three hours—and I still don't care that he is pissed at me about something. Sometimes, I apologize without even arguing my side—me, not arguing my side. Can you imagine? I don't even care to win. I think it's the beginning of the end."

"You can work on that, Pru. Get to the bottom of it," Lisa counseled. "When couples stay in a rut, it becomes harder to dig out. Keep it light. Ask if he's noticed that things have been a little wonky between you lately."

"Yes," Kizzy preached, "don't let it get ahead of you. Look at me!"

"You look pretty OK, Kizzy," Pru commented.

"Don't let my calm, chill demeanor fool you. I'm in lobotomy mode."

All three looked intently at Kizzy for further explanation.

"My grandmother taught me how to do it. It's a temporary vacation from reality, until you get your strength back."

Addison and Pru turned to Lisa, who just shrugged, while Kizzy continued.

"This is the hardest thing I've ever dealt with. Whenever I really think about it, my heart races, my hands tremble, and I feel like vomiting. Get your fire back, Pru, you don't want this. This is the worst!"

"She's right, Pru—about how hard it is. The lobotomy method, I'm not so sure about. You know I'm working on my life coach workbook. I am happy to send you the couples worksheets. Everyone I tested them on so far has found them really helpful. And I can always give you the names of some great marriage counselors."

"I would try those worksheets first. I'm not sure I could get Tom into therapy right now."

"And I thought our twenties were hard," Addison moaned.

"You know, marriage is a social construct. If Pru gets divorced too, we can switch things up—all move into Aunt Gicky's house and grow old together," Kizzy suggested, only half-joking.

"We can construct our own happily ever after. Sisters are doin' it for themselves!" Addison declared, internally cueing up the Annie Lennox and Aretha duet of the same name.

"I'm not getting divorced," Pru responded dryly, before playing along.

"But if I did, could we each get a puppy?" She turned to Addison. "Are you a dog person now?"

"Maybe, and yes, we can each get a puppy."

"And a fetching dog walker!" Kizzy joked.

"Done!" Addison agreed.

They all laughed, before staring out at the ocean's waves in silence for a good long while, lost in their own thoughts. Except for Addison, that is, who seemed to be happily bopping to the aforementioned feminine anthem playing in her head.

Chapter Nineteen

That night, after Pru and Lisa had left for the city, Addison and Kizzy walked over to Shep's for the barbecue, where Addison was greeted with a hero's welcome. It was the first time since being fired that she had felt part of a community, and she had to admit she was digging it. She thought again about what keeping the house would look like—maybe turning the art studio into another weekend rental to make it more profitable. But that art studio was her favorite part. It was kind of absurd for her, of course, with no job, no partner, few savings, and no primary residence, to own a beach house. But there was no denying that this place was sticking to her soul.

The barbecue featured all the usual suspects—hamburgers, hot dogs, corn, watermelon salad, and lots of beer. She knew most of the people from the game and was introduced to a bunch of others she had never met before.

She found herself guessing who was who from Ben's last book. The handsome guy from the market was working the

grill—well, not working it literally. He was clearly a guest helping out. The ferry captain popped in, grabbing a burger and a
beer. Everyone was giving him the third degree about his daughter, who was spending the summer in the Galápagos—apparently
for the second year in a row. Even Addison was interested in her
whereabouts after putting it together that she and Matty from
the ball game were the characters from the big coming-of-age
plot in Ben's book. She was introduced to Matty's mom, Renee,
who seemed to be currently single, but also seemed to light up
when the ferry captain plopped himself down next to her.

Addison made a plate and brought it outside.

"Hey, Slugger," Ben called out to her. She smiled. She liked
the nickname better than Addie—though she was warming to
that a little too. He tapped the seat next to him on the oversized
sectional on Shep's back deck. It surprised Addison how chic Shep's
house was. Chic and Shep did not go together.

"This house!" she noted upon sitting.

"I know. Shep's wife Caroline had beautiful taste."

Shep belched as he walked by.

"In most things," Ben added dryly. He was funny when he
wanted to be.

"Where are your friends?" he added, looking around.

Addie pointed to Kizzy in the corner, having her ear talked
off by one of the ballplayers—Eddie.

"It's just Kizzy. The others made the five o'clock."

She was finally getting the insider lingo down.

"I think Eddie has a crush," Ben observed.

"Everyone has a crush on Kizzy. He won't get very far, I'm
afraid. She's not ready to date. Just last week, she was a happily
married woman. Or at least she thought she was."

"Ugh. I knew there was something up. I could see it in her eyes."

Addison was surprised that Ben was so perceptive. Also, she wasn't surprised.

A lull fell on the conversation, and they both took the opportunity to eat their corn on the cob. A few rows later, Ben broke the silence with, "Good corn."

Addison smiled in agreement, revealing a kernel wedged between her teeth. The two of them did that dance that people do when trying to home in on the location of a wayward morsel till Ben gave up and stuck his finger in her mouth. He held the errant kernel on the tip of his finger.

"You want it?" he asked. She pushed on his shoulder and laughed the way one does when both embarrassed and happy.

Kizzy made her way over and joined them.

"How long are you staying, Kizzy?"

"I'll probably leave before the weekend. You have a guest coming, right, Addie?"

Addison gave her a look.

"Sorry. I kind of like calling you Addie. It seems to fit suddenly. But don't worry, I will get Addison—not Addie—a fabulous job in the fall."

"Kizzy is a headhunter and I am out of work—the Page Six incident," Addie added sheepishly.

"She was on track to be the first female head of the art department at a top Madison Avenue ad agency," Kizzy embellished. Her pride was adorable.

"What about you?" Addison asked strictly out of politeness. She had already completed an online course in Ben Morse 101. And Kizzy was close behind her.

"I write for *Sports Illustrated*," Ben responded.

Kizzy and Addison both shook their heads in acknowledgment, as if they didn't already know where he worked, where he was born, and whether he wore boxers or briefs. Aside from Addison being present for the Spice Girls interrogation, there were a million interviews on the internet with this guy.

"Actually, your guest next weekend is my next subject. Terrence Williams—the Vagabond Surfer. He's at the tail end of a year of surfing across the country, and he's stopping here before heading to a big contest out in Montauk. Claims to be sleeping on people's couches, but rumor has it he has a girl in every port."

"I've heard of him! He's a hottie." Kizzy winked at Addison. "The first Black surfer to win the US Open of Surfing."

"I didn't know you were into surfing," Addison remarked in surprise.

"I'm not. I'm into black people breaking stereotypes. How old is he?" she asked Ben.

"Pushing forty."

"Perfect for that one-night stand you've never had, Addison."

"Kizzy!" Addison shoved her. "Look who's talking!"

"Well, I have been married since, like, the tenth grade. What's your excuse?"

"It's not happening," Addison insisted before going back to busying herself with her corn.

Ben piped in, clearly feeling like one of the girls, "They serve a purpose, you know. No commitment. No feelings. Just sex. I've only had one-night stands since my wife passed away."

"What if you develop feelings?" Kizzy asked, sincerely curious.

"In one night? Not a problem for me."

"What about for them?" Addison asked.

"So far, no complaints."

"That's gross," Addison said.

"There's nothing gross about it. It's totally transactional. Tit for tat."

"You're the tat, I presume."

"I think this is my cue to leave," he said, a bit flustered. "I'm going to take a lap. Receive some accolades for my winning run today."

"*Our* winning runs," Addison pointed out with a flirty smile.

"Our winning runs." He smiled back at her as he stood, causing the sweet dimple to appear on his cheek. She felt like she was on an emotional roller coaster with this guy.

"Why did you bring that up, Kizzy? So embarrassing!"

"Sorry, what do you care? You're not interested in him anyway, remember?"

Addison's thumbnail went right to her mouth.

"Don't sleep with the slightly manic, emotionally unavailable neighbor, under any circumstances, Addison. That is not a one-night stand. That's a see-him-every-day-afterward-and-regret-it stand."

Addison agreed, but fought the urge to cross her fingers as she did.

Week Five

Chapter Twenty

Addison and Kizzy sat on the beach for most of the week, reading, drinking wine, searching for job listings for Addison, and blowing up pictures of Terrence Williams's abs.

The tide suddenly rolled in, taking out an older couple sitting by the shoreline. The seniors jumped from their chairs, grabbing their flip-flops from the surf and laughing as the cold water shocked their toes. The husband gave the wife a swift pat on her rear, causing Kizzy and Addison to react in unison.

"How sweet!" Kizzy exclaimed.

"How mortifying," Addison scoffed.

They both laughed.

"I'm glad Rome didn't squash the hopeless romantic in you."

"Me too, I guess."

Lisa had given them each a Life Assessment Worksheet before she left. It had annoyed them both when she handed them off, but they spent the afternoon contemplating their answers. Specifically:

What do you want out of life?
What are the obstacles to achieving your goals?
What are the steps to reaching them?

They shared their answers to the first question over sunset and rosé.

"I want to get my career back, but in a way that leaves more room for other things."

"I love that for you! Though it may be difficult, given your tendency to take it all on." Kizzy paused before admitting her answer.

"I want the family at the ferry dock."

When Kizzy said it, *the family at the ferry dock,* it made Addison feel like she was lying to herself. She wanted some iteration of that too, though she worried she was too controlling to dream of something that seemed so hard to control.

Their deep thoughts were interrupted by Sally running toward them with a tennis ball in her mouth. Ben stood tall at the top of the steps, causing Addison to fumble her throw. He walked down to them, barefoot in jeans with an open button-down. His abs were not as insane as Terrence Williams's, but they were nothing to shake a stick at. His hair was all over the place, and between that and the outfit, he was a bit of a mess—a sexy mess.

"I like what you did with your hair there," Kizzy joked, motioning to the part that was standing straight up. Ben licked his fingers and flattened it. It was undeniably adorable.

"You two want to go to town tonight?"

"Maybe. Where to?" Addison asked.

"It depends if you want to stay out of trouble or if you're looking for it."

"We're looking for it!" Kizzy shouted, like a college kid on spring break.

"OK, then!" Ben laughed, and joked, "We can search for your one-night stands. I can be your wingman!"

At least, they thought he was joking.

They shared a conspiratorial look, and when he added, "It's one-hit wonder night at the Sandbar!" they both agreed. Neither had heard of such a thing, but it certainly went with the one-nighter theme. It sounded like the perfect antidote to their introspective day.

The night was fun, just the kind of fun they all needed. It wasn't wingman-like at all. Simply three friends drinking and laughing and dancing together. When "Come On Eileen" came on, they screamed on the dance floor like drunk teenagers. Half a dozen songs later, ironically during "I Melt with You," by Modern English, Ben excused himself to get some air. Kizzy ran off to the ladies' room. Addison followed Ben out to the street, where he sat on a bench. She slid down next to him, appreciating the cool night air—she was also melting.

"Wow! What a fun night!"

"Yeah, you never know what to expect on this island."

"I haven't danced that hard in so long!" she gushed, while catching her breath. "My mom used to blast music—all disco—and make my sister and me help her straighten the house before the housekeeper came. We would dance hard like that. It's one of my best childhood memories."

Ben was quiet, kind of staring straight on at nothing.

"You OK?" she asked, tapping him on his knee, and catching her breath.

"I'm not much of a wingman, sorry—not that either of you needs a wingman."

"You'd be surprised."

"I'm surprised that you're single, to be honest. What's up with that?"

"I never met the right person, I guess. My friends say I choose poorly."

"Oh—you like the bad boys?'

"The opposite. I pick painfully nice guys who end up boring me to tears. It sounds awful, but I think I like to have the upper hand."

"You should definitely look for a main character type—a side guy could never be worthy of you."

"Noted." She smiled at the compliment, but on second thought, it gave her pause. Why was he doling out dating advice and playing the wingman?

"What about you?" she asked instead.

"Well, that was the first time I've really danced. You know, without Julia."

And voilà—the man from the book appeared right before her eyes.

"I'm sorry," she said. "How long has it been now?"

"Three years, forty-three days."

He laughed at his preciseness, and his humility tugged at her heart.

"But you've dated?"

"I haven't dated. Just, you know—had the tit-for-tat sex."

Addison laughed. "Are you always so open about these things?"

"Not at all, actually. Not only have I not danced with anyone since Julia, I also haven't talked to anyone since Julia. I mean, really talked. Julia was a major league listener."

"I can't imagine how much you miss her."

"Talking about her helps. Not that anyone lets me. It's nice to talk to someone about Julia who didn't know her. Someone who doesn't find it painful to talk about her—or laugh about her. Her sister, Nora, and I manage to do it sometimes. Just bring up funny stories, or her amazing laugh. But her parents, or her best friend—they still look at me like I will break in two if they even say her name."

"Was Julia funny?"

"Not particularly. I mean, once in a while she would come out with a real zinger. But she had a great sense of humor. When she laughed, when she really laughed, her entire face would contort, and her eyes would fill with tears. Her laugh was everything. Complete strangers would laugh, watching Julia laugh."

"Well, I don't feel like a complete stranger—after reading your book."

"I don't even recognize the guy in that book anymore. He was so angry."

Addison was quiet. Ben mistook her introspection for judgment and apologized again.

"I'm really sorry about the bungee cord thing. I have a hard time with change—like things to be a certain way. You should have seen the fit I threw when they tried to replace the sidewalk on our block."

Addison thought to say, *I heard*, but the only thing worse than throwing a fit about something is throwing a fit about something with witnesses. She saved him the further embarrassment.

"It's fine," she said, falsely adding, "I forgot about it already."

It wasn't completely false. Her eyes were open, but the more time she spent with him, the more she trusted he was a good guy. Possibly even a great one.

The night had definitely taken a turn. The first beats of "99 Red Balloons" echoed from the club. She wondered if she should steer him back inside.

"It's so nice to be with someone that doesn't look at me with a pained expression," he said with a somewhat pained expression.

She sank further into the bench and placed her hand on his knee in comfort as he continued.

"It's not just here, you know. Anyone I meet who has read my book knows my pain. It's like I'm wearing a scarlet *W* on my chest. I think it's why I didn't properly introduce myself to you. I was so excited to be anonymous."

And although the sweat on her back was not completely dry, she could think of nothing better to say than, "I think you could use a hug."

"I'm still a little sweaty," he said, as if reading her mind.

She shrugged, stood up in front of him, and motioned for him to do the same.

He did, and she wrapped her arms around him and squeezed with all of her might, not even cringing when her hands reached the sweaty spot on his back. After a solid minute of their bodies pressed together, Ben nuzzled into her neck and whispered in her ear, "I am really sorry, Addison."

It brought her an odd sense of comfort that wiped out the last threads of distrust she had previously felt for him. She broke away and looked into his eyes. She was sure she saw something warm and loving in them, under the sadness. Like looking into the sun, it suddenly became too much.

Ben clearly felt it too. He broke away.

"Want a tour of the ice cream flavors at Scoops?"

"Absolutely." She blushed, embarrassed by the sudden intimacy.

Soon, they plopped down onto the stoop in front of the ice cream shop with two cones. On one side, two kids were selling painted shells out of their wagon; on the other, a couple seemed to be breaking up. It was hard not to listen to them fighting, and Addison and Ben were happy when the girl stormed off and the guy followed.

Ben got up to check out the painted shells.

"What's your sign?" he asked Addison.

"Sagittarius."

"How much for the painted Sagittarius shell?" he asked the two young proprietors. They consulted with each other for longer than contestants on *Shark Tank*. Both Ben and Addison were holding in laughter.

"Two dollars and fifty cents," the older of the two (who couldn't have been more than eight) finally announced.

Ben handed him a five. "Keep the change," he said. "Two fifty, each."

Their eyes nearly burst out of their heads. Ben handed Addison a gold-painted shell with the sign of an archer decoupaged onto it. It was pretty.

"I'll keep it always," she joked—though she meant it.

Am I a hoarder now?

"What's your sign?" Addison inquired.

"Couldn't you tell on the dance floor? I'm an Elaine," Ben said, waving his hands in the air in imitation.

Addison laughed. He was an Elaine. "I see that. I think everyone wants to be an Elaine."

"You?"

"I'm a Jerry. I really love cereal."

Speaking about the friends from *Seinfeld* reminded her of her own friend.

"Kizzy! We ran out on Kizzy!" Addison suddenly remembered, adding, "She's very fragile right now!"

As if on call, Kizzy came flying out of the club, covered in foam.

"Guys!" she shouted. "It's a foam party! Come back!"

They joined Kizzy back inside, where copious amounts of frothy bubbles were blasting out from a contraption on the ceiling. As the volume rose and the lights dimmed, they belted the lyrics to "Stacy's Mom." At first, the foam situation felt kind of good—cool and wet and decadent. But soon the three began to slip and slide and feel genuinely ancient compared to the rest of the crowd, who now looked to be about 99 percent fake ID holders. They shook off as much lather as they could and made their way to the front door. Riding home, side by side by side, they laughed about their fun night and analyzed whether Stacy's mom really had it going on or if she was a bit of a perv.

"Would you describe these walks as wide sidewalks or narrow streets?" Addison asked Ben when they stopped between their houses.

"Depends on the day," he responded, leaning off his bike and placing a sweet good night kiss on the top of her head.

Chapter Twenty-one

The next morning, Friday already, Addison woke up early to take out the recyclables only to realize that in her drunkenness she hadn't locked the gate the night before. She looked for her bike in a panic and soon discovered that it was gone. Her heart raced and her hands shook as she ran around the property, double- and triple-checking. She acknowledged that she was irrationally upset, but she loved that bike. She loved how it was so unique to her aunt and how everyone recognized it and smiled at her as she rode by. She thought of waking Kizzy, but decided she needed someone who knew the deal. She ran to Ben's and banged on his front door until Sally greeted her.

"Go get Ben," she instructed her furry friend, who clearly understood both her command and her duress. Ben arrived quickly, and in T-shirt and boxers. His eyes still sleepy, his hair sticking straight up, again. Addison fought the urge to lick her fingers and run her hands over it, smoothing it out.

"Gicky's bike was stolen," she lamented, near tears.

"Annette Kellerman! Give me a sec."

He returned a minute later in sweats and a baseball cap and led her to his shed, where he pulled out two bikes. He instructed her to follow along as he spouted all the right things.

"We'll find it. Don't worry. It's usually some drunk groupers. I know all the best places to look." And finally: "It couldn't have gone too far."

Ben and Addison spent the next hour weaving in and out of the streets to the north and south of their own. Every once in a while, Ben would hop off his bike and look around back at random houses. Addison couldn't tell if he chose them from previous bike-hunting expeditions or just on a hunch. Whichever the motivation, he always returned empty-handed.

"A few more places to check," he said, adding, "Don't lose hope."

"Forget hope, I lost Annette Kellerman."

They disembarked in front of the Schooner Inn and searched the bike racks both there and at the ferry dock. Nothing.

"One more spot," Ben promised.

Addison followed him to the last block in Oceanview, where a towering, rather ramshackle share house sat on fifteen-foot stilts. They could see her from the sidewalk—Annette Kellerman tossed in the sand underneath the house among a pile of ordinary beach bikes and chairs.

"Oh, the humanity!" Ben cried out, laughing.

They pulled out the bike, which looked no worse for the wear—except that something was missing. The garland of shells that Gicky had strung together like popcorn at Christmas and draped over the front basket, was nowhere to be found.

"I'm going in!" Addison declared.

"Into the house?" Ben responded. "I don't think that's a good idea."

"I don't care. I'm going in."

"You know I'm going to follow you and end up in fisticuffs."

"I can't believe you just said *fisticuffs*. Maybe you shouldn't follow me, Grandpa."

But of course, he did.

The two quietly climbed the wooden steps to the side door of the house, trying not to creak as they did. Addison ever so gently opened the door, and Ben popped in front of her to save the day. If she weren't trying to be invisible, she would have given him a piece of her feminist mind plus a good shove out of her way, but the goal was to get in and out unnoticed. Like two kids late for curfew, they stepped gingerly into the living room, where a gaggle of twentysomethings lay passed out in every corner. And there, on the mantel over the fireplace, in all its glory, hung Annette Kellerman's shell-covered garland. Addison gasped, which caused a few of the culprits to stir and one rather large specimen to open his eyes. She didn't care. She grabbed the laurel in one hand and shook her finger at the big one with the other.

"This is mine," she said, draping the string of shells around her neck like a scarf. "And don't steal!" she added, making Ben chuckle.

They ran out the door, laughing and stomping down the stairs, not caring that they too had been breaking and entering. It was a big thrill, and they spun around outside like two kids on a sugar high, till they collapsed with dizziness and happiness on the sidewalk.

"That was awesome," Ben shouted, reaching for her hand to pull her up.

"It really was," Addison agreed as she jumped to her feet. They held hands after that for a little longer than necessary, and for a quick second Addison thought Ben may kiss her. He had leaned forward and looked into her eyes in a way that made it obvious that he wanted to. As she leaned in to encourage him, one of the share house guys, the big one, came barreling down its stairs.

"Let's go," Ben warned.

Addison held up Gicky's bike so that Ben could steer it aside his, and then jumped on the other one. They smiled all the way home, partially from the charge of success, partially from the thrill of adventure, and partially from imagining the kiss that hadn't happened yet but felt inevitable.

Chapter Twenty-two

Terrence Williams opened his eyes and looked around the room he woke up in at the Folly Beach Motel with no memory of where he was. It was a common occurrence given the lifestyle that had led to his nickname, the Vagabond Surfer. It was his sixth location that month.

Folly had done him right though. The people were nice, and the best surfing spot, the Washout, had been consistently heavy since his arrival two days earlier. He wished he could stay. Even flipped through real estate listings in the local magazine he picked up at the entrance to the diner where he ate the night before. He had been feeling that way often lately. Dreaming of putting down roots somewhere, and with his parents now retired abroad, South Carolina seemed as good a place as any.

The magazine had been his companion until his server recognized him and wrote her name and phone number on the back of his check.

"I'm off at ten," she said, in her thick southern drawl. He put her number in his pocket, unsure whether he would or wouldn't take her up on her southern hospitality. She would be the third woman that month who had propositioned him. Southern girls seemed to really know what they wanted, and while each was more fun than the last, he was tiring of it. Tired of living out of his duffel, tired of repeating the same stories and answering the same questions, even tired of the meaningless sex. He thought about that a lot lately. Suddenly longing for a greater attachment than his board being leashed to his ankle. After twenty or so years on the circuit, he was ripe for change.

The waitress, Carly, came out of the motel bathroom and fixed her name tag in the mirror.

"Breakfast?" he inquired hopefully.

"Nah, I have to get home." She held up her phone and kneeled down next to him in bed. "Selfie?" she asked, snapping one before he could answer. He winced at the thought of her posting it—being that he was shirtless under a white sheet in a motel bed. Not that anyone would be surprised. His reputation preceded him.

Carly left, and before showering and getting ready to head to the airport for his flight to New York, he looked through the questions that the reporter from *Sports Illustrated* had sent. Basic things about his childhood, riding his first wave, and whether his race was ever a factor for him. He figured the reporter was a white guy. A black man would never word the question that way, unless they wanted the answer to be *Duh*. Though there was no denying, as the first black surfer on the cover of *Surf* magazine, and the first to place in the Olympics, he had excelled in a sport dominated by blue-eyed, blond-haired Americans.

Terrence didn't catch his first wave till he was sixteen—but once he had, he didn't stop. The son of a navy doctor, Terrence had moved with his family four times by the time he was in high school, when they landed at the naval base outside of LA in Ventura County. He had learned to swim in the ocean at an early age, while they were stationed in Jacksonville, and took to it like a fish, but had lived on landlocked bases in the years that followed in DC and Georgia. The ocean was the only consolation prize for leaving his friends and girlfriend in Atlanta. His dad promised him a surfboard and as soon as they arrived, they headed over to the Ventura Surf Shop to make good on his promise.

It didn't take long before Terrence mastered the waves and ingratiated himself with the tight local community that stretched from Carlsbad to Pelican Point. He was a natural, and along with winning a couple of local competitions, Terrence was known as a really nice guy. The combo led to his first sponsorship. He traveled to competitions, making friends and sleeping on couches wherever he went. Soon, his nomadic ways led to a local newspaper reporter naming him the Vagabond Surfer. After that, he kind of leaned into the nomadic lifestyle.

The notoriety was fun, but didn't really matter to Terrence. He was in it for the thrill and had been since his first nose-ride. Though lately there was no denying that the thrill had faded.

Terrence shook out the bedspread and looked under the bed one last time to make sure he hadn't left anything behind before calling an UberXL for the airport.

Chapter Twenty-three

There was no amount of scrolling through Terrence Williams's Instagram and YouTube videos capturing "great swells, man" that could have prepared Addie and Kizzy for the perfect specimen that walked off the Fire Island ferry. A vision in flip-flops, jeans, and a paper-thin tee that revealed a veiled view of his abs.

"That must be him. Is that him?" Addison enthusiastically asked Ben.

"The one with the surfboard? You must be psychic," Ben grunted. His attitude made them lay it on even thicker, bugging him for sport.

Terrence approached and smiled, causing his dark brown eyes to crinkle at the sides. Addison and Kizzy both went weak at the knees. Not as a metaphor. They both had to steady themselves while simultaneously resisting poking the other to death in that *oh my God, do you see this man?* kind of way. Ben stood aside like a tree, or a pole, or something that has always been there but you had never really noticed, until he stepped in, giving both women a *get it together* look.

Ben introduced himself with an outstretched arm, which Terrence ignored, coming right in for the bro hug. Kizzy stepped in line after Ben, and he hugged her as well, which made Addison laugh out loud with no regard for this poor, gorgeous guy. She imagined he was used to it.

He had a duffel bag and his surfboard. The two women pulled both in Gicky's wagon behind the two men, whispering ridiculous things to each other and staring at Terrence's butt. Two intelligent, grown-ass women transformed into surf groupies on the set of *Beach Blanket Bingo* in less than the time it took to hang ten.

After settling in, Terrence asked the women to point him to the beach and, of course, they jumped at the chance to show him personally. They were really just goofing around with all the attention they were giving him, partially to annoy Ben, partially to keep things light for Kizzy, who was trying her best to circumvent the disaster waiting for her at home. Rome had been searching for her for days now and was no closer to finding her than when she had stormed out of the Mark Hotel. He had left Addison near a dozen more messages, all of which she ignored. Still, it was only a matter of time.

It was a green flag day—good for swimming but not so good for surfing—and Terrence was quick to drop his chair in the sand and dive in. Kizzy whipped off her now favorite caftan and followed while Addison stared longingly from the sand.

"What's with her?" Terrence asked as he and Kizzy bobbed up and down over the mild waves before the break. "Can't she swim?"

"She can swim," Kizzy shouted. "But she's not a fan of waves. Of any kind actually."

"I can fix that," Terrence declared, heading back to shore as Ben and Shep were making their way toward the chairs. The sand was scorching, and they each plopped down on one to save their feet just as Terrence approached Addison.

"I'm teaching you to swim," he said, offering her his hand.

"I swim," Addison protested. "In a pool, or a lake. Waves are too unpredictable for me."

"That's because you never learned how to ride them—c'mon, these are ankle busters at best." He reached his hand out again, and she let him pull her up.

"It's far better than stepping in that swampy muck at the bottom of a lake!"

She certainly didn't agree but followed him anyway.

Ben crossed his arms over his chest as he watched them descend to the shore. He calmed down after a minute, when it was quite obvious that Addison would not make it past the first break. Five false starts later, Terrence lifted her up in his arms and carried her in. Ben seemed as if he might explode with jealously. Shep looked him over before declaring, "Hold on, son. I said to be nice to her, not to sleep with her. You're gonna have to change the name of your house from Love Shack to Heartbreak Hotel."

Ben laughed—hard.

"It's not funny, son. You're a little loose with the goods. I worry you're gonna get the clap."

"For your information, I am not sleeping with Addison. In fact, I'm pretty sure that until yesterday, she may have hated me. And not that it's any of your business, but I haven't slept with anyone all summer."

"Listen up, Hot Lips. She will definitely hate you if she becomes another notch on your 'Make a Widower Happy' card. She will sell that house to the highest bidder before you can say *chlamydia*."

"Oh my God, Shep, I don't have chlamydia. And look who's talking. Don't think I haven't noticed you slipping out the back of Ruth Ingram's house early mornings."

"You know I hate sleeping alone."

Addison and Terrence were bobbing up and over the waves, her hands visibly wrapped around his neck, her legs, no doubt, wrapped around his waist. Ben's face reddened at that realization, and he stood to flee the scene.

"This is ridiculous. He's supposed to be surfing, not babysitting Addison. Tell him to come by when he's done doing whatever this is."

Shep looked at him knowingly. Ben mumbled "Shut up" under his breath as he hightailed it back over the hot sand.

Addison soon emerged from the water, her wet skin catching the rays of the sun. Clearly proud of herself, she squinted, watching Ben walk back up the stairs, dousing the gleam in her eyes. She wrapped herself in a towel and plopped down next to Shep.

"Good job," he offered, patting her on the back.

With the fear removed, the sea water felt invigorating. Even now, with its remnants glistening on her skin, she relished in the aftereffects. She planned on going in again for sure and wanted to tell Ben how much she loved it—but alas . . .

"Where did he run off to?" she asked Shep.

Shep shrugged, sighed, and changed the subject.

"Have you found my painting from Gicky yet?"

"Not yet. But I'm planning on doing a major purge next week. I'm sure I'll find it then."

That afternoon, Terrence and Ben took off to the east, where the waves were said to be gnarly (OK, not really gnarly—but at least bigger). They ended up having dinner on the east end of the island with a couple of surfers that Terrence had met in Baja a few years back.

Disappointed by the late return of the Big Kahuna, Addison and Kizzy went to bed early, each reading another one of Ben Morse's books. Sunburnt and seaworn, they both dozed off after a chapter or two and remained asleep till about 2:00 a.m., when Kizzy awoke to a noise in the kitchen.

"Do you hear that? There's someone in the kitchen," she whispered, nudging her friend awake.

"I'm sure it's just Terrence. Go back to sleep."

"You should go out there, Addison. Be the girl in this port!"

Addison seemed to contemplate it.

"C'mon, you must want more of his hands wrapped around you like in the ocean this morning!" Kizzy insisted.

But she didn't. In fact, her mind ran to Ben at the suggestion of it.

"You go," Addison responded.

"I couldn't," Kizzy countered.

"I think you can. I think Terrence is your one-hit wonder! Rip off the Band-Aid."

As if on cue, there was a light knock on the door. They both jumped two feet in the air and landed, laughing. Kizzy prudishly pulled up the blanket while Addison barely squeaked out, "Come in."

"I heard chatting in here so thought it was OK to knock—I can't figure out your toaster oven."

"Kizzy will help you," Addison declared, physically pushing her out the bedroom door.

What are you making?" Kizzy asked, while futzing around with the knobs on what may have been the oldest working toaster oven in existence.

"Pizza bagels—they were in the freezer—I hope it's OK."

"God knows how old they are, but it's fine."

Kizzy twisted the timeworn dials and pressed buttons until the red oven light went on.

"Voilà!" she exclaimed, before standing there awkwardly, not knowing whether to leave or stay. She looked into Terrence's red eyes, contemplated his choice of 2:00 a.m. snack, and came right out and asked.

"Are you stoned?"

"Maybe a little."

He pulled a bright yellow vape out of his pocket. It had been years since Kizzy had smoked pot.

"Want a hit?"

"It's been so long—years."

"You know it's legal now?"

"Yes, I heard that," she laughed. "That's not the reason. The last time I smoked, my husband made me crazy paranoid." She remembered the awful night, fighting with Rome about his flirty behavior with a woman they bumped into at the Smith restaurant.

"It turned out that I wasn't paranoid after all. My husband was having an affair. I only left him a week ago."

"Oooh, I'm sorry. That stinks. But good that you can partake again—right?"

He handed her the vape.

"Why not?" she acquiesced.

A few hits later and she too was staring down the timer on the pizza bagels.

"What's your husband's name?"

"Rome."

"Rome is an odd name."

"Yes, and he took it literally," she answered, laughing.

"Can I ask you a personal question, Kizzy?"

Kizzy nodded and held her breath.

"How long were you with your husband?"

"Seventeen years."

"Wow. Was it always bad?"

"No, of course not. Before the last couple of years, I would have said it was always good."

"How old were you when you met?"

"Fifteen."

"Fifteen! Were you a virgin?"

"Is that the personal question?"

"Well, fifteen?"

"Yes, we both were. That was his excuse for cheating—the first time at least. When we were getting back together, my shrink asked if I would feel better getting even—you know, having an affair of my own."

"Did you?" He smiled like a teenager, in contrast to the speckling of gray hair sprouting from his temples.

"I didn't." At least that's what she tried to say—the words got caught in her throat and came out garbled. Terrence noticed.

"So, if I were to kiss you, I would be the first person other than your bad Rome-ance," he joked, adding, "Since you were fifteen?"

Kizzy laughed. She loved a good Rome pun, but had never heard that one before. Terrence laughed too.

"Yes, and before that, I only kissed Charlie Schwartz and Bobby Sweeney. And Charlie wore a retainer."

"He didn't take it out?"

"I guess he didn't know."

"Poor guy."

They were still standing a few inches apart, but now the space felt electrified. Kizzy tried to control herself from rocking forward—she was drawn to him. She silently willed him to kiss her, but after what seemed like an eternity, she couldn't wait any longer. She leaned in and gently brushed her lips against his. That was all he needed. He kissed her back, at first gently and then passionately.

The toaster oven dinged.

"Are you still hungry?" Kizzy asks.

"I am," he said, turning off the oven and leading her by the hand out the back door to the guesthouse. He shut the door behind them and whispered in her ear, "Are *you* still hungry?"

"Ravenous," she answered, wondering who this willing seductress was.

Terrence took off his shirt, and Kizzy ran her fingers over his abs. He smiled at her and took her face in his hands, kissing her softly on the lips before running his fingers down her torso and lifting her tank top over her head. He wrapped his hands beneath her bottom, scooped her up, and lifted her with ease onto the bed. Starting with her ear, he kissed and nibbled, sending a long-forgotten yearning down her body. She was happy she had vaped a little. She wasn't feeling stoned really, more so just relaxed. If it weren't for the pot, she would probably tense up her whole body.

Ever since Rome's affair, Kizzy couldn't help but question herself in the bedroom. If it was taking a long time, she would be completely insecure, wondering if it was the same with the other woman. If Rome didn't seem interested, she would wonder if there was someone else again. If his eyes were closed, she imagined him imagining the other woman instead of her. Her mind was always running in bad directions. It wasn't conducive to having an orgasm, that was for sure.

Somehow, this stranger who was feasting on her skin one quivering inch at a time had her feeling things she hadn't in years—both desirous and desired. She held her breath, anticipating where his mouth would go next. You would think she would feel more self-conscious with a stranger, but she didn't—she felt hot. And that felt good. She broke away for a second, not one to wham bam thank you, ma'am, even with all of this talk about one-night stands.

"You know I have to leave first thing tomorrow morning, right?" she mentioned breathlessly.

"It's all good." He placed his finger on her lips. "Don't think of anything else but how your body feels right now."

He pulled her forward so that her legs dangled off the front of the bed, and slid down to the floor between them.

Just relax, Kizzy, she coaxed herself, focusing her eyes on a cloud-shaped water spot on the ceiling like she did when trying to balance at yoga. She should tell Addison about that, she thought, gazing at the spot intently until Terrence buried his face between her legs, his tongue circling and darting and teasing until a wave of ecstasy rolled over her so intensely that she couldn't take it anymore. She grabbed his head in her hands and directed him to climb back onto the bed and inside of her.

They lay on top of the covers afterward, sweaty and satisfied. Kizzy fell asleep contemplating whether she should stay in his bed or go back inside. As she dozed off, she heard Terrence whisper in her ear, "That man of yours is a fool."

Chapter Twenty-four

Kizzy awoke the next morning feeling great. She felt strong. New. Ready. She slipped out quietly and walked, naked, to the outdoor shower.

Addison saw her through the kitchen window, knocked on it, and smiled. Kizzy turned around and mooned her before happily skipping into the shower. Ben walked in as Addison spun back around, a ridiculous blushing smile on her face.

"What?" Ben said.

"Nothing . . . I'm just . . . happy, I guess. That Terrence is really something else."

Ben helped himself to a crisp piece of bacon, avoiding further commentary.

"Where's he at," he asked, faking indifference and adding, "Still asleep? I kept him up pretty late."

"You're not the only one." Addison hummed to herself with a little grin. "He's in the guesthouse. Can you tell him breakfast is ready?" She broke off a piece from her latest batch of scones, tasted it, grimaced, and dumped them in the bin.

The door to the guesthouse was cracked open, so Ben let himself in.

"Hey," Ben called out upon entering.

"Hey," Terrence responded from the bathroom.

Ben sat on the edge of the bed, waiting, until he noticed a condom wrapper on the floor. He jumped up like the bed was on fire, contemplating whether to flee, when he saw a second one mere inches from the garbage pail. That Terrence was a bad shot was of little consolation. Ben was mad. Mad at himself, mad at Terrence, and mostly mad at Addison. The first person he had truly felt something for since Julia died, the first brunette whose hair he could imagine running his hands through. Could he be that out of touch that he misconstrued the chemistry between them?

Terrence ascended from the loo and, without further ado, Ben confronted him. He pointed to the condom for a visual.

"So, is that what this is all about? Your thirst for another wave is all just BS?"

"No, man. Lighten up. We were just having fun."

Ben clenched his fists and rolled his shoulders back.

"You know—there are women throwing themselves at me everywhere I go. It's, like, beyond consensual," Terrence added, clearly confused by Ben's nunlike reaction to two consenting adults having relations.

Ben controlled the urge to sock the guy and decided, right there and then, he would hit him where it would hurt more—in his piece in *Sports Illustrated*. It was irrational, and he knew it, but he didn't much care.

And then Terrence dropped the real bomb.

"It's getting old, man," he complained, adding, "and I'm getting old too," before flipping himself onto the bed like a teenager would.

"I'm thinking of asking if I can see her again. You think she would want to? I know she's in a transitional time in life—lots to figure out."

Ben weighed his options. He could do his best to thwart it right now, but where would that leave him?

All he could manage was, "Go for it, man."

Terrence's face lit with promise, and Ben felt a spark of happiness for him before remembering it was at the price of his own.

"You need anything else from me before I go?" Terrence asked cluelessly.

"No. I got all I need," Ben answered, and reluctantly received Terrence's bear hug goodbye.

Week Six

Chapter Twenty-five

Usually, when Ben Morse had to leave the island midsummer, he was immediately filled with dread. Today, he was filled with relief. He couldn't get away fast enough.

The woman next door had cracked his hardened resolve, crawled under his skin, and then jumped back out, leaving an open, festering wound. OK, it wasn't quite that dramatic, but that's how the novelist in him perceived it. Even the fact that he could work up that over-the-top sentiment alarmed him. The closest he got to writing with emotion lately was this past winter when the petulant goalie he was writing a feature on stopped a goal at the buzzer and won the Stanley Cup. Even that only garnered the sentence "Grown men blinked away tears as he circled the arena with the legendary trophy." It figured that the first time he had enjoyed talking to, even flirting with, a woman since Julia for reasons other than purely carnal satisfaction had left him broken and rejected.

Lesson fucking learned, he thought, before burying his nose in the *Fire Island News*, hoping to discourage early morning conversation on the ferry.

Ben had turned in his first draft of the Terrence Williams piece the night before and was meeting his editor at the *Sports Illustrated* offices late that afternoon. Enough time to grab lunch with his agent first at one of his favorite downtown haunts.

The Paris Cafe was a dark waterfront restaurant circa 1873 where Thomas Edison, Teddy Roosevelt, and even Butch Cassidy are said to have dined. After eating at the same handful of places all summer long, he was definitely looking forward to mixing it up a bit. At least his tastebuds were excited about something.

He arrived first and ordered an iced tea from the bar. He didn't like to drink before meetings. His agent, Elizabeth Barnes, arrived before his beverage did. Ben's sportswriting gig had little to do with his formidable book agent, but she kept close tabs on him since Julia died. Her greeting lacked the pity-based warmth she had presented with as of late.

"What the hell, Ben? You skewered that surfer."

And there was the woman he remembered! He summoned the bartender. "Make that a Bloody Mary instead."

"It wasn't that bad," he moaned.

Elizabeth pulled out her phone and quoted him.

"At first, one may be fooled by the seemingly sincere surfer, but in the end, I doubt a wave is the only thing Terrence Williams is hell-bent on riding."

"Really? You usually love a good alliteration."

"Benjamin!"

"Let's see what my editor says."

"He already called me. He's not publishing it."

Back to the bartender. "Drop a vodka floater in this, please."

"Wait, he wants me to edit the article?" he asked defensively.

"He wants you to throw it out and start again. Every sentence is laced with acrimony."

"He said that?"

"No. I said that. He said, 'It's a bloody hack job that isn't worth a dog pissing on it.'"

"That sounds more like him."

"He canceled your meeting. There will be a car waiting at your apartment at four to bring you and a photographer out to Montauk. He wants you to cover the tournament. Speak to other surfers about Terrence's legend. Report with zero bias."

She put her hand on his arm. No one brought out her faint thread of maternal instinct more than the widowed Ben Morse.

"What happened, Ben? When we spoke, you were all keen on this guy."

"I don't know," he said unconvincingly.

She raised her eyebrows. In the old days she would have scared a confession out of him, but little scared him anymore, aside from possible heartbreak. He read her expression and threw her a bone.

"Fine. I do know, but I don't want to talk about it except to say things got personal. I was wrong to be so harsh and judgmental, and I will do the rewrite."

"OK. Let's sit in a booth and eat like two human beings, please."

And they did. But Ben barely spoke.

Chapter Twenty-six

The aftereffects of the vodka (and possibly not giving a crap) caused Ben to ignore the photographer and sleep for most of the ride out to Montauk. He was sure that his editor had set up the four o'clock departure time just to punish him. No one sets out for the easternmost tip of Long Island at rush hour. What usually took two and a half hours under these conditions took five.

They arrived at the Born Free Motel, a no-frills twenty-four-room inn within walking distance of the beach. He fell asleep in his clothes, with the unfortunate words to "Born Free" running through his head on a loop. The loop being a recap of the first few lines—"Born Free / As free as the wind blows"—because he couldn't remember the rest.

The next morning, he was set to meet Terrence at the tournament. Word was, he had already made it to the semifinals.

If Ben were ever to leave Fire Island, Montauk would be the place. All the beauty, none of the poshness that makes the Hamptons the Hamptons. Montauk people surfed and fished and drank clam chowder from coffee cups. The vibe was analogous to the vibe on Fire Island.

Bottom line: he didn't mind being there so much—especially since he needed to get away from Addison.

The farther out east you went, the bigger the waves, and this was as east as you could get. Ergo, the town's tag line, Montauk: End of the World. The excitement of the annual surfing contest vibrated in the air, but it barely permeated Ben's sad-sack state. He sat on the shore, watching the waves crash onto the beach. Looking out past the break, the water was dotted with brightly colored boards as the surfers paddled out, each hoping to catch the perfect wave. The photographer walked toward the shore to capture it.

The contest was well underway, and the surfers were in the middle of the round. If Terrence made it to tomorrow's finals, which was expected, Ben would stay around, write the piece, and never look back. Unless, of course, Terrence asked to hitch a ride back to the ferry, to see his girl on Fire Island. Ben's stomach rolled over at the thought. Suddenly, someone buying Gicky's house, knocking it down, and building a towering monstrosity that would steal his light seemed like the best outcome.

He put it all out of his mind and got down to business. He wasn't letting this guy take more than he already had.

For many of Ben's readers, surfing was an unknown sport, unlike, let's say, football. So, Ben felt the need to explain the basics in a way he usually would not. He spoke quietly into his mobile phone's microphone, describing the scene. Writing about sporting events came naturally to him. It was practically as easy for him as writing out the alphabet.

"The judges sit in a tower on the beach, watching the action through binoculars, carefully evaluating each surfer's performance. The semifinal round of the contest is underway, and the surfers show varying degrees of skill and confidence. Some ride the waves with grace and ease, executing impressive maneuvers and displaying incredible balance. Others struggle to stay upright on their boards, wiping out and disappearing beneath the water. With each round, the competition becomes more intense. The surfers pushing themselves harder, attempting riskier moves, and taking bigger chances. Experience is the key to squashing one's nerves and moving in and out of the waves with fluidity, and Terrence Williams—at a couple of years shy of forty—has been competing since he was sixteen. He has more experience than most, if not all, of his competition."

The photographer came back, and the two men made their way through the excited crowd of onlookers in search of their subject. Terrence suddenly appeared before them.

Ben briefly considered punching Terrence, arm swung back, right hook to the jaw. The image ran through his mind, puncturing his melancholic mood with a small spark of joy. He was bigger than Terrence, and in pretty good shape. He could take him, he thought.

Terrence's big bear hug quickly extinguished Ben's animosity. It was the kind that was followed by a drum roll of sorts on his back. Oh, how he wanted to hate this guy.

"I'm glad you're here, man. I have a whole new angle for the story, if you're willing." Terrence ran his hand across the sky as if the magazine headline would be up in lights, and announced, "The Last Ride of the Vagabond Surfer."

Terrence's retiring wasn't a bizarre notion. Most professional surfers "hang their leash" by their midthirties. And for Terrence, with multiple championship and world titles to his name, it would make sense to go out on top. Ben thought about this slant as it related to his story. It would certainly make his job easier.

"I'm tired of worrying about heats and scores and mostly of the constant travel. I want a family. One that I have dinner with every night, not one I see between chasing waves across continents."

That morning, while on his third cup of coffee, Ben had thought about what had gone down between Terrence and Addison. He contemplated the alternative to spending the rest of the summer hiding in his house, avoiding the little vixen next door, and tried his best to banish thoughts of this guy kissing Addison's perfectly tanned shoulders. Or worse. Now he worried that it wasn't just the one-night stand that her friend Kizzy had suggested. He worried that Terrence's sudden hankering for a family had something to do with Addison. After all, she had made him, the widowed Ben Morse, feel things he was sure he would never feel again. He tried to discourage Terrence.

"That's a very quiet life," Ben cautioned, "and I think you have a bunch of good years left in the spotlight!"

"That's just it. The spotlight, the adrenaline, the adoration from my fans has all begun to feel empty and unfulfilling."

And just then, as if by magic, Kizzy Weinstein—the antidote to Terrence's empty and unfulfilled life, pranced (yes, pranced) over to greet them. Ben was shocked.

Terrence further explained their plan.

"After the finals tomorrow, I'm gonna stay with Kizzy for a bit in New York City. I've been approached by a sportswear manufacturer in the Garment Center about starting a new clothing line called the Vagabond Surfer. I want to see what they have in mind."

God, it was worse than Ben had even imagined. And Kizzy!

Could no one resist this man's abs? He kissed Kizzy hello, even though he was pissed for Addison.

Instead of pulling Kizzy aside and asking if Addison was OK sharing their concubine, he unsuccessfully joked, "How Crocodile Dundee of you."

Clearly neither of them had seen the eighties rom-com of the same name where an Australian cowboy moved to NYC, and he didn't bother explaining. He settled on "I'm so happy for you both!" Possibly meaning it—as he now had another chance with Addison. They all hugged, basking in Ben's good wishes.

That night at a local surf bar, three tequilas in, Ben came out and asked Kizzy, "You're not concerned about how Addison will feel about your getting with Terrence?"

"Why would she care? She just wants me to be happy!"

To each his own, he thought.

The next day, as the final round of the tournament approached, the tension on the beach was palpable. Terrence and a kid named Jack Morgan were neck and neck for the top spot, but it was really anyone's win. The wind was picking up, the waves were getting bigger, and though it added an extra element of difficulty to the competition, this was nothing that either of them hadn't experienced before. Terrence came by and gave Kizzy a sweet kiss on the lips before picking up his board.

Kizzy seemed nervous as she watched her guy paddle out to sea. Ben was surprised by how much she cared about Terrence in such a short time. He tried to get her to sit down next to him, but she insisted on standing, fidgeting in the sand, bouncing from one foot to the other.

It may be good that the guy was retiring. Kizzy did not look like she would survive the circuit.

Ben watched in awe as Terrence paddled out to the lineup, ready to take on the next wave. There was no denying his bravery and skill. Even when faced with the tough conditions, younger competition, and waves that could easily take him down, he seemed calm and collected. Ben quietly recorded his thoughts for safekeeping.

The competition went on for a while, and after two sets of eliminations, Terrence Williams and Jack Morgan were still on top. Ben stood up tall as Terrence caught a particularly enormous wave. It was quite remarkable to see, until he suddenly vanished from sight. Ben asked the photographer for his camera and used the zoom to get a closer look, but there was no sign of him. He held his breath as Kizzy yelled out, "Do you see him? Do you see him?"

"I'm sure he's OK, just wait."

But he wasn't sure of anything. Had Terrence wiped out? Had he been injured? It was pretty agonizing to watch. He looked through the camera lens again and scanned the water, searching for any sign of Terrence. Nothing. And then, as suddenly as he had disappeared, he reappeared, popping up from the water with a big grin on his face.

Epic relief flooded them all.

As Terrence completed his final professional ride, they made their way over to greet him. The judges were busy tallying up the score, and Terrence happily signed autographs and took pictures. From the joy on his face, it was hard to imagine he was serious about quitting, until he saw Kizzy, that is. And then it was quite obvious that he was.

The head judge stepped up to a microphone and tapped on it,

getting the crowd's attention before reading off the final scores. It was a close call, but Terrence emerged as the winner. The crowd cheered and showered him with congratulations, and as he collected his trophy, he took the moment to announce his intention.

Terrence grasped the microphone, and the crowd went silent again.

"Thank you, thank you! It means so much to me to take this cup home today, on my last ride as a competitive surfer."

The crowd reacted to the news with both cheers and boos. After all, the Vagabond Surfer was a legend.

"The decision to retire is a tough one, but in my gut, I know it's time. I want to take a minute to thank my fellow surfers, fans, sponsors, and supporters, who have been by my side throughout this incredible journey. I have had the honor of riding some of the most off-the-hook waves in the world, sharing the lineup with some of the most talented surfers on the planet, and being part of a community that has become family. The stoke and the bond that we share as surfers is amazing. I love you all, man."

The crowd cheered, and Ben looked around in amazement. There was no doubt about it—Terrence Williams was truly loved.

"While my competitive days may end, my love for surfing never will. Keep following me—there's more to come!"

He held the trophy over his head, and the crowd went wild.

The story was indeed writing itself.

It was some speech. And it prompted Ben to contemplate retirement as well.

Retirement from misery, that is.

Chapter Twenty-seven

Addison had spent the week thinking up ways to bump into Ben that didn't involve her staring out the window all day, waiting to pounce. By now there was no denying, even to herself, her attraction to her ornery neighbor and nothing stopping her from pursuing him. That almost kiss had been playing out in her mind ever since it didn't happen. Though she would be hard-pressed to admit it, she now believed he truly did not know that she was Gicky's niece when they began their little flirtation. Still, it was hard to align flirty Ben, with Ben from the book, with the ill-tempered Ben who berated her on the sidewalk. He was an enigma, and she was determined to crack his code.

With no luck in the bump-into department by Thursday, she decided she would bake more scones and bring them over for a taste test. Surely Gicky had shared her renowned culinary creations with her neighbor, rendering him the best person to judge.

While the scones were in the oven, Addison went to the studio to meditate. She had been diligent about it for the past three weeks, and it had been getting easier every day. Plus, she couldn't deny the positive effect it was having on her. She had transitioned from admonishing herself to "be in the moment" every few minutes to actually being in the moment.

The oven timer went off and, for the first time, the results of her baking looked like actual scones. She put a few on a plate and headed next door, filled with hope and curiosity. She had never been inside Ben's home, even if from the pages of his novel she felt as if she knew every inch of it.

"Knock, knock," she said out loud, while rapping on Ben's porch door. Sally was the first to greet her, obsessively offering her paw.

"Good girl." She kneeled down and scratched the dog's ears. Then she broke off a piece of scone and gave it to her. Sally quickly spit it out and ran into the house.

These fucking scones.

She heard footsteps approaching and swiftly tossed the evidence of her failure over the railing into the garden. Shep appeared before her, immediately focusing on the empty plate. Addison stared at it too before handing it to him. "Hi, I'm returning this plate," she said, oddly proud of the cover that was sure to eventually backfire. He took it.

"Ben went to the city for a few days. I'm watching Sally. I'll tell him when he returns."

Addison felt overly foolish. She took back the plate.

"It's my plate," she mumbled, before embracing next-level foolishness.

"What's going on here?" Shep inquired.

"Nothing. Really, nothing."

"That's what Ben said when I asked him about you—you know I was most certainly *not* born yesterday."

There was a woman's sun hat hanging on a hook shaped like a mermaid next to the doorway. Shep saw Addison's eyes turn toward it, the hat's meaning sinking into her face.

"He hasn't cleaned out even one of his wife's things from this house," he said. "I broached it once, and he bit my head off. He puts on a cocky face when he is out and about, but he's still mourning Julia far more than he wants to admit. His anger is really just grief dressed in wolf's clothing."

He took a deep breath in and sighed, adding, "I'm not telling you this to discourage you—I'm telling you because he is worth it, and I don't want you to give up. You know, Gicky really adored him. This would make her so happy."

Addison did not know what "this" was but noticed it was the second time the old guy had mentioned Gicky's happiness as it related to her and Ben. It was strange. Her mind was running in a million directions. She needed quiet, to clear her head, but she also didn't feel like being alone.

"Can Sally come over for a little?" she asked.

"Sure," Shep replied, fetching the pup from inside. He ruffled both their heads before they took off.

In the studio, Addison revisited her self-portrait. She had done an OK job, she thought, replicating her figure in the clay. If she were less self-critical, she might have said it was excellent. She would say that the experience of looking at herself naked in the mirror, molding the clay into her image with no thoughts of the world around her, was intimate and powerful. Maybe Paresh had gotten into her head, but she indeed felt an inner connection that was new to her. A sense of peace, even while being completely confused about every detail of her future.

She soaked a brush and wet down the torso of the sculpture,

using a fine tool to draw out the lines of two sleeves, transforming the naked breasts into a shirt. She decorated the top with a pattern, testing out checks and florals and geometric shapes before dabbing them with the tiny damp brush and gently erasing them with her thumb to begin again. Thoughts of doing the same with the mistakes she had made in life filled her head—leaving them behind, starting over, making new mistakes with little consideration of the old ones.

In the end, she chose a simple chevron and began slowly and meticulously carving the light pattern with a tiny V-tipped blade, repeating it over and over. Hours later, the figure appeared to be naked only from the waist down, like some kind of free-loving floozy. It made her laugh.

Sally barked at the studio door, startling Addison and alerting her that someone was there. She wiped off her hands and headed to the front of the house. Regardless of what Shep said, she hoped it was Ben. To her great surprise, but also not surprising at all, Kizzy's husband was standing on the other side of the screen door.

"Rome, I told you she's not here."

"That's nice, but I know she is. I told her parents what happened. Apparently, they still track her on her iPhone."

"Of course they do." Kizzy's parents were definitely the helicopter type. "She left a few days ago."

"Well, her phone didn't."

Addison had texted Kizzy a few times since she had left, and hadn't received an answer. She had even checked with Pru and Lisa, and neither had heard from her. She hadn't really been worried; Kizzy was not the most responsive on her phone. Unless she was working, she wasn't tethered to it. Which was admirable really, unless you were looking for her.

Addison opened the door and let him in, determined to give him a piece of her mind as she led him to the guest room. She hadn't straightened it out yet. No one was due to come until her parents' arrival the following weekend, and she'd gotten too caught up in sculpting to think of anything else.

Addison and Rome had been friends nearly as long as Addison and Kizzy had, and while there was no denying where her loyalty lay, and that she was furious with him, she did still have love for him. But right now, fury won.

"What you did is awful, Rome. How could you betray her like that?"

"I don't know."

"You don't know?"

She really didn't feel like lecturing him. Aside from her zen and all, she had always had a soft spot for Rome—mostly for the way he looked at Kizzy.

Rome looked at Kizzy like she hung the moon. Even lately, while he was apparently having an affair, he still looked at her that way. Addison had noted more than once that if she were to settle down, it should be with someone who looked at her like that. She thought again of the way Ben had looked at her when they were about to kiss, and her heart physically dropped to her stomach. She pressed her hand to her belly, as if to catch it.

"You OK?" Rome asked.

"Yes," she lied. She wasn't about to share her relationship woes with another disappointing version of the male species.

She shook out the linens. No phone. And looked under the bed.

"I'll call it," he said.

"If it's here, it's dead by now."

The telltale vibrato buzzed through the room. And there it was, plugged into the bathroom outlet.

He took it in his hands and stared at it almost longingly.

"Do you still love her?" Addison asked.

His eyes welled with tears. She didn't feel bad for him.

"You must be hungry," she said. "Would you like a scone?"

"No, thanks."

She stared at him for a minute longer before offering, "I'll make you a deal. You can wait here to see if she calls me or comes back for her phone if you help me clean this place out for the white elephant sale next week."

He agreed. And though she knew it might seem weird to some, hanging with her best friend's cheater of a husband, Addison knew it was what was best for Kizzy. And that was all Addison cared about right now. Addison was determined to get to the bottom of what was going on with this guy in order to give her friend the proper advice. She needed to explain to him that Kizzy deserved big love—heart-stopping, earthquaking, unwavering big love. Kezia Weinstein was too extraordinary for anything less. And she knew that if Rome were being honest with himself, he wouldn't want anything less for her.

But first—she would use the extra set of hands.

Apparently hard, mindless labor was just what the doctor ordered, because Rome was all in.

If this had been a few weeks earlier, Addison would have thrown it all in the giveaway pile, but now it felt like her Marie Kondo sensibilities were being choked by sentimentality. She had begun to love the aunt she had barely known by living in her home, on her island, among her things, and from meeting the people she loved. As if reading her mind, Rome said, "You can get a fortune for this place, Addison, it's like you won the lottery."

The conflict raged in her brain. She did a few deep cleansing breaths and evicted it. Progress.

"Let's start with the attic. Wanna go up?"

She said it real casual, as if fear were not a factor. In truth, she hadn't been able to bring herself to open the door since she arrived. She feared bats way more than dogs.

"Sure," he said.

"OK, let's get the ladder."

Addison held it while Rome climbed up. Even from below, she was scared of what may jump up out at them. He put his hand on the lever and let go of it like it was on fire.

"What's wrong?" she panicked.

He looked down at her from the top of the ladder and admitted, "I'm scared."

Addison laughed. "Just come down."

They decluttered the kitchen, with its multiple waffle makers, juice presses, strange-looking items that Rome guessed were potato scrubbers, and air popcorn makers.

"She was like the Noah of kitchen utensils. There are two of everything!" he joked.

She didn't want to laugh at anything Rome said, but a chuckle escaped her lips and reminded her of what was good about him.

"Can we talk, Rome?" She didn't wait for an answer. "Why do you want to stay married to Kizzy?"

"What kind of question is that?"

"It's a good question."

He didn't answer until they moved on to the storage closet in the studio.

"You know, I barely remember not being with Kizzy."

"Yeah, that's not a reason."

"Well, I love her. I love her very much."

"Yet not enough to resist breaking her heart, again, right?"

"Didn't you love that broken-engagement guy when you broke his heart?"

"Betraying someone you still love and ending a relationship because you've fallen out of love are two very different things." When she said *falling out of love*, she felt like a liar. She wasn't about to admit to Rome that she may have never been in love before. She had barely even admitted it to herself.

"Mine was the right thing to do," she added, for Rome's benefit. She paused to let it set in. She knew in his heart he would want to do right by Kizzy. He held up a broken clock.

"Keep or toss?" he asked.

"That is the question."

He climbed off the step stool and sat on it. His eyes filled with tears.

"Let me ask you something," Addison said. "What makes you think that this time would be any different? I mean, you cheated, then promised it was a onetime thing, then cheated again—with the same woman. Are you still in touch with this woman?"

"Yes."

"Then what are you doing, Rome? If you love Kizzy, as you claim to, then let her go. She's young. You're *both* young. You have endless days of happiness ahead of you. "

"I don't know how to live without Kizzy. I barely remember a time when she wasn't by my side."

"I'm sure you will figure it out. Let's take a break—go to the market to pick up stuff for dinner."

"It's OK if I stay here tonight?"

"It's fine. You can leave in the morning. And if I hear from her, I will ask her to call you or reach out myself."

She knew Kizzy would want it this way. Even with everything that had happened before and now, Kizzy didn't hate Rome. She wasn't a hateful person.

After dinner, they sat down to watch a movie. Before it began, Rome asked, "Addison. Do you think we will remain friends after this?"

"Me and you?"

He nodded a yes, and she smiled at him sweetly, even put her hand on his knee before saying, "Absolutely not."

Chapter Twenty-eight

Ben spent the next few days holed up in the Montauk motel crafting the piece on Terrence. He polished it up on the train back to Bay Shore. Ben loved writing on trains. He once took a fifty-one-hour ride from Chicago to San Francisco when behind the eight ball on a deadline. By the time they had reached the plains of Nebraska, he was halfway through, and he finished up somewhere in the Nevada desert. Now, as the conductor announced, "Next stop, Bay Shore," he proudly closed his laptop. He was satisfied that he had given Terrence his due as the legendary and barrier-breaking athlete that he was.

Ben boarded the ferry, sat up top, and thought about his next move with Addison. He had escaped unscathed, really, and contemplated chickening out. He didn't have to open himself up like that again. As he walked home in the dark, he tossed both options around in his brain—deliberating between letting it go or pursuing her. Though he knew it was really a matter of the heart. The brain could come up with a thousand reasons not to do something, but it was the heart that held the presidential veto.

When he turned onto his block—their block—it became obvious what would come next. The draw was almost magnetic, and his feet were barely touching the ground. The light was on in her living room, and he could see her through her window, curled up on the couch watching TV. One look at her, and he was sure he had no choice but to tell her how he felt. He walked quietly onto her front deck, contemplating knocking, knowing full well that she would jump ten feet in the air when he did. With that in mind, he pulled out his phone to text her first.

As he was about to press Send, a man appeared in her living room with a big smile and a bowl of popcorn. He plopped down next to her on the couch with a casualness that couldn't have belonged to a paying guest. Ben looked closer. The man said something that looked to be deep. Addison answered, placing her hand on his knee.

And Ben turned around and headed home to Sally, the only living thing that had never disappointed him.

The next morning, Ben woke with a familiar ache in his stomach, but refused to give in to it. Instead, he threw on his wet suit, grabbed his paddleboard, and headed to the beach. Watching all of that surfing reminded him how good it felt to be out on the ocean, to clear his mind. Sally followed and sat dutifully waiting for him on the shore, dipping in and out of the waves, becoming a wet, salty mess. She did her usual meet and greet on steroids when he made his way back onto land.

They headed back home together, him carrying his board, her running ahead and then circling back behind him again to make sure he was OK. She was in tune with his feelings and always had been. And while he was nowhere near the depths of grief that he had been in the past, he was most certainly bummed, and Sally most certainly knew it.

"Good girl," he said, running his hand over her back as she passed.

Sally looked back at him knowingly and made a beeline for Addison's house.

"Bad girl, bad girl," he mumbled under his breath.

Ben kneeled down in front of the doggie door—ass in the air—and peeked through at Sally. She was wiggling her back all over Addison's living room rug, doing the doggie mamba.

"Get out of there!" Ben coaxed, before changing his tone to a high pitched, "Here, girl!" Neither worked. He knocked on the front door. No answer. So he kneeled back down, his head through the doggie door, when Addison arrived behind him.

"Ben?" she called out.

Smack, boom. "Ow!" he said, flipping back on to his butt. He ran his hand over his forehead, grimaced at the blood on his fingers, swooned a little, and pushed himself against the door to settle down.

"Oh boy," Addison said. "Let's get you inside."

The cut was nothing much, but Addison broke out Gicky's first aid kit (a metal box painted to look like Clara Barton) and went to town while Ben whined on the couch. "This may sting," she said, wiping a cotton ball with hydrogen peroxide over the wound. It did.

"Where's your boyfriend?" he stung back.

"My boyfriend? Do you mean the guy who was here last night?" Addison laughed. "That's Rome, Kizzy's husband. He left on the morning boat."

Ben's expression said it all—followed by his words.

"Wow. Do you two share everything?" he asked.

"Yuck. Don't be ridiculous. Kizzy was missing, and she left her phone behind—possibly on purpose. He came looking for her."

"Kizzy is fine. Actually, more than fine. I'm sorry to be the one to tell you, but she's in Montauk with Terrence Williams. They're in love."

"C'mon."

"Yup. I asked her how she could do this to you—she said you'd be happy for her."

"Of course I'm happy for her, but they're in love?"

"For real. He's giving up the road for her. Moving to the big city."

"Who is he, Crocodile Dundee?"

"That's what I said, and nobody got the reference."

"Another gift from my mother. What's your excuse?"

"I had a thing for reptiles—I was a Teenage Mutant Ninja Turtle for Halloween four years in a row."

She smiled, squeezed some Neosporin onto a Q-tip, and gently traced the cut with it. It had been so long since anyone had taken care of him. His eyes widened as he stared into hers.

"So, you and Terrence? Was that just your big foray into the one-night stand?"

He wasn't happy about it but knew he could deal with it if it meant being with her.

Addison laughed, "Oh my God, Ben. That wasn't *me*. It was Kizzy. You just saw them together—how could you think that?" She laughed again until she realized he was particularly serious.

"I thought it was you. That morning, when I came over, I thought it was you who had been with Terrence."

"Seriously?"

"It's not that crazy. You thought I traded sex for an autograph!"

"Well, I may have been wrong about that—but you had sex on the beach with that Sex on the Beach girl—I saw you saying goodbye to her on the stairs."

"I was saying hello to her. She saw me walking Sally and called out to me."

Addison laughed at all of the confusion. So did Ben.

"If conclusion jumping was an Olympic sport, we would have won gold," he joked.

"Synchronized misunderstanding!" Addison added before carefully placing a small Band-Aid onto his forehead. When through, she rested the back of her hand on his cheek in a particularly loving way. It made his heart shake.

"You're good to go," she said, the words getting caught in her throat.

He blushed and looked into her eyes. "Do I have to?"

"Do you have to what?" she said, barely audibly.

"Do I have to go? I'm still a little dizzy, you know, from the gash," he said, pointing to his forehead.

"I don't know if I'd call it a gash." She smiled. "It's more like . . . a boo-boo."

"Maybe you should kiss it, then, make it all better."

She leaned over and kissed the tip of his nose instead, which had clearly been broken once or twice. He took her hands in his and pulled her onto the couch next to him.

"Not like that," he whispered, running his finger across her lips as if silently asking for permission. She gave it and kissed him straight on. Their positioning was awkward, so she brazenly climbed onto his lap and wrapped her long legs behind him.

And they kissed.

They kissed like two teenagers who had never kissed before but also, so perfectly, and so in sync, as if they had been kissing each other for their entire lives.

She kissed the salty skin behind his ears and down his neck while running her hands through his disheveled hair. And he responded with a hunger that the small collection of women he had slept with since Julia hadn't touched. He hadn't truly desired any of them. It was just a primal urge. This was also primal, but from his heart. She had indisputably awoken his dormant organ.

He wanted, actually needed, to feel her skin against his. Needed to scoop her up in his arms, carry her to her bed, and make love to her. But with every inch of him pushing for that to occur, he knew that there was still one enormous obstacle. He was, in fact, wearing a wet suit. There was no graceful way of getting out of a wet wet suit. It was one of those things that needed to be done in private—nothing even minorly sexy about a grown hairy man peeling himself out of a spandex suit. Logic and humility stepped in and curbed the hunger.

He broke away.

"Are we doing this?" he asked quietly.

"It seems so," she answered, clearly not interested in a break in the action.

"I'm going to bring Sally home."

Addison looked down at the dog. Seeing her little snout resting on the coffee table and her human eyes staring at them was more than mortifying.

"That's a good idea. Come right back?"

"Give me a half hour—I want to feed her and rinse off the ocean."

The need to take off his wet suit made him seem cool and collected when, in fact, he was anything but. Her eyes longed for him, but she nodded yes. He almost stopped to tell her the truth—but that longing in her eyes was too good to squash with intimacies that usually aren't revealed until at least the first anniversary. An anniversary—he flinched at the thought. The thing he had sworn against felt inevitable with this woman. He worried about going home, breaking the spell.

Chapter Twenty-nine

The minute the screen door slammed and Ben was out of sight, Addison stuck her nose under her arm and took a whiff. Not awful—but certainly not the essence of lilac that Gicky's bottle of shower gel assured. She stripped off her clothes in the outdoor shower, washed her body, and even ran a razor over her lightly stubbled legs. Inside, she followed the whole thing up with a coat of moisturizer and threw on a cotton sundress and a pair of sexy undies.

She was feeling vulnerable, which was new to her. Vulnerability may have been the number one thing that Addison had steered away from in her dating life. Granted, she had felt a host of emotions this summer that were unusual for her—beginning with failure—but this type of raw emotional exposure felt exceptionally risky. She brazenly slipped off her panties, knowing that when Ben reached under her dress and realized that she was naked, it would make him crazy. That's not why she did it though; it would also make her feel as if she were in control. And with that thought, she felt more at ease.

Get out of your head, Addison.

She knew only one way to do that. She went to the studio to meditate, leaving the door ajar so that she would hear Ben return.

As she sat on the floor counting back from one hundred, everything released in her head. Her heart, her mind, even her pores were all open. When she finally opened her eyes as well, she found Ben sitting on the floor—staring at her. She did not know how long he'd been there.

"What are you doing?" she asked, amused.

"Counting your freckles."

"There are forty-seven," she laughed.

"You counted?"

"My sister counted when we were kids."

"You have a sister?"

"Yes. Ivy. Three years younger than me."

"I guess we put the cart before the horse. Should we fix that?"

"OK, go!" she said with a funny sense of urgency.

"Where did you grow up?"

"In a suburb of Chicago. You?"

"Jersey. College?"

"School of the Art Institute of Chicago."

"Nice! Wesleyan undergrad, then Columbia for journalism."

"I may have guessed both, smarty-pants."

"Favorite author, aside from me, of course?"

"John Irving. You?"

"Same."

"C'mon."

"Pinky swear," he said, holding out said pinky.

They looped their pinkies together, and the tiny touch sparked ripples of warmth.

The cross-examination changed course.

"You're very beautiful," Ben whispered, placing his other hand on her leg, its smoothness resulting in a shy smile. She nodded, a permission of sorts, and he released her pinky and slid both hands upward, beneath her dress. Her nakedness registered on his face, and his smile widened. His hands grazed her bottom before he rested them on her torso, pulling her toward him and realizing how they were somewhat lined up. Toes against toes, lips against lips.

"And tall," he added with an even wider smile. He brushed a wayward hair from her eyes and kissed her gently on her lips. When he reached his hand between her legs, he was the one who moaned. He pulled her dress over her head, and even with the bright light flooding the room—making her all the more naked—she completely gave in to it. She anticipated every movement of his hungry eyes and even hungrier mouth. By the time they actually made love, she couldn't control her body from shaking.

She had seen the words *quivering loins* in books, and it always made her laugh. *Quivering loins*, written by men like Ben, only to be topped in the humorous category by a throbbing member. But there they both were. Her loins quivering, his member throbbing. Her thoughts stopped.

They lay spent on the floor afterward, and he whispered, breathlessly, "Addie?"

"Yes, Ben?" She suddenly liked her nickname.

"Was this your one-night stand?" he asked. She couldn't tell if he was serious or joking.

She rolled over on her side to face him.

"It's not even noon—ask me again in the morning."

They both laughed, and he tickled her side, which led to them starting up again. She wrangled away from him, stood, and stepped back into her dress.

"Come with me," she said.

He took her hand as she led them to her bedroom. The room was still cold from the air she had blasted the night before. The unmade bed, with its white rustled sheets and linen duvet, was crisp, delicious, and inviting. Addison pulled her dress back overhead, and they found each other, under the sheets. Entwined in each other's arms, they drifted off.

An hour or so later, Addison slipped away to the bathroom. Ben didn't flinch. She wondered if he always slept so soundly, especially in the middle of the day. On her return, she watched him sleep for a minute or two—his broad chest rising and falling and rising and falling. A faded suntan line cut across his triceps. She traced it with her finger before leaning over him and depositing butterfly kisses on his eyelids. Still, he didn't stir. She kissed the place where the dimple usually appeared on his cheek. No movement. She straddled her legs around his torso again—careful not to put her weight on him—and planted more kisses, circling his chest and tracing the line that divided his abs with her mouth. He finally stirred, and she continued kissing and teasing and running her hands everywhere but where he wanted it most.

He opened his eyes and looked up at her mischievously, before scooping her up and flipping her onto her back. He couldn't wait a second longer.

"Should we get dressed—go to the beach? It's gorgeous out," Addison asked afterward. The pressure to enjoy the beach on a sunny day always weighed on her. Ben didn't seem to care. Addison was still a newbie, but after all his years on the island, Ben was an old schooler at this point. Old schoolers knew better than to reproach themselves for missing a great beach day. It happens. Plus, there was no doubt that the two of them sitting together on the beach would fuel the gossip mill.

"Or we can watch *Love Is Blind*?" he suggested instead.

"Shut up, you watch *Love Is Blind*? I may love you," Addison said, not thinking much of her revelation.

"I may love you too," Ben said before searching the nightstand for the clicker.

Somewhere in the middle of episode two or three, they made love yet again. This time slowly, and with their eyes burrowing into each other's souls. For real, it felt like that. Addison, in particular, couldn't remember ever having felt that unguarded before.

"Want to help me with something?" she asked afterward, with a hint of seductiveness.

"Are you seriously not satisfied yet?" he asked. "I need a little time."

She laughed. "It's about the attic. I need to get up there before the white elephant sale."

"Ugh. I should definitely take part in that this year," he moaned.

"Well, if you help me, I can return the favor and help you."

The color drained from his face, and he looked suddenly nauseated. She noticed, and thought of the sun hat on his porch and what Shep had said about him. She redirected the focus from his dead wife's belongings back to her dead aunt's.

"Don't worry, I have most of it sorted. I just can't bring myself to look in that attic."

Her redirect worked. Ben laughed and declared, "By all means open up the attic, let the bats fly free," before explaining that her aunt Gicky loved to say that. He thought it hysterical.

"I even put it in a novel," he joked.

"Well, I hope she didn't mean it literally. That's kind of what I was afraid of."

Now, a melancholy look settled on her face.

Ben clocked it.

"Don't worry. I got you."

"That's not it. Everything I have learned about Gicky makes me so angry that my parents kept her from me. You know I hadn't seen her since I was a little kid?"

"I know all about it. That's how I went about convincing her to let me have the house for a song."

"And what song was that? Was it something by Cheap Trick?"

"Very funny. C'mon. Let's do this."

Ben wiggled back into his shorts and took up the challenge. The attic was surprisingly bare—no bats, no raccoons, and very little stuff. He handed her a box of empty votives, a couple of throw pillows, and something resembling a polka-dot-covered papier-mâché deer's head.

"Can *I* keep this," he asked, "as a consolation prize?"

"Sure."

"Thank you!"

Addison laughed. "What's up there—on top?"

"Hold my legs," he asked, before standing on his tippy-toes and pulling down what looked to be a painting that was balanced on the attic's wood frame. It was wrapped in brown paper, same as the two that Gicky had left for her friends. Ben read the names written on it as he passed it down to Addison.

"Beverly and Morty."

She shook her head in disbelief. "It's for my parents. Gicky left a few pieces of art for friends," she added in explanation.

"And enemies as well, it seems," Ben quipped.

"I don't know if you would call them enemies. My dad once told me that his relationship with his sister, or lack thereof, was his biggest failure in life."

"And you don't know what caused it?"

"Something so awful that they never told me."

She held the picture up in the air. "It's heavier than the others were."

"Are you gonna open it?"

"They're supposed to come next weekend. It can wait."

"All right." He waited for her to put it down before moving on to the next thing, but she didn't.

"Maybe take a peek," he suggested. A mischievous smile spread across his lips.

"I can't. I mean, I'm beyond curious. Even so, it feels wrong to open it."

Ben climbed off the ladder. "I'll do it."

"Oh, you shouldn't," she said, following up with an exaggerated wink.

She leaned the picture against the wall, and Ben carefully untied the string that held the brown paper in place, and took a peek inside.

"Well?"

"It looks like one of those mosaics. You know what I mean?"

"I think so. But there must be more to it. Show me the corner."

Ben pulled down one corner, and Addison saw that it was a collage made of broken china. Not just any broken china, but her mother's pattern, famously passed down to her by a wealthy aunt on Addison's father's side. Her mother loved to say the only thing they ever got from Morty's side of the family was indigestion and a pristine fifty-two-piece set of fine Ginori china.

Addison ripped off the paper with a vengeance. The china—which was broken into a hundred tiny pieces—was set in cement in the form of a broken heart.

She was mad with a rage she'd never remembered feeling before. If she were an emoji, she would be the one where a head explodes. Could the Big Terrible Thing be about a broken plate? She picked up her cell phone to call her parents, taking a small beat to get rid of Ben. Yes, they had sex multiple times, and yes, she was feeling all kinds of feelings that she had not felt in a long, long time, if ever, but there was no way she was blowing this by turning into a raving lunatic in front of him. The Irwin family's particular brand of insanity should not be revealed in the honeymoon phase. She told it like it was.

"You don't want to be around for this discussion."

"I don't mind."

"Well, I kind of do. I'll catch up with you later."

He wrapped his arms around her, engulfing her in a big eye-to-eye, rib-squeezing, belly-bumping hug. It made her even more annoyed with her parents—for tainting the perfect day.

As soon as he was out of earshot, she dialed.

"Hello, darling," her mother said, picking up on the first ring.

"Mom. I need you to tell me that the whole Big Terrible Thing between you and Aunt Gicky wasn't over a plate."

Her mother laughed, "Of course it wasn't over a plate."

Relief exuded from every inch of her body, every inch. Between the meditating and ocean swimming and the sex and the freedom of being unemployed, she had been feeling, well, blissfully unaware. She knew it couldn't last forever, but the Summer of Addison was still in session, and she was not interested in cutting it short with family drama. She took a deep meditative breath to seal in the relief and then . . .

"It was a soup terrine," her mother said, with zero emotion.

The words brought her right back to the spring of 1998.

The scene from the last time she saw her aunt flashed before her eyes. It was a Jewish holiday—Passover, the second night, with only the immediate family plus Aunt Gicky. The evening before, at the first Passover Seder, they had had a full house. Given her mother's tendency to behave like a Stepford Wife in front of company, the whole thing may have turned out very differently had there been a bigger crowd present on day two. Addison's mother had "the help," a lovely Polish woman named Anya, serve the matzah ball soup directly from the pot in the kitchen. Once everyone had a bowl, her mother took her seat, while quietly lamenting, "If I had the soup terrine that went with this beautiful set, I could have served right from the table."

It was a statement that Addison and her dad and sister had heard before, one that didn't need a response. Even at that young age, Addison knew all about the missing piece in the set. She knew that her mother had flown to New York to retrieve the blessed china when said aunt passed and how the fifty-two-piece set was inexplicably missing the pièce de résistance: the soup terrine. Beverly had famously ransacked Morty's aunt's apartment before it was sold, searching every corner for it. She referred to the china from that day forward as the fifty-two-piece set of china minus one.

Beverly brought a spoonful of soup to her lips and gently blew on it as Aunt Gicky casually announced, "Oh, when you come to my house for a holiday, I will serve you from it."

All eyes went from Aunt Gicky to Beverly, who stood up, pushed in her chair, and said, "Morty, take care of this."

If you have ever been to a Passover Seder, you know that the timing of this dramatic revelation couldn't have been worse. Everyone was on their third cup of wine, and had been waiting patiently for the meal to begin after sitting through an hour's explanation of their ancestors fleeing slavery. Meaning that everyone was both tipsy and hangry.

Addison and her sister were handed a couple of pieces of matzah and dismissed to the basement to play Barbies. The two girls sat on the top step instead and listened as best they could. Over the crunching of their cardboard-like meal, they heard shouting and crying, and things said that most definitely should not have been said. And while they were too young to really understand what was up, they knew it was bad.

When they were finally fetched from upstairs, Aunt Gicky was gone. To this day, Addison never, in her wildest dreams, put two and two together. In fact, the only reason to think that the soup terrine was the trigger of the Big Terrible Thing was that she still remembered the incident vividly, considering she was all of six years old at the time.

All she managed now was, "Put Daddy on the phone."

Addison was furious. Not so much at her mother, the most Waspy Jew on the planet, who avoided drama and confrontation at all costs, but at her dad. Beverly Irwin would rather write someone off than work through a conflict. But Addison expected more from her father. Her father was a wuss who literally kicked his only sister to the curb to save himself from dealing with his insufferable wife.

As she held the phone, there followed a lot of painful yelling (hers), and a lot of painful silence (his). For Addison, it was hard to process, after a lifetime of thinking otherwise, that her parents, particularly her father, were just people. Flawed people. They didn't always have the right answer; they didn't always do the right thing. And they in fact could stop talking to their closest relative over a gold-leafed floral soup terrine.

Morty Irwin was undeniably a wimp.

Maybe it wasn't her grandfather's infidelities or the humiliation of Jeffrey Pearlman kissing Sofie Bonelli that had shaped her future with men. Maybe it came down to the old adage about girls marrying their fathers. Or in her case, dating them.

Or maybe it was a combination of all three.

In the end, she disinvited Morty and Beverly for the following weekend, which was met with obvious relief on their part, and hung up. She went directly to the clay, relishing in the powerful sense of connection and escape. Losing herself in it once again, she gave her girl a skirt. A long flowy skirt, which she carved with tiny flowers, not unlike the pattern on the infamous china. Sometime after dark, Sally appeared at the studio door with a note tied around her neck that read *Miss me?*

She cleaned the paint-splattered washbasin that had become,

for some inexplicable reason, her favorite thing in the house, and
scratched Sally behind her ears. She pulled out her phone and
texted Ben.

Want to go out on the town?

A few minutes later, her phone vibrated.

I'll pick you up at nine.

Addison looked through the suitcase that she hadn't fully un-
packed yet and paired a bright strappy camisole dress with high-
tops. While she sat in front of the mirror doing her makeup, she
realized she'd barely even worn mascara since being there. She
put on an extra coat and smiled at herself in the mirror.

This happy state she had found herself in came with a natural
glow.

Ben arrived promptly at nine with a bouquet of cut flowers
from his garden tied together with string.

So sweet.

He explained their options while she put them in water.

"There are two choices here. We go to town, and by morning
the entire island will know that we are, you know—"

"What? Doing it?"

"I was going to say *an item*."

"An item? Addison laughed. "What century were you born in?"

"You sound like Julia." He smiled. She did too. She was
happy that he was comfortable reminiscing about his wife in
front of her. She hoped it would continue.

"It's just I'd rather keep this between us—get to know each
other a little more before fueling the rumor mill."

Addison was really beginning to feel like she knew him, the
man who had carried her bags onto the ferry and counted her

freckles, that is. Though she realized she didn't even know whom he voted for in the last election.

"Makes sense," she said, thinking of when to bring up politics.

"OK. Grab a jacket. We are taking a water taxi to the Ice Palace in Cherry Grove."

Chapter Thirty

The Ice Palace, named after an F. Scott Fitzgerald story by the same name, was Fire Island's first disco. It could easily fit a thousand people—a thousand sweaty people, and as Ben and Addison entered, it felt like a thousand and two.

Aside from a recent rebuild following a fire, the club had been the center of nightlife at the gay enclaves of Cherry Grove and the Pines, on the east end of the island, for decades. There was no better place to dance on the island, if not arguably the world. They entered to the tune of Chic's "Good Times" and immediately hit the dance floor. It was crowded and steamy and, thanks to her mother, Addison knew every word to the seventies classic. As she crooned, "Clams on the half shell and roller skates, roller skates," moving her hips from side to side to the beat, Ben couldn't help but laugh. She was like a different person.

They stayed on the dance floor straight through "He's the Greatest Dancer," during which Addison continued dancing and singing along like she was the fifth member of Sister Sledge.

She spun around Ben, taunting him with, "Halston, Gucci,

Fiorucci" and teasing with, "Do you wanna funk with me?" They joined forces with Barbra Streisand and Donna Summer for the duet "No More Tears (Enough Is Enough)," dancing in slow motion to the ballad-like beginning before pounding it out when the disco beat kicked in. By the time the eight-minute extended version was over, they were both dripping with sweat.

"Air!" Addison shouted over the intro to the next song. They had been dancing for at least an hour.

Ben followed her out to the back deck of the hotel that housed the club, to a double-decker horseshoe of rooms with a pool in the middle. There they cooled off, sipping frozen Rocket Fuels and dipping their feet in the water until the notes of another Donna Summer hit, "I Feel Love," beckoned them back inside.

They danced and sang the title lyric over and over again until the intensity and absurdity of it all became too real. Ben took Addison's hand and led her outside, stopping to get their hands stamped on the way out.

The ridiculously spot-on soundtrack of their night continued with the disco classic "Babe, We're Gonna Love Tonite." The fading chorus could still be heard in the distance when they reached the beach, where they took the stairs, two at a time, eager to feel the August breeze coming off the ocean.

The beat still resonating in her eardrums, Addison yelled, a little too loudly, "Thank you for taking me here! I love it."

Beyond the fun factor, the night had cut into the anger she was feeling at her parents. The memories of her mother dancing around the house to those same disco songs diluted her animosity toward her with every note. She wondered for a second if Ben had done that on purpose. She doubted it. She was probably giving him too much credit.

Either way, she felt so appreciative that she wrapped her arms around his neck and hugged him. And though they had been dancing together for over an hour, they had not really touched since briefly holding hands on the water taxi. Her hug seemed to break the seal.

"Come on," he said, leading her to a shadowed spot on the beach, out of sight from the lit-up houses above.

She was nervous at first, but Ben promised her that no one would know or care.

They made love in the sand, with Addison feeling thankful that she had worn a dress and that the ocean was as loud as it was.

Afterward, she asked, "Should we walk home?"

"We can," he replied.

"How long is the walk?"

"Around an hour twenty, or a water taxi leaves in . . ." He wrestled his phone from his pocket and checked the time. "In six minutes!"

"Let's go!" they said in unison, quickly putting themselves back together and racing to the dock.

They sat on the small open bench at the back of the boat, staring straight ahead at the other passengers, who were packed onto the three small, covered benches inside. The wind blew Addison's hair all over the place. Her thoughts were following the same trajectory. This was all happening so quickly. They held hands on the way home from the dock to their street and shared a kiss between the two houses.

"I have to go walk Sally," Ben said.

Still thinking about how quickly things were moving, Addison made the choice to close out the night. She yawned, a big exaggerated yawn.

"I'm so tired. Can I see you in the morning?" she asked tentatively.

"OK. See you in the morning," he responded, with a quick, sweet peck on her lips.

Week Seven

Chapter Thirty-one

To say that Addison was feeling things she had never felt before was an understatement. She opened her eyes on Monday morning with what could be best described as a giddy sensation. She couldn't remember her body ever seeming this light, and her mind this hopeful. She began to question herself—to analyze whether this mood was due to the man or the zen or maybe the clay. She was loving the clay, the feel of it in her hands, the freedom to create and destroy and then start again with no repercussions. But the man—he confused her and challenged her and excited her. Still, she refused to believe this feeling was just about a guy. She vowed to spend the day alone, sculpting and baking and finishing up sorting out the piles she had created of Gicky's things. Gicky's gallerist was set to arrive that Saturday, and the white elephant sale was on Sunday.

Yes, she would spend the day alone evaluating the source of her happiness. She heard the rumble of the garbage truck and ran to take her cans to the curb. And there was Ben, doing the same. One look at him destroyed her resolve.

"Want to come over?" she called out to him. Her cheeks flushed. She covered up her excitement by adding, "To taste my scones?"

Sally chose that moment to roll over and play dead, and Addison couldn't help but take it personally.

Even with that warning, Ben lit up. He looked up at the overcast sky and approached.

The closer he got, the more charged the space between them felt.

"Let me take this girl for a beach walk first, before it rains."

Standing there on the sidewalk, not touching him, felt brutal. It was as if they hadn't spent the entire weekend binge-reading each other's bodies. The longing in her was immense. She took a step back to breathe.

"All good—whenever," she said, trying to sound casual, even though games didn't seem necessary. She was struck by how after six weeks of flirtations and miscommunications, their coupling suddenly felt like a given, as if they were an old couple now. As if she were home.

Addison watched him walk down the block with Sally and fought the urge to follow them. She had things to do. Things just for her. She would sneak in a morning meditation in between tackling the scones. This time, she would set the oven timer for fifteen minutes. Twenty had been a disaster.

She followed the recipe exactly and put the perfectly shaped spheres in the oven, set the timer, and went out back to meditate. Within minutes of doing so, a bolt of thunder literally rocked the room. The studio darkened, and the sky opened up.

Her mind went to Ben and Sally on the beach.

She already felt possessive of them both, like they were hers.

The feeling swallowed her until the timer buzzed, breaking her out of it.

Ben and Sally walked in while the scones were cooling, and stood in the doorway—soaked, but safe.

"Oh my God—come in, come in," Addison cried.

She threw a kitchen towel at Ben and then ran off to get bigger ones.

"I should have gone home first, but I couldn't take another step," Ben said, apologizing for the puddle at his feet. "It came out of nowhere."

"It's fine. It's fine." Addison threw a large bath towel over his shoulders and got to work on Sally with another one. A few minutes later they were sitting at the kitchen table—Ben happily dressed in one of Gicky's caftans, sipping tea and tasting scones, Sally at their feet.

Ben cautiously took the first bite while Addison looked on. The pressure was palpable.

"Do you want me to tell you the truth?" he asked.

"No, I want you to lie to me."

"OK. They're too dry. And kind of grainy."

"I just told you I wanted you to lie to me! I'm a very literal person!"

"Sorry."

Addison dumped the batch in the pail and all out moped.

"Want to climb into bed and watch *Love Is Blind* again?" Ben asked with the confidence of a sixteen-year-old girl.

She weighed whether to give in to his delightful request or to finish packing up and organizing. It was pouring out, after all— the perfect day to do either.

"Or we can finish boxing up Gicky's stuff and then take the leftover boxes and tape to your house to do the same."

Her cell rang, and she grabbed it. She barely got out "Hello" before the voice of Nan, the real estate agent, blasted out of it.

"Great news. I have a hot buyer coming on the ten o'clock ferry tomorrow. They're looking for a double lot—so it's as good as done! Have it clean, please, not that it matters."

And she was gone.

Ben had obviously heard.

"So, you're selling?"

She contemplated telling him how she had reached out to the real estate agent right after they had their falling-out at the block party, but the insanity of selling a house because your crush hurt your feelings seemed too great to admit.

"I'm considering my options, is all."

"So, can you consider mine?"

"Sure. Lay it on me."

"OK." He looked down at the flowery caftan and tied it tightly around his waist. Addison laughed.

"Gicky offered me the house for half a mil. I have it in writing—on a clamshell."

"On a clamshell?"

"Yes. And I don't know if you know this, but Native Americans in this area used shells for money—wampum."

"Oh, then it's totally legit. Silly me!"

"I have a totally legit idea. I give you the half a million for half the house. You keep the main property and the studio. And I take the guesthouse and the property between us for a pool."

He took in her blank expression and threw in, "That you can

use!" before standing up in his caftan and doing jazz hands. Addison laughed again.

"Let's just take it one day at a time—starting with tomorrow. I haven't even shown the place yet."

The imminent visit from the agent put a fire under Addison to finish up. As soon as the rain let up, she sent Ben and Sally home. Sally used the front door, while Ben escaped out the back dressed like the ghost of Aunt Gicky.

She tackled one of the last two closets left—the towel closet. It was as much a trip through Gicky's travels as her matchbook and toiletry collections were—though bulkier. She separated the plusher towels from the threadbare ones, tossing all of those but a bathmat from the Plaza and a pool towel from the Taj Mumbai. On the bottom shelf sat a big Frye boot box that looked older than Addison. One look inside and she knew she would be sitting on that spot for at least the next hour.

It was packed with old photographs, letters, and keepsakes. She pulled out a forest-green autograph book with the words *School Daze* embossed in gold on top of an image of an old schoolhouse, like the one in the painting that Gicky had left for Margot. Addison admired her aunt's perfect penmanship on the first page.

This book belongs to Gloria "Gicky" Irwin, Sixth Grade P.S. 449. Teacher: Ruth Glass

In Addison's time, autograph books like this—or yearbooks, really—were filled with short sentiments like *Stay Cool!* or long diatribes from your bestie detailing every inside joke or tiff you ever had, but this was filled with adorable little ditties written in cursive. One was funnier than the next.

Your album is a garden plot
Where all kind friends sow seeds
I plant the sweet forget-me-not
Please keep it free from weeds.

Cows like clover
Pigs like squash
I like you, I do, by gosh!

And others that had stood the test of time, like:

2 good
2 B
4 gotten!

There was a cute one from her dad, just a hand-drawn heart and his name, Morty, with a backward *R*.

And the one that made her think the most, from Gicky's sixth-grade teacher.

To Gloria, a nice little homemaker. Love, Mrs. Glass

And while Addison knew that all the girls probably received similar encouragement from Mrs. Glass, poor Gicky was likely already knee-deep in homemaking activities—parenting her kid brother and getting dinner on the table nightly. She had deserved more than she got from Addison's father.

The next thing she pulled from the box really sealed the deal: a pile of cards and whatnots, neatly tied up with an old satin ribbon. She carefully pulled it loose, hoping to replicate the perfect bow when she put it back together, and was amazed to see that the pile was all Morty. She carefully unfolded a couple of letters home from sleepaway camp.

Dear Gicky,

My friend Bernie cries every night. I don't do that, but I do miss you. Please bring me a salami on visiting day.

Love, your brother, Morty

Dear Gicky,

I passed my swimming test. I'm a minnow. Bernie is only a guppy. He cried. Please bring me Vanilla Charleston Chews and Cherry Sours on visiting day.

Love, your brother, Morty

His fifth-grade report card, filled with marks of Unsatisfactory and Needs Improvement versus his seventh-grade straight As, had her thinking about what Margot said regarding Gicky teaching Morty to read. Her disappointment in her father was really getting to her—breaking her heart. She decided to call him back. If anything was really to be learned by what happened between the two Irwin siblings, it should be not to let things come between family.

The minute Addison heard her father's remorseful tone, it broke her resolve. What good would berating him really do? He was clearly doing that enough on his own.

"I'm sorry I was mean on our call, Daddy, I know this all must have been so hard for you, and with Gicky leaving me this house—well, I can't even imagine what you're feeling."

The other end of the phone was quiet until Addison realized her father was crying. She gave him a minute to get it together. In the end, it was more like three.

"I—I—I," he finally stammered, "I wish I could do it over again. All the emails I wrote and didn't send. All the time, I was more concerned with who was right and who was wrong. It all feels so pointless now. What did it all matter? I never got to tell her I forgave her. I never got to ask her for forgiveness."

"She forgave you, Daddy."

"How do you know?"

"I know. She made a broken heart out of that soup terrine. She only made things for the people she loved."

As she said it she thought about Shep's claim that there was a painting for him too, somewhere. He didn't seem to fit into the same category as the others. It gave her pause. And while she still put off having her parents visit and would always be disappointed in what had transpired between the older Irwin children, she forgave her father too.

Maybe she was on the path to enlightenment after all.

She forgot about the scones in the oven.

"Fuck me," she cursed, while dumping a burnt batch in the garbage.

Maybe she had a ways to go on that path.

The day went by in the way it does when you get caught up in things and time passes quickly. Like one of those high-speed trains from London to Paris—whoosh—suddenly it was five o'-clock.

Just as she realized the time, there was a knock on the back door. Her heart smiled, and she jumped him—all five foot nine of her leapt into Ben's arms. His tall frame was planted so solidly in the ground, he didn't even rock. It really turned her on.

They made love on the braided living room rug, and though, most of the time, Addison was feeling and moaning and pleasing and being pleased, the fact that she was having sex on the floor of her aunt Gicky's living room interrupted her pleasure more than once. If she stayed, she thought, she would update the living room a bit, make it more her own. Maybe a new couch, and definitely a new rug.

"What are you thinking about?" Ben asked, staring up at the ceiling afterward.

"That I wish those people weren't coming to see the house tomorrow."

"It looks good." He spun around, adding, "Even that pile of boxes looks neat."

"Well, that's Addie's fault. There should be twice as many cartons. Addison would have hoovered through this place, leaving little in her wake, but Addie seems to be a sentimental fool." She turned onto her side to face him and reintroduced herself in the vernacular of an AA meeting.

"Hi, I'm Addie, and I'm a hoarder."

He laughed. "Hi, Addie."

She was happy that she avoided discussing the deeper meaning of her statement. She was not ready to decide whether to stay or sell. The words from Gicky's letter ran through her head. The part that read *I hope that the house stays in my family—and you are my family. I see you don't have one of your very own.*

Then she pushed it all aside.

"I'm sorry. When you walked in the door, you were about to say something when I so rudely interrupted."

He jumped up, remembering his grand gesture.

"Oh shit. I ordered us dinner from the market. Get dressed. It will be here any minute!"

With that, the word "Delivery" rang out from the direction of the front door, followed by Ben's bare ass disappearing into the bedroom.

Addison zipped up her cutoffs and answered the door to the delivery boy holding a large tinfoil tray of food.

"Rack of ribs?" he asked, panning the house behind her for more mouths to feed, no doubt.

"Yes, yes. So hungry, thank you."

The kid walked in and placed it on the counter like he had been in the house a hundred times. He probably had. Addison realized she should tip him and searched her pockets habitually. It was useless. She hadn't touched money since arriving on the island.

"Give me a sec to find some cash, please."

"It's OK," he said, his cheeks suddenly flushed. "You don't have any of Gicky's scones, do you?"

For fuck's sake, she thought, duly frustrated.

"Nope, sorry to say. I do not."

"You know, I never even tasted scones till I met your aunt. Really, I used to only eat plain bagels before that, maybe a corn muffin if they were fresh from the oven at the market. She dared me to taste one, and now I have a very diverse palate."

Of course the delivery boy was quirky. *Just like everyone else around here*, Addison thought. He continued singing Gicky's praises.

"She was pretty cool, Gicky. But I don't have to tell you that."

Sadness squashed her frustration. He seemed to notice.

"Don't worry about the tip. You'll catch me next time. And sorry for your loss," the kid added before leaving.

Addison shook off her emotions and called out, "The coast is clear!" while pulling two plates from the kitchen cupboard.

After dinner and a delicious bottle of merlot, Addison made a fire. She had been waiting to do so since she arrived, and the night was just cool enough to warrant one. She had also bought all the ingredients for s'mores in anticipation of the occasion.

Ben was engulfed in Gicky's bookshelves.

"Take anything you want," Addison encouraged. "Except for that little shelf over there with that hot Fire Island author's books. Those stay put."

He sat down on the floor with his back against the couch and thumbed through a collection of short stories by Gay Talese. On the inside cover it read:

With admiration and thanks, Gay

"For someone who was so humble, your aunt lived some life."

"It seems so," Addison agreed, before plopping down in between Ben's knees and pushing back into his chest to admire her roaring handiwork. Ben was quiet for a beat. She tilted her head back so as to see his face.

"What?" he asked in response.

"Nothing. You're kind of quiet, is all."

"Just thinking."

"Just thinking 'bout what?" she pushed.

"Just thinking how I am *not* sitting here coming up with excuses for why I can't stay over."

"That's nice. I usually would want to run by now too."

"Well, it is your house."

"I'm nowhere near thinking of this place as my house. I'm still in shock about the whole thing. My life changed in a minute."

"Do you miss your job?"

"I'm not sure. You know, I never had a break like this before. I started working at the agency right after college. Well, not exactly right after. I got engaged my senior year and . . ."

"Wait—your senior year?"

"Yes, kind of crazy, right? We started dating sophomore year and were inseparable throughout college. My parents were so happy, a nice Jewish boy from a nice midwestern family."

"What happened?"

"I panicked, broke off the engagement after the invites were already sent, and fled to New York. An old camp friend introduced me to Kizzy, who was interning with a headhunter while still at NYU. I was her first placement."

"What camp?" he asked, as if that were the point of the story.

"Mataponi in Maine, you?"

"Lokanda—upstate New York."

"Wasn't it the best?" she gushed.

"Yes, it was, heartbreaker."

"Don't even joke about that. It was bad, really bad. Not only did I break my fiancé's heart, but my mother—she took to her bed for weeks."

"A southern lady like me?" Ben joked.

"Midwestern born and bred. But she should have been southern. Beverly is a big drama queen."

She changed the subject again—to something sweeter.

"S'mores?" she said. Now that she had determined he was a camp person, she was even more excited to break out the ingredients.

While gobbling up their sandwiches of chocolate, marshmallows, and childhood memories smashed between graham crackers, they talked about a million different things. Ben shared a couple of funny camp stories and similar antics from his early days as a sportswriter covering minor league baseball. He spoke about boyhood days on the Jersey Shore and about meeting Julia, and their love story. Addison thought she already knew his perspective from the book, but she could see how much he had grown since then. His attitude now seemed to come less from anger and frustration and more from pure love.

She talked a lot about the Chicago suburb she'd grown up in, how she was both different and the same as her sister, and the stress of her broken engagement—which of course felt weird in comparison to what Ben had gone through.

"That sounds freaking awful," he said. "I think I would have gone through with it just to avoid the conflict."

"Good to know," Addison responded. In truth, she loved his empathetic, validating responses.

When the fire died, they moved into the bedroom and crawled under the covers, where Addison snuggled into the crook of Ben's arm to watch *Love Is Blind*.

Two episodes later, and they were both having a hard time staying awake. Sally was already out cold on the pile of old towels that Addison had yet to bag.

"Should I turn it off?" she whispered.

He nodded and pulled her in closer, his arms wrapped around her torso, her head resting on his chest.

"*Love Is Blind* is kind of stupid, no? Falling so quickly," she mumbled.

"Preposterous," he agreed.

They were both lying.

Addison woke up the next morning, still in Ben's arms, and the fact that they had fallen asleep like that—without having sex, just holding each other for the entire night—felt like the most intimate act they had experienced together.

They were both surprised to see that it was still raining. Well, Addison was surprised. Ben insisted it was a sign.

"It's Gicky crying because you are going to sell her house."

"I'm not going to sell the house," Addison insisted, and then waffled. "I don't think so, at least. Maybe I should make a pro and con list."

"That's smart," Ben said before diving under the covers and nibbling on the inside of her thigh. He peeked out his head for a second, announcing, "First pro. Where else are you going to find a neighbor who does this?"

She had no qualms about kicking Ben out, even after his delicious performance. The prospective buyers were due to arrive around eleven o'clock, and Addie needed to straighten the place up. She traded in her new beachy look for a more city-like outfit. When she looked at herself in the mirror, she saw Addison staring back at her in the heels she had arrived in. After being barefoot for over six weeks, she couldn't wait to take her shoes off again. She kicked them aside and went out back to meditate. For the first time in weeks, she found it impossible to wrangle her thoughts, so she lit a couple of candles in the living room and waited for the prospective buyer's arrival.

It turned out that there had been no reason for her to dress up. The first words out of Nan's mouth were a whispered, "Make yourself scarce. People don't like to talk in front of owners."

She left and walked barefoot down to the beach, where Ben was sitting on a blanket reading the *Times* with Sally. He nudged her off to make room for Addison, and they sat there in silence, neither wanting to address the big elephant on the beach. Addison grabbed the Science section and fell into an article about butterfly migration, but found it hard to concentrate. A strange tension filled her chest. She tried to breathe through it, but it felt impenetrable. Her phone vibrated, and she took a second to think of what she hoped it would say. The words *sorry, they didn't care for it*, popped into her head first, and she got that unsure feeling, like you might have when expecting the results of a pregnancy test.

It read, **They're gone. Let's talk.**

"Gotta go," Addison said before planting a quick kiss on Ben's cheek. His hand went right to the spot where she kissed him, and it melted her. He was so soft inside for someone so hardened.

"Should I come by later?" she asked.

She said it deliberately that way, since it bothered her a little that she hadn't been inside his house yet. It was feeling purposeful, though of what purpose, she wasn't sure. His response soothed her.

"Yes. I have to work today, but how about dinner? I make a mean lasagna."

"Great. Sevenish?"

"Perfect."

She spoke to Nan briefly. The people were very interested, and she was confident they would come back with an offer.

That night, Addie collected her extra packing supplies, some made-up boxes, and a couple of rolls of tape and headed next door. Sally and Ben greeted her on the porch. Neither hid their excitement upon seeing her. She felt . . . loved.

"Boxes for the white elephant sale," she said, laying them in the corner of the porch.

"Thanks," Ben said, unceremoniously lifting the sun hat belonging to his wife off the hook it had probably been sitting on since she passed and tossing it in the box. A casual toss, but a monumental step.

The house was cozy and simple, and permeated by the delicious smell of warm lasagna and garlic bread. Addison's stomach rumbled loudly, and she put her hand to it, embarrassed.

"Hungry?" Ben asked.

"I guess so," she replied, and blushed.

"Let's eat!"

The table was already set with a big salad, the bread, and a bottle of wine. It was very sweet that he had made such an effort. She had a feeling he had not done this for his other female guests. He seemed nervous as he transferred a hearty portion of lasagna from the baking dish to her plate and watched as she took her first bite.

"It's delicious," she said with a smile. He poured two glasses of wine and held his up to toast.

"To my first lasagna—and yes, I lied before, to impress you."

"Wow. I am impressed."

"Don't be. I just followed the recipe on the box. The hardest part was separating the noodles."

"Next time, put a little olive oil in the water—my mom used to do that."

Both of them ate greedily, and Ben suggested they leave the dishes and take their wine down to the Bay Beach area to watch the sunset. A bunch of teenagers were there, taking selfies and a zillion pictures of the sun's red haze as it sank into the Great South Bay. Addison and Ben sat down on one of the swinging benches that hung from wooden pagodas, sipped their wine, and watched the sun paint the sky. Ben reached down and took her hand in his, seemingly not caring if anyone saw the subtle intimacy. The bliss of it all made Addison smile for so long that her cheeks grew tired.

At home, they bypassed the dishes and headed for the bedroom, where they made love slowly, as if it were the first time. Ben's eyes locked onto Addison's with an expression of utter amazement. At least that's how Addison read it. When they were through, she lay on top of him for a long time, her head buried in his chest, their breath rising and falling in synchronicity.

They heard Sally getting into trouble at the table, and Ben realized he had forgotten to feed her. They threw on clothes and bolted to the kitchen to do so, and to wash the dishes. It all felt very domestic and comfortable. Ben stopped and wrapped his arms around her.

"I can't believe this," he said.

She didn't ask for clarification. She couldn't believe it either.

That night they made love one more time, and as she drifted off to sleep in his arms, she felt something she never had before. She felt anchored.

Chapter Thirty-two

Addison opened her eyes as the first hint of sun peeked through the bedroom window, and reached out her hand to feel for Ben. The bed was empty. She sat up and called out his name, trying to make sense of her feelings as she realized she already missed him, missed his skin and his smell and the safe feeling she had lying in his arms. He stepped out of the bathroom, dressed in jeans and a button-down shirt.

"I have to head back to the city," he said, without even a hint of regret. "My editor summoned me."

When? Addison thought, but thought best not to ask it out loud.

He hurried around his bedroom, getting his stuff together like the house was on fire, and Addison suddenly felt very out of place.

"I'll get out of your way," she said, grabbing her clothes from the floor and slipping them back on under the covers.

"No rush," he said. "Shep will come to fetch Sally around ten—so you may want to be out of here before then."

"I could have taken Sally," she said.

"I wouldn't want to impose."

Impose, she thought. All he ever did with Sally was impose.

And with that, he kissed her quickly on the cheek, quipped, "Have to make the boat," and left.

She convinced herself that he was just stressed about work. She gave and received a bit of love from Sally and headed out through the front porch.

Julia's sun hat was sitting right back on its hook.

Addison sat down on her meditation rug. She felt awful, heartbroken, and guilty. Why had she brought those boxes over so flippantly? And why was she being so flippant with her own heart? Ben's wife's things were all over that house. Her books were clearly still sitting on her nightstand. Her clothes still hung in her closet. Ben had shown her how much pain he was in over and over again, and yet she'd ignored it. Anyone in their right mind would have left right after dinner, feigned a migraine, saved themselves. A month ago, she was someone who wouldn't even go in the ocean, and now she had ignored every red flag. She was angry—with herself.

She went back inside the house, determined to make "those fucking scones" as she was now referring to them in her head.

Addison floured her work surface, pulled out the leftover scone mixture from the fridge, and ran it through her hands, kneading and squishing, forgoing the round cookie cutter and forming the dough into random shapes—a circle, a triangle, a square—placing each haphazardly on the baking sheet. She had gone rogue. She stared at the pan for a minute, when inspiration hit and she ran back out to the studio.

Uncovering her creation from the day before, Addison put

her hands through her scalp, her clay scalp, and opened it up like the crater of a volcano. She molded a piece of fresh clay into an abstract shape—as she had with the scones, and slowly and meticulously attached it by wetting the clay with a small brush and using her thumbs to seamlessly mold the pieces together. She stood back and looked at it. She was onto something. Hours later, the sculpture resembled Medusa, except instead of snakes, she had abstract shapes jutting from her skull. It looked like she felt.

Utter confusion.

Her phone buzzed, and she hoped it was Ben, but it was Nan with an offer. A very good offer. Addison texted her back. **Should I counter?**

If Addison had been keen on selling, she wouldn't even have thought to counter; she would have just said yes. But she wasn't doing so for the money—the offer already felt like she would be winning the lottery. She was countering for the time the negotiation would afford her. In her heart, she was sure that what she felt happening between her and Ben was real, but a few seconds later, she was equally sure that it wasn't.

Again, she needed time. They needed time.

She walked down to the lifeguard stand and took a dip in the ocean without even hesitating at the break. She hoped the confidence it inspired would give her a good dose of fortitude. It didn't.

That night, she wrote and erased six different iterations of "just checking in," ranging from the literal, **Just checking in,** to **How did it go with your editor?** to **Tomorrow is recycling day. I can bring your cans out too if you want,** to **I understand that things went very quickly with us. We can slow down if it makes you feel better,** to **What the hell Ben? Come back,** to the crowd favorite, the hi emoji. (Yes, she had consulted her posse on the group chat for more texting material.) She decided to send nothing. She would have to give him the space he clearly needed.

Addison was surprised when she woke up feeling even sadder than she'd felt the day before. She hadn't slept well and had barely eaten since Ben left—she found it tough to swallow.

After dragging out the recycling, Addison went for a long beach walk, hoping to clear her head in the beauty of it all. There was a light mist coming off the ocean. It was too early for the throngs of homeowners and day-trippers to have set up their chairs in purposeful configurations. The mornings belonged to the beach walkers and the anglers and the dogs. She walked for a couple of miles, stepping in and out of the ocean and watching the sandpipers scurry back and forth in the foamy surf. It was really something.

"The Walrus and the Carpenter," the Lewis Carroll poem she had been tasked with memorizing in the sixth grade, played on repeat in her head, providing relief from her thoughts and quandaries. *The mind is funny that way*, she thought, reflecting that sometimes a song or a poem gets stuck in your head for no reason but to take up room and allow your brain to rest. She couldn't remember her Amazon password but could still recall every word of the humorous verse from *Through the Looking-Glass* about two old friends taking a walk on the beach, weeping to see such quantities of sand.

> *"If seven maids with seven mops Swept it for half a year,*
>   *Do you suppose," the Walrus said, "That they could get*
>   *it clear?"*
> *"I doubt it," said the Carpenter, And shed a bitter tear.*

When Addison arrived back at her block, a record-breaking (for her) two hours later, Sally came running toward her onto the beach. Addison's heart jumped from her chest at the sight of her. It sank, just as quickly, when she spotted Shep following a few steps behind.

"Have you heard from Ben?" she asked at his approach. She couldn't help herself.

"No. But it's not the first time he has wandered off."

Her face said it all. He cut to the chase.

"You seem like a nice girl," Shep said kindly. "At first, I was all in on this love connection, but now—maybe he is too broken?"

Addison shrugged. She had certainly never wanted a broken guy before. She could accept the offer on the house today, clean out the place by Sunday, and never look back.

Sally took off after a seagull, prompting Shep to chase after her.

"I'm sorry, Addie," he said as he jogged off.

"It's Addison," she said to no one.

She typed a message to the real estate agent.

Counter with whatever you think is right.

It was met with a thumbs-up emoji.

She followed it with a text to Kizzy.

Anything on the job front? September is coming quickly.

Kizzy wrote back right away.

I was about to reach out! Word is Ogilvy is looking for fresh blood. Should I set up an interview?

Now Addison gave the thumbs-up.

Two thumbs up on my new life plan, she thought. Both prospects should have made her smile. They didn't. She was miserable. Possibly more miserable than she had ever been.

She went to the studio and continued molding abstract shapes and attaching them to the piece she was now calling *Utter Confusion*.

At around three in the morning, it felt done. She left it to dry.

Too exhausted to think, she fell asleep quickly that night and woke the next morning with *Utter Confusion* calling out to her. It had been so long since she had that yearning to make something with her hands—even longer since she had felt the pull of creativity calling her back to a piece she was working on. She didn't have that same draw at work. Yes, she was proud of many of her ad campaigns over the years, but those collaborative efforts felt very different from this. She remembered the feeling from college, remembered skipping parties when a piece she was working on had total control over her. She poured herself a bowl of cereal and ate it while staring down her creation, taking it all in before choosing the colors to paint it with.

Gicky had a nice selection of glazes arranged by shade along the shelves of an antique corner cupboard. Addie opened each jar to see which were dried up and which were fresh. She mostly leaned into the more muted colors, blues with names like Dawn and Isle and Yonder, Lettuce Green, Green Thumb, and one vibrant and shocking tangerine. She took her time with each section of the sculpture, only stopping to eat a second bowl of cereal and to use the bathroom. It was nearly midnight when she was done.

Despite the hour, Addison couldn't wait to fire up the kiln. She gingerly placed her piece in the center and closed the lid. She set the timer for noon the next day and nervously went to sleep.

Chapter Thirty-three

Addison paced back and forth at the Saturday morning ferry, waiting for the gallery owner and her entourage to arrive. She was nervous about meeting the illustrious CC Ng, her aunt's contemporary and longtime friend, and the proprietor of the CC Ng Gallery. CC was about as innovative and well respected as they come in the art world. She had opened her first gallery on Prince Street in 1970, a few years before the sketchy downtown neighborhood south of Houston Street was rebranded as SoHo. It soon became evident that CC had an infallible eye not just for what was beautiful, but for what was marketable. By the eighties she had expanded into the space next door, and in the nineties, CC moved her gallery, ahead of the curve, to a fabulous ten-thousand-square-foot space in Chelsea. The CC Ng Gallery had been thriving there ever since.

Her upcoming show, *Gicky Irwin, a Retrospective*, had been in the works for over a year—well before Gicky fell ill and was diagnosed with leukemia. The other pieces in the show, some dating all the way back to her time in India with Paresh, had already been photographed and archived and were safely stored away in a climate-controlled facility in Long Island City. Addison didn't know whether CC had seen the paintings in the house, or if she would be surprised by them. The whole thing was quite thrilling, and Addison vowed to hold on to her excitement, at least for the day. She could go back to being sad about Ben afterward. Meanwhile, she practiced her happy face.

She did, in fact, have plenty to be happy about.

Kizzy had set up an interview for her at Ogilvy for Monday afternoon. Word was that they were eager to meet her, and she was eager as well. Her excitement wasn't just based on interviewing at the firm *Ad Age* recently dubbed the comeback agency of the year. She was feeling excited about going home—about seeing her friends and taking a real shower in her own bathroom. She hadn't felt really clean since she arrived. It was time to wind down the Summer of Addison and think about what the rest of her life could look like. Still, while the anticipation of her first bite of short rib pappardelle at Bad Roman put a smile on her face, thoughts of Ben sank her.

She could see the ferry in the distance. *Get it together, Addison*, she admonished herself.

She redirected her mind, picturing herself opening up the kiln when the timer went off—to see what *Utter Confusion* looked like. Hopefully, it would look better than it felt.

A slight woman with blunt-cut bangs grazing painted-on eyebrows stepped off the ferry, followed by an entourage carrying an assortment of wooden crates and packing supplies. Addison would recognize CC Ng anywhere, her jet-black helmet as famous in the art world as Anna Wintour's signature bob was in fashion. And while CC's reputation was not as scary as Wintour's, still, she was quite the ball of fire—especially in view of her diminutive size.

Addison approached the group. She was surprised that CC herself was carrying a painting wrapped in brown paper. Though nervous as hell, Addison followed her introduction with a joke.

"I thought you were picking up—not dropping off?"

CC flashed the tiniest of smiles.

"This is for Gicky's friend Shep. She had strict instructions that it should go to him and only him."

Aaah, the mysterious painting had been located. At this point, she was sure the old guy had invented its existence. She was beyond curious to see what was inside, but resolved to mind her own business.

CC introduced her people: a photographer named Ryan, who snapped a picture of Addison in lieu of saying hello, and her handsome schlepper, Marco. The latter insisted on pulling the wagon back to the house. Addison let him. It was, after all, in his job title.

She could not get a word in on the walk home, and neither could Ryan or Marco. A deluge of thoughts spilled from CC's brain, many regarding Gicky, and she barely bothered to finish one sentence before starting another. If Addison weren't feeling so intimidated by her presence, she would have had a hard time controlling her amusement.

"Can I get you something to drink?" Addison asked them upon entering the house.

"Let's look at what Gicky left us first. I'm bursting to see it all!"

Addison quietly handed the two men glasses of water. Each thanked her with a smile.

CC began with the few pieces of Gicky's that were hanging

throughout the house. She didn't need a tour, and it was obvious that, like Paresh and Margot, she had visited the house before. Most of the art in Gicky's personal collection was not her own. Addison had googled some pieces with little luck. CC's comment when glancing at them confirmed Addison's suspicion.

"Gicky was a sucker for a starving artist."

Back in the studio, CC went through the pieces slowly and meticulously, taking them out one by one and bringing them into the outside light for a better look. She was restrained, saying little more than *ooh*, *aah*, and *oh* as she perused each piece. Addison could see that among this collection of old and newer paintings was some of her aunt's best work. The brushstrokes were bold and expressive, the colors vivid and intense. There was a wealth of beauty here—it would be some show.

"When is the exhibition?" Addison asked.

"The end of October. It will be up for six weeks. You'll be invited to the opening, of course," she noted, as if this weren't the most meaningful thing Addison had heard all summer. She could feel the color drain from her cheeks. CC saw it as well. She stopped looking at the art and focused on the artist's niece, standing before her. Even Marco and Ryan took in the emotional moment. It was obvious that CC didn't often go there.

"I asked Gicky if she wanted me to reach out to you, and even your dad, when she fell ill. But she was adamant that I should not. I pushed it, a little, but she was a stubborn woman, your aunt. And quite prideful. I don't know which of those emotions drove that decision. It could have been love, for all I know. She still loved her brother, and obviously, she loved you too. Maybe she didn't want you to have that image of her. Maybe she liked the way she would remain young and vibrant in your eyes."

Addison refrained from admitting that she barely remembered her.

The twelve o'clock siren went off just as the alarm sounded on Addison's phone, startling her and signaling that her piece was all fired up. Addison wiped away the tears that she hadn't even realized had sprung from her eyes and exclaimed, "It's done!"

She was all fired up too, until she remembered she was standing next to one of the most discerning pairs of eyes in the art world.

Addison pictured herself opening the kiln and gently attaching the piece to the stand she had created for it out of driftwood. She imagined CC pulling down her cat-eyed glasses and peering at it from every angle before declaring Addison a modern Rodin.

"What's done?" Marco the schlepper asked.

She blurted out the first thing that came to mind.

"Um—Gicky's scones," she lied, adding, "but don't get excited. I've made the recipe taped to her fridge a million times since I got here, and I can't get it right."

CC let out a cacophonous laugh. It completely filled the room. When all eyes landed on her, she explained herself. "That's because Gicky's famous scones were frozen, ready to bake from Costco. She left that recipe taped to the fridge to impress renters. She never baked a scone from scratch in her life."

And Addison felt like a fool again.

She excused herself to fake check the oven. When she returned, CC had her head in the kiln. Apparently, it buzzed when its timer went off as well.

"What's this? This isn't Gicky's," CC declared correctly.

"Oh—oh," Addison stammered. "It's just something I've been playing around with." She laughed awkwardly, peering in at her creation and lifting it from the kiln as delicately as Mary lifting Jesus from the manger. She couldn't help but smile. The colors were brilliant—even better than she could have imagined, better than anything she had made before. She remembered Paresh's story about the weaver and the princess and wondered if unrequited love counted toward producing good work.

CC pulled down her glasses and studied the sculpture intently. It brought Addison right back to art school, and she found herself holding her breath until CC spoke.

"The cubist distortion of the female form is quite inspired."

Addison exhaled, and a small laugh came out with it. She resisted admitting that the self-portrait had been inspired by scones.

"It conveys such emotional intensity," she said finally, adding, "such a profound sense of vulnerability."

"That's what I was going for," Addison joked. CC was clearly not joking.

"I'm putting together a group show in December supporting emerging artists working in ceramics. Do you have others I can see?"

She knew better than to break out the silly vases she had created. They didn't exactly go together.

"That's my first, I'm afraid—since studying at SAIC."

She didn't know why she had suddenly thrown in her credentials. Well, that wasn't really true. CC Ng had just called her piece "inspired." Of course she was throwing in her credentials.

"If you can have a few more for me to see, I would consider them for the December show. Let's say in eight weeks' time?"

"Oh, I am not a professional artist. I'm in advertising."

"That's not what I heard."

Addison blushed, and CC softened it with, "There are worse ways to make Page Six."

"I'm contemplating going back to Madison Avenue. I have an interview on Monday."

"How about just a few more pieces, then?" CC asked.

She took in Addison's contemplative expression and threw in a few more compliments. "Look," she said, "I've been doing this a long time, and it is rare to find such natural talent. The way the organic shapes burst from the sleek lines, it's both graceful and strikingly modern. I have a feeling about you. And my feelings are often right."

CC stepped back and admired the work from a distance.

"You should think about it."

"I will, thank you."

At the very least, this brightened her mood. Though she wasn't sure that the sculpting, meditating, ocean swimming, free-to-be-you-and-me Addie would ever even show her face in Manhattan, much less survive more than a day there. And Manhattan Addison would never quiet her mind long enough for her hands to work so freely. She was pretty sure she was a one-hit wonder, like Dexys Midnight Runners or Fountains of Wayne. One and done.

Chapter Thirty-four

While watching CC and her crew fade into the distance on the Great South Bay, Addison texted her friends: **Who's free for dinner Monday night?**

Soon an array of hearts and exclamation points confirmed that everyone was available. Addison called in a favor for a res at Bad Roman and smiled.

I'm back, she thought happily.

She was confident she could forget about the roller coaster of nonsense she'd been riding for the past seven weeks. She was not Addie; she was Addison Irwin.

Back at the house, Addison went through the final closet for the white elephant sale. She would bring everything over first thing tomorrow and then head back to the city for her Monday meeting.

When she walked into the living room, she noticed Shep's package peeking out from a now empty corner and looked at her watch. It was too late to visit him. She would head over there in the morning.

Early Sunday morning, Addison made two trips to the ferry dock, where the white elephant sale was spread out along the sidewalk. She now realized that she could have left everything for the new owners to deal with, in the Fire Island tradition—though if she had, it would probably have all ended up in a dumpster. While she was unhappy that she had fallen for Ben in the short time she'd been on the island, she was happy that she had also fallen in love with her aunt. Gicky's things should go to other Fire Islanders. She was sure they would be snapped up by both sentimental and eclectic-minded residents as the treasures that they were. She slipped a set of handmade black-and-white poodle-shaped salt and pepper shakers into her pocket, suddenly unwilling to part with them.

Addison loaded the last boxes onto the wagon and placed Shep's painting on top. She had enough time to make a quick stop at his house before dropping off the goods and catching the next boat, though she was cutting it close.

As she rang Shep's bell, Addison decided that, if he wasn't home, she would open the door—islanders seemed to leave their houses unlocked—and place it inside. In fact, she hoped he wouldn't be home. The old man had won her over, and she didn't feel like explaining where she was off to. Also, she knew that whatever she said would probably go right back to Ben, if he even cared to inquire about her whereabouts when he returned—if he returned.

Shep answered his door and immediately noticed the painting. "You found it! I told you she left something for me!"

"Actually, she left it with her gallerist."

"It's a masterpiece, no doubt."

Addison handed him the painting. He took it and joked, "OK, Don, let's show him what he's won!"

Addison smiled. She would miss this guy.

He untied the string, and the paper fell behind it. One look at the painting and his face became red and contorted. He quickly covered the canvas back up and put it down facing the wall. From his reaction, Addison reconsidered her plan to ask to see it. She again questioned what her aunt's relationship was with Shep. It was a question she didn't need to know the answer to.

"I have to run, Shep," she said. "I have to bring the rest of this to the sale and make the next boat."

Shep looked at his watch.

"Go!" he said. "I'll bring this stuff for you and lock up your wagon by the dock. You're never going to make the boat pulling that thing."

She knew she would make it, but loved the thought of not arriving like a sweaty zenless mess. She took him up on his offer to bring the final round to the sale and headed to the boat with nothing more than her purse. Once on board, she took a seat up top and thought about how she had felt when arriving, compared to how she felt now. If anything, the heartbreak had proven that her former priorities weren't so bad after all.

Chapter Thirty-five

Back in the city, Addison felt immediately happy to be home. Happy to greet her doorman, to rustle through weeks of mail, and to be among her own things.

She added a layer of glittery gold shadow to her usual basic daytime makeup in order to distract from the remaining sadness in her eyes. She had yet to hear word one from Ben, and being ghosted by him was a lot to bear. She was starting to feel as if she had imagined it all until his words—*I can't believe this*—ran through her head. She thought about her mother's favorite piece of advice: "When someone shows you who they are, believe them the first time," and it confused her even more. In her heart, she knew Ben wasn't a bad guy—maybe just a bad guy to start a relationship with. Her eyes threatened to well up and ruin her makeup, so she changed the subject on herself.

"Hey, Siri. Play Beyoncé's 'Best Thing I Never Had'!"

The interview that afternoon was flawless, and it was obvious from the first line spoken—"Addison Irwin, finally!"—that it was just a formality. If she wanted the job, it was hers. And while the whole exercise filled her with pride and confidence, once in the privacy of the elevator, she found herself gnawing on her thumbnail again. She was suddenly wistful regarding everything she would be giving up if she were to accept an offer.

The strap on her shoe pinched at her heel. She loosened it.

The bare feet had sure felt good.

The sculpting had felt good; the meditation had felt good; the ocean had felt good; and the love, the love had felt great. Even if the latter had been in her imagination, there was no denying how it made her feel. She thought of a prophetic meme she had read on Instagram that morning.

"It only takes one decision to change the entire direction of your life."

She couldn't wait to monopolize the conversation at dinner that night. She knew she would have to wrestle it away from Kizzy, with her "out with the old, in with the new" shenanigans, but she was in desperate need of all kinds of advice.

She predicted that each of her BFFs would listen to her options, toe the feminist line, and propose that she should accept the forthcoming offer, sell the house, and throw not even a backward glance in Bad Ben Morse's direction ever again. The last to arrive, she sat down at the table, ordered a gin martini, and presented her case. They went at her laundry list of issues—starting with the opportunities with both Ogilvy and CC Ng.

"Being that this is my department, can I go first?" Kizzy asked, in full headhunter mode.

Everyone agreed.

"I have been fielding offers to poach you from Silas and Grant for years, so let's just say—I'm invested in this career of yours. And yes, a generous offer from Ogilvy is as good as done. But I watched you with that clay and I thought it was remarkable. I mean, you all should have seen her. It was like everything was connected to her hands: her heart, her mind, her image."

Pru wasn't having it.

"That's all fine and good, but unless she's going to relocate to somewhere like Portland, I don't see her supporting herself, here, as a potter!"

"She's not a potter, she's a sculptor," Lisa said sharply, adding emphasis to the word.

"A ceramicist?" Kizzy corrected.

"I'm not any of those things," Addison protested. "Yes, Kizzy is right that I loved it, but it's not a job. At least not yet."

"Well, it will never be if you go back to advertising full-time and let them suck the life out of you again. What do you think about asking for more time to explore the other option? It's such an incredible opportunity to be in a CC Ng show," Lisa fired back. "Or maybe wait for the next offer?" She turned to Kizzy for backup. "She got the first job you sent her on. Can we assume there will be others?"

"Well, not as prestigious maybe, but it's safe to say—yes."

"That's a good idea. And selling the house will let you afford to try out sculpting!" Lisa added. It was obvious where her head was.

"Not so fast. Why are you so quick to jump on the first offer for the house?" Pru asked.

"I think that has something to do with the guy next door," Kizzy quietly interjected.

"I agree with number three on your list—not looking back in Bad Ben Morse's direction, but I want to hear all the terms for the job and the house." Pru had always been the most logical of the four of them.

"That's fair, "Addison agreed.

"I'm sorry, but I don't agree with number three," Kizzy insisted.

She was so obviously love spoiled right now, even while going through a divorce. Addison questioned her reliability on the issue.

"Don't take this the wrong way, Kizzy," she said, "but I'm not sure you're that levelheaded about matters of the heart right now."

"I hear you, but I'm not basing my opinion on my own thing. I'm basing it on yours. Before Ben walked out that morning, what were you feeling for him?"

The question took Addison aback when she was leaning toward moving forward. She looked at Lisa for a therapist's support.

"Just answer her. You shouldn't sweep your feelings under the rug."

"I may have been falling for him," Addison began. They all shot her a look of doubt. It was impossible to deny that she loved him. "OK, I fell for him. Hard. It's not easy to explain, because his whole up-and-down vibe is the opposite of anything I usually go for."

Lisa mixed a cough with the word "boring," and everyone but Addison laughed.

"The Ben Morse who came to Montauk was already completely in love with you. I'm sure of it," said Kizzy. "His face, when he saw that I was with Terrence, was indescribable. I've never seen someone so happy to see me in all my life."

"Wow, you described it pretty well," Lisa said, with a hint of longing.

"I thought he was kind of jerky, honestly. Not a fan," Pru admitted.

"He's not a jerk. He's amazing!" Addison jumped in, realizing she had switched right into defending him.

"I'm not talking about sex. I've read his books and I doubt someone could make up all of that without a good amount of carnal knowledge," said Pru. "But being good in bed does not make a good mate."

Addison surprised herself, becoming over-the-top protective. "He's good out of bed too. And he's funny, and caring, and I could tell from the way he treats his dog that he would make a great dad. He's scared, is all. I scared him. He lost his wife!"

She knocked back the rest of her drink in one huffy gulp.

"Look at that, you answered your own question. The first guy we have ever heard you passionate about, and you ran away as soon as it got hard," Lisa said.

"I didn't run away. He ran away."

"Well, if you care about him so much, maybe you should be waiting for him when he returns," said Kizzy.

Addison found it a bit rich, given the circumstances of her own love life.

"I bet the man I saw in Montauk, whose whole face lit up when he spoke about you, is working through his shit and coming back. If you give him the chance."

Suddenly, Addison pictured Ben and Sally knocking on her door at the beach, waiting for no one to answer, and walking home with their tails between their legs. It broke her, totally broke her.

"What time is it?" she asked, not even waiting for an answer. She barely made the ten thirty boat.

Addison took off her heels and ran to her street in full third-act rom-com mode. She waited till she'd reached the corner ball field to stop to catch her breath so that she wouldn't walk in like a hot mess.

The street was asleep—literally every house was dark. She didn't care. There was no way she was waiting until morning. She looked at her watch. It was 11:11 p.m. She made a wish before knocking.

Chapter Thirty-six

Ben was tossing and turning in his lonely king-size bed. He had composed and deleted ten different apologies to Addison since returning to the beach the day before. For an author, he was having an unusually hard time putting his feelings into words. He had gone home to the city to get away from her but, apparently, out of sight, out of mind was ineffective when it came to Addison Irwin.

In the city, the day before, Ben had stopped at Zabar's to pick up a babka before heading over to Julia's parents' place on Central Park West for their sacrosanct Sunday brunch. After her death, Ben had continued the tradition whenever he was in town. At first it was out of guilt, because Julia's father had asked him to, but later, after Julia's sister, Nora, had had a baby, it was more about his wife's adorable little namesake, Juliette.

Ben's heart had been like a bear in hibernation until the first time he held Juliette. The love he felt for this little brown-haired, blue-eyed baby, who shared Julia's DNA, poked at the cold, dead organ in his chest and alerted him that it was still viable. Of course, now, after having met Addison, he was fully aware of the viability of his heart—or more accurately, of the chance of it being broken again. He was sure if that were to happen, he would drop dead on the spot, or worse, have to live once more with the unyielding misery he waded through for so long after Julia had passed.

"Hi, Henry," he greeted his in-laws' doorman with a casual wave as he entered their building. Henry, who had been the doorman ever since Julia was a baby, wore his heart on the sleeve of his uniform for everyone to see. He had watched Julia and Nora grow up and was devastated by Julia's death. He once told Ben that he always thought he would go first. At the time, Ben was in his asshole stage of mourning and had to stick his fingernail into his arm, nearly drawing blood, to stop himself from laughing. He still had more than a little of that "screw the world and everyone in it" sentiment running through his veins, but those feelings that once ruled his every thought were seldom now.

"They're not here, Mr. Morse," Henry informed him.

Ben corrected him for the seven hundred thousandth time—"Call me Ben"—before looking at his watch. He was a bit early.

"I have a book, I'll wait," he said, moving toward the couch in the lobby.

"No, no. They're really not here, they're in Italy. Back Labor Day weekend, I think."

Ben felt overly embarrassed. He hadn't been in touch much that summer. It wasn't unusual to arrive on Fire Island and forget that the rest of the world existed.

"I forgot," he fibbed.

He took his babka and headed out of the building and then out of the city.

An hour later, Ben parked his car at the Wellwood Cemetery out on Long Island, to visit Julia's grave. It had been seven weeks since he had been there, a record for him. He wondered if Nora, who often stopped there on the way home from the Hamptons, had visited in between. Each of them gave a beachcomber's twist to the Jewish custom of leaving stones and pebbles on the graves of their loved ones by placing shells and beach glass on Julia's headstone instead.

It had become obvious that the two of them were the only regular visitors. Both believed that, while their relationship with Julia had moved from physical to spiritual, it still very much existed.

A few months back, Nora had begun arranging their now massive collection of tiny sea treasures into words. She'd started out with mundane greetings like HI, to which Ben responded, YO, and advanced from there to more ghostly sentiments like BOO, to which he added HOO. It worked well for each of them, sandwiching their sadness with the giving and receiving of laughter.

Today, the new phrase that Nora had last left Ben felt a little judgy. It read: GO AWAY.

Ben analyzed what Nora meant by it and deduced that she thought him too long at the fair. He smiled as he thought it. "Too long at the fair" was the kind of saying that Julia would have edited right out of one of his novels.

Who are you? Mother Goose? she would have teased, before suggesting something like, *Her sister thought it was time that Ben move on in life.*

"Go away?" Ben had repeated it out loud before contemplating whether he had the patience, and sea glass, to spell out his reply—"Piss off, Nora!"

"Ooh, inappropriate cemetery language, Ben Morse!" Nora scoffed in the flesh. Juliette was strapped into a front carrier, kicking her feet in the air as if they were at a playground. It was the first time Ben and Nora had ever bumped into each other in the graveyard, though both of them carried on like it was a regular occurrence.

"Says the woman holding a baby in a cemetery."

"Says the man holding a babka, like he is still sitting shiva."

He laughed. He didn't know why he had taken the babka from the car, except that he was hungry and thought maybe he would stay for lunch. It wouldn't be the first time he'd eaten a meal there.

"The babka was for your parents."

"Who are in Italy."

"Yes, Henry informed me."

Seeing Nora, and now Juliette, was as close as he could get to being around a live version of his late wife. He hoisted himself up off the ground and gave his sister-in-law and nine-month-old baby niece a kiss.

"Should we worry that your parents are sitting on lounge chairs in the Mediterranean and we are still sitting in the cemetery?"

"That was kind of why I wrote *go away*—though in my heart I think Julia is happy that we both visit."

"I think so too," he said, changing the subject.

"How was your summer?"

"Not over yet," she laughed, "but good, thanks, though Lars has been working a lot—he's on a call in the car."

"Better than not working, I guess."

"True. He would be in the car, regardless. He's not a fan of coming here really—thinks it's weird. But he's always good about stopping for me. How about your summer? Same old, same old?'

Nora always joked that every day on Fire Island, and therefore every summer there, was exactly the same, like the movie *Groundhog Day*. Ben was fine with her teasing. That kind of attitude kept out the riffraff—the riffraff being the fancier folks of the Hamptons. The same breed, Ben noted, that had been coming to Fire Island and building huge houses as of late. It was a generalization, of course, and Nora was really as down to earth as Julia had been.

"Good, good," he replied with little enthusiasm to back it up.

Nora took a hard look at him.

"Really? 'Cause you don't look so good."

"I'm OK."

"You left the beach on the weekend and missed your sacred ball game to have brunch with my parents—who are out of the country?"

"I met someone."

"You met someone? That's fantastic! Why don't you look happy?"

"The question of the hour."

Ben sat back down on the grass in front of Julia's grave. Nora carefully kneeled down next to him. He opened up the babka, ripped off a piece, and handed it to her, before taking another piece for himself. They sat like that for a beat, thinking and chewing on the sweet braided bread, and putting little pieces into Juliette's mouth, waiting for Ben to elaborate. He finally did.

"Hard as I try, I'm still married to your sister. And I'm not complaining about that. I want to still be married to your sister. But what if I fall in love and there is no room for her anymore?"

"It sounds like you've already fallen—and since you are sitting here with Julia, there seems to be room for both."

"I wonder how the woman at the beach would feel about that?"

"It's not about the woman at the beach, it's about you."

He looked skeptical. Nora placed a hand on Julia's headstone.

"Look, Ben, here is my sister, Julia, and here is my baby, Juliette. One did not replace the other."

Ben smiled down at the baby, who reached out for him with her chubby little baby fingers—tapping on his heart again.

"People thought I was crazy naming her Juliette—so close to Julia. My parents begged me to name her Jane or Jordyn or Jenna."

She rubbed her hand over Ben's back and smiled.

"But I knew Juliette would heal me. You may say that's a lot to ask of a baby, but it turns out I wasn't asking anything of her at all. I was asking something of myself. To love again. Love heals, Ben. Find someone who will sit in the car while you say hello to Julia."

"I think I already have. But I screwed it all up. I'm scared. The last night we were together, I held her so tightly, as if she may slip away."

"Lightning never strikes twice in the same place, you know," Nora insisted metaphorically.

"That's actually not true. It often strikes in the same place twice. Sometimes more."

"Well, then, it's a good thing you ran," Nora joked.

"I thought that I got past the fear. Really, I did. I was all set to pack up Julia's things and make room for Addison—literally and figuratively. But in the morning, I choked and ran."

"Well, run back. What are you waiting for?"

Nora took her hand and, in one fell swoop, cleared off half of her snarky last message to him. The beach glass and shells that spelled out the word *away* fell to the floor, leaving just the word GO.

And he did.

Chapter Thirty-seven

Sally heard her first and barked. It began as a low grumble and grew to a distinct warning that someone or something was there.

"What is it, girl?" Ben asked, swinging his feet off the side of the bed. He was relieved to have a reason to stop tossing and turning.

He switched on the porch light and looked out, expecting to see a raccoon or a fox. His eyes focused in the dark and settled on the image of Addison. It took his breath away. He leaned both hands on the glass door between them. She did the same.

Ben slid the door open, and they held each other for what felt like an eternity, with Sally jumping and nudging her nose between them, desperate to be a part of it. When they gave in to her request, breaking away to allow her in, they both had tears in their eyes.

They asked each other the same question, "Where did you go?"

And laughed as they both tried to answer.

Addison took a breath and said, "I went to the city, for a job interview."

"Did you get it?"

"I did. But I don't think I want it. At least not right now."

"It doesn't matter," Ben said. "As long as you're back."

"And you?"

"I ran away."

He held her face in his hands and looked straight into her eyes.

"I'm so sorry I left. I was afraid," Ben admitted.

"And you're not afraid anymore?"

"Oh, I'm still afraid."

"Afraid I'll leave you?"

"Yeah."

"I can say the same thing, you know?" Addison pointed out.

"I'm not going anywhere," Ben assured her.

"Well, if you do, I'm telling you right now, I'm coming with you."

They both laughed and wrapped their arms around each other.

Ben whispered in her ear.

"I love you."

"I love you too," she whispered back.

Ben took a step back to look into her eyes and spilled his heart out.

"I think I've loved you since I saw you sitting on the sidewalk with your tossed salad. But I'm broken. And you're not. And I'm not sure it's fair of me—to love you."

"It's not fair not to," Addison barely whispered, before taking his hands in hers and kissing him gently on the lips.

"I thought my world had to be big in order to be fulfilled.

And then I came to this tiny beach town, and met you, and suddenly a hundred feet holds more happiness for me than the entire universe."

The next kiss was more passionate and ignited a hunger in them that had to be quenched immediately. They quickly made it to the bedroom—a trail of shoes and shirts, pants and sweats in their wake. All the tossing and turning that Ben had been doing before Addison's arrival felt like a distant memory. As soon as they were done making love, he drifted off to a peaceful sleep, as if he hadn't slept in days. The truth was, it had been years.

As the morning light filled the room, Addison woke first. She sat up and stretched her arms overhead before patting Sally on her belly. Ben woke too and pulled her toward him, kissing her gently all over her face.

"I owe you an apology, Ben. I really do."

He shot her a quizzical look.

"I never should have pushed you to clean out Julia's things, I'm so sorry."

"You didn't really push me; you brought boxes. It's just, when I woke up that morning and saw Julia's sun hat in that box—I don't know how to explain it, but seeing that hat on the hook, especially when I've been away from here for months, makes me feel like she's still here, waiting for me. Sometimes I even say, 'Hi, Jules,' when I walk in the house. I know it sounds crazy—it *is* crazy."

"It's not at all crazy."

"I packed everything up—look."

There were boxes lined up between the bed and the wall. Addison rolled over to look at them.

"I know the sale is over, but I'm going to tape them up and

send them back to the city for her mom and sister to go through. That's where her stuff belongs, anyway."

"Never apologize for loving Julia. I love that you still love your wife. I love that you want to keep her alive. I wouldn't want it any other way."

Addison and Ben took Sally for her morning walk on the beach, holding hands for anyone and everyone to see. By lunch, the news of their pairing traveled to the checkout girls at the market, where Les stood at the grill, making Shep a bacon, egg, and cheese on a roll. He eyed Shep over the griddle and said, "You kept a good secret, my friend. I'm impressed."

"What you talking 'bout, son?"

"Ben and the new girl, the neighbor?"

"That gal is long gone. I was hoping, so was Gicky. She had it all planned out, you know. She set the whole thing up from the grave. But Ben blew it."

"That's not what I heard." Les called over one of the register girls. "Ginger, come here—tell Shep the gossip?"

"You mean about him and Mrs. Ingram?"

Shep turned bright red and Les laughed.

"Didn't know you could embarrass, Shep. Wow!"

Les redirected, "Not about him, about Ben."

"Oh, sorry. Ben and Gicky's niece walked down the beach this morning holding hands and sometimes kissing."

Shep took off without his sammie and pedaled home as fast as his old legs would take him.

He entered Ben's house a few minutes later to find Ben and

Addison lying on the living room couch. They peeled themselves off each other and sat up, but not in an *oh no, we're busted* kind of way. They sat up as if their coupling were the most natural thing in the world.

"We didn't hear you," Ben said.

"What a shock," Shep said, raising his hands to his chest in jest.

They gave him a laugh.

"I have something for you two. It's a gift from Gicky," Shep announced, handing the rewrapped painting to Ben.

Addison turned to him and whispered, "Say no thank you. I think it's a nude. I think he and Gicky were—you know—an item."

Ben laughed. "They were most definitely not an item."

Still, Addison covered her eyes and giggled, peeking out between her fingers as Ben unveiled the painting.

They both gasped at the image. It was a painting of the two of them together, sitting on the beach staring out at the ocean, with Sally sitting similarly at their side.

Neither of them spoke for at least a minute. Shep was miraculously patient, letting them take in the image before speaking himself.

"I don't understand, Shep, what's going on here?"

"Well, it's subjective, but I think she was trying to capture . . ."

"Shep!" It was obvious from Ben's tone and clenched jaw he was not amused. Addison's jaw, on the other hand, remained agape. She was amazed at her dead aunt's ability to turn her life on its head.

"Gicky came up with an entire plan the night she promised

you the house on the clamshell. She already knew she was dying, had already thought through her estate and put everything in place. Before I knew she was sick, she and I got to talking about a far-off time when I'd be gone, and she'd be gone, and it would be up to Ben to stand up for the integrity of our block. But when I visited her in the city, when we'd all gotten word of the leukemia, she joked that I should push Ben to meet her beautiful niece. She even showed me pictures of you. She followed your whole life on that Instaface thing."

Addison couldn't believe her ears. She felt a bit duped, like a pawn in a chess game.

"You think she left me the house as some grand scheme to fix up Ben and me?"

"No, not really. She always wanted to leave you the house. It's a thing we would talk about—you know, 'cause my daughters are estranged from each other. So, when she would say, 'Who am I going to leave this place to? I should have had a kid,' I would say, 'Look what good that did me.'" He grimaced, adding, "My two are definitely going to fight over my house for eternity."

"I can't believe this," Ben said, clearly not loving being manipulated. Addison wasn't feeling as annoyed, though in all fairness, annoyance seemed to come easier to Ben. Shep stuck up for himself as best he could.

"What did you want me to do? Gicky was torn between leaving each of you the house. She thought you two young Turks had what it takes to save our block from ruin—got it in her head that if you two were a couple, she could leave it to both of you. I went along with it, humoring her, given that she was dying and all—but wouldn't you know it? She was right!"

"I feel like a damn puppet," Ben groaned.

"Yeah. I can see why you're mad, seeing as how you were doing so well on your own."

Shep took a purposeful step back. "I'm gonna go—leave you two to admire your original Gicky Irwin."

"That's a good idea, Shep," Ben grunted.

He left, and the two of them gazed at the painting for a long while. Ben eventually calmed down and even smiled.

"Unbelievable," he said.

"Truly unbelievable," Addison agreed.

"Where should we hang it, your place or mine?" Ben asked.

"About that." Addison inquired, "Can we discuss your offer, to buy half of my place? I am thinking of taking some time off to sculpt. And that money would allow me the freedom."

"Yes! And you can rent out your half—minus the studio— and stay here next summer."

What he said was not crazy. She had never felt like this before—as if it were written that they would still be together next summer. Either way, she didn't need all of that house and property. The house and studio were more than enough.

"We'll see," she said, in contrast to what she was feeling. She had zero intention of going anywhere.

Ben dug out his tool kit, and they hung the painting over the fireplace to the usual picture-hanging banter of "a little to the left, to the right, a little lower." They stood back and stared at it. In the end, it was just right.

"I want to hang one more thing," Addison said, "if you don't mind."

She went into the bedroom and took Julia's sun hat from the open box and out to the porch, with Ben and Sally following her.

She carefully placed the hat back on the mermaid hook, where it belonged.

"Hi, Julia," she said, and smiled.

Ben laughed, wrapping his arms around her and whispering, "Thank you," in her ear.

And while it may have been the corniest rom-com ending ever—it felt very much like a beautiful beginning.

After

Chapter Thirty-eight

Addison changed a half a dozen times in front of her bedroom mirror to the soundtrack of a Spotify Christmas playlist. The scene, reminiscent of a nineties movie montage, wrapped with her in the first outfit she tried on. The black pencil skirt, color-blocked sweater, and high suede boots were a perfect balance between standing out and blending in.

She slipped in her EarPods and bounded down the stairs of her downtown apartment to the tune of Darlene Love's "Christmas (Baby Please Come Home)." At the corner bodega, she paused to inhale a big whiff of evergreen from the line of fresh Christmas trees that had been delivered the day before. She loved the short period of time when the scent of the city was elevated from *What's that smell?* to a delightful blast of pine and maple syrup. It was the hap-hap-happiest time of the year, and Addison was feeling it, along with a bellyful of butterflies.

Overly zealous, she decided to walk the twenty or so blocks to Chelsea in an attempt to wrangle said butterflies. It was tough to tame her emotions, and she soon found herself nearly skipping. Nearly skipping made it worse.

She spotted the for-hire light on an approaching cab and raised her hand.

"CC Ng Gallery, 500 West Twenty-Ninth, please."

She slouched back into the black leather seat of the taxi and lowered her gaze.

Be present, Addison.

Meditating didn't seem possible, even though she had gotten so very good at it. Nothing could contain the excitement in her belly.

"I'm heading to my first show," she told the cabbie, leaning forward. "I'm an artist."

It may have been the first time she had said those words out loud. *I'm an artist.* It was for sure the first time she believed them.

"Very nice, very nice," the cabbie replied. "What kind?"

"Ceramics," she said proudly.

She sat back and closed her eyes again, thinking of Paresh's first lesson in meditation.

Focus on your breath. Notice the sensation of the air as it enters and exits your nose. Place your left hand on your belly, and lose yourself in the rise and the fall—the rise and the fall.

Miraculously, calmness enveloped her, until she pulled open the heavy door to the CC Ng Gallery and saw her name typeset on the wall with those of five other emerging artists.

ADDISON IRWIN, WORKS IN CLAY

Addison had spent the last four months actively working in her Fire Island studio, creating similar sculptures to the first piece that had caught CC's eye—*Utter Confusion*. She named each of the other ceramic sorority sisters she was showing after emotions she had felt over the past six months—in no particular order:

> *Stark Gratitude*
> *Pure Pride*
> *Total Panic*
> *Complete Madness*
> and *Sheer Joy*

She'd made *Sheer Joy*—a wild-haired woman dressed in a rainbow, dancing with her arms raised above her head—just the month before, the day after Ben had written, *Marry me?* in the sand and placed the perfect emerald ring on her finger. It was a surprise, but it also wasn't a surprise. Their future together had been sealed the day they hung Gicky's portrait of them over the fireplace. They had barely left each other's side since.

Today, Ben was coming straight from an interview with a baseball player in Atlanta. Addison tried, unsuccessfully, not to let her brain go toward him and the precarious timing of his arrival. When she saw him across the room, her heart jumped. She wondered when and if that would stop happening.

Ben wrapped his arms around her and whispered in her ear, "So proud of you, baby."

The sweet, intimate moment was cut short by Kizzy, Lisa, and Pru's boisterous entrance, with Pru's husband, Tom, and the metro version of Terrence Williams following staidly behind.

Kizzy squealed at the sight of Addison's work laid out on bright white rectangular pedestals in the center of the concrete-floored room. Much like Addison herself, some of the pieces were playful and whimsical, and others felt more serious and contemplative. And while many of the other artists there were displaying works ten times the size, Addison's women demanded attention.

Addison's parents soon followed, her mother, like Kizzy, gasping in delight. It was ironic; if Beverly Irwin had been this supportive of Addison's art ten years earlier, Addison might now be less starving and more artist.

"Hold up your engagement ring in front of your sculptures," her mother instructed. "I want to take a picture."

Addison was about to say, *Stop!* but Ben mouthed, "Just let her," so she acquiesced.

As soon as Beverly realized that her sister-in-law Gicky was responsible for marrying off her older daughter, she forgave her for absconding with the soup terrine. When Addison had called and said she was engaged, Beverly had looked up toward the heavens and yelled, "I forgive you, Gicky!" at the top of her lungs. She didn't do it in front of Morty. He would find no humor in it. He was still working through his guilt, and probably would be for a long time.

Addison posed for a few pictures, then warned, "That's it, Mom. Chill!"

Chill was usually a trigger word for Beverly Irwin, but she let it go. It was too good a day. Morty stepped in with a kiss for his daughter, followed by a wink.

"C'mon, Bev, let's check out the other artists."

Addison paused for a moment to take in the room.

Pru and Tom canoodled in the corner; they were big fans of Lisa's worksheets. The last time Addison asked, Pru told her they were back to passionately arguing and making up again. They weren't the only ones to praise Lisa's method; one of her clients was a bigwig at a publishing house and swore that Lisa's approach had saved her marriage. She offered Lisa a book deal— and *The Lisa Banks Method* was set for a late spring pub date. It was already in the top one hundred self-help books on Amazon, a great sign.

Another great sign was the pictures that Kizzy had texted to the group chat just the day before: a photo of her signed divorce agreement followed by a couple of tag choices for Terrence's new surf-wear line. They all hearted the photo of her new marital status and placed three thumbs-up emojis on the second iteration of the Vagabond Surfer logo.

Finally, Addison landed on CC Ng, deep in conversation with Roberta Smith and Jerry Saltz. The power couple were legendary art critics, Roberta for *The New York Times* and Jerry for *New York* magazine. She feared Jerry would compare her work to souvenir models of Michelangelo's *David* in a Florentine gift shop. She remembered him making a similar judgment about a sculptor once before. Roberta, she worried, would label them banal.

"Look at the couple talking to CC, are they smiling?" Addison asked Ben, her thumbnail going right to her mouth for the first time in ages.

Ben wrapped his arms around his fiancée's waist. He knew a thing or two about critics and reviews.

"It's gonna be fabulous," he said.

And it was.

First in line at the corner newsstand the next morning, Ben and Sally raced home in the rain to the apartment the three now shared.

Ben called out, "Where you at, nepo baby?" as they entered.

Addison yelled back from behind the bathroom door, "Aah!" before busting out with, "Nepo baby? No way! Let me see that!" She read the review out loud.

Masterful and exuberant, the newest nepo baby of the art world.

"Aaaah, the irony," she squealed before continuing.

Addison Irwin, niece of the late, great Gicky Irwin, brings her own kind of whimsy to clay. At first glance, the intense color and playful forms of Irwin's work will all but guarantee a smile, but there is more to them than meets the eye. A closer look reveals the complexity of the young Irwin's work and its astonishing detail in texture, pattern, and glaze.

"Oh my God, this is crazy!"

"No, it's not—you're amazing! I can't wait to see what you're going to make next!"

"Well, you're gonna have to wait a bit. Less than nine months, though."

Ben paused and contemplated her words for a moment, before his expression erupted in an incredulous smile.

"Wait, what? Are you . . ."

Addison pulled the telltale plastic pregnancy test wand from the pocket of her robe and showed him the plus sign. He took it and studied it.

"Are you sure?" he said, tears instantly running down his face.

She reached into the other pocket of her robe and pulled out two more positive tests.

"I'm sure!" she laughed before joining him in his tears.

Ben kneeled on the floor, placed his hands gently on Addison's belly, and planted a sweet kiss on the place where their baby grew.

"You can't believe it?" Addison laughed, quoting his usual reaction to extraordinary things.

"Actually, I can believe it," he uttered. "I believe it with all my heart."

Sally came charging between them, knocking them onto the couch and licking the remnants of happy tears from their faces.

"We're having a baby!" Ben told Sally, who took off in circles of zoomies around the apartment.

"She can't believe it," Addison said, laughing, ignoring the fact that it was Sally's usual reaction to a wet coat.

They watched the dizzying spectacle in silence, each thinking about where they were and where they were going. Ben took Addison's hand in his and brought her into his arms.

"Thank you for saving me."

"Thank you for saving me right back."

And the rain stopped.
      And the birds chirped.

And somewhere in the sky, there was most definitely a rainbow.

ACKNOWLEDGMENTS

To my wise and wonderful agent, Eve MacSweeney: may we be comrades in arms until we both pop our clogs! Thank you for it all!

Boundless gratitude to Amanda Bergeron and Sareer Khader, editors extraordinaire! You make it all look so easy, though I know it's not. Thank you for your thoughtful brilliance, direction, and steadfast belief in me.

To everyone else at Berkley: the dynamic duo of publicity, Danielle Keir and Tina Joell; my newest team member, Elisha Katz; and my ride-or-die, Jin Yu. To Claire Zion and Craig Burke, and all who have lent a hand or even just a finger—thank you for all of your effort and support.

Many thanks to the talented Vi-An Nguyen for the beautiful cover design and to Katharine Asher for the stunning illustration.

Thank you to my middle daughter, Melodie Rosen, my husband and best friend, Warren Rosen, and his best friend, Linda Coppola, for being such smart first readers. And to all of my cherished readers and cheerleaders—endless thanks for your endless support. Extra shout-out to the best cheerleaders of all— the bookstagrammers. You have no idea how encouraged I am by your enthusiasm and positivity. And to all of my author friends as well—thank you for making the solitary pursuit of writing a book somewhat sociable.

Finally, to my family and friends who still respond with accolades each time I declare, "I turned in my book today!" I know I say that many times during each run. You are the very best for pretending each time deserves a toast. I love you all.

Seven Summer Weekends

JANE L. ROSEN

READERS GUIDE

Behind the Book

My goal—after breaking your hearts a little with *On Fire Island*—was to present my readers with a full-on happy ending. And nothing says *happy ending* quite like a romantic comedy.

You may or may not know this about me, but before I was a novelist, I was a screenwriter—specifically a screenwriter of rom-coms. And while all of my novels are sprinkled with romantic tropes, including love triangles, long-lost loves, and fake relationships, romance is not their main theme. I wrote *Seven Summer Weekends* with the goal of writing a pure romantic comedy.

Like many young women, I grew up in front of a constant feed of funny fairy-tale-like films where the princess always landed the prince. I would watch and rewatch them so often that I could recite their scripts as easily as if I had written them myself. I knew every line of *Pretty Woman* and *Dirty Dancing* by heart and could match famous quotes to famous movies faster than a winning *Jeopardy!* contestant.

"Alex, what is, 'You had me at hello'?"

But even though I would never forget Julia Roberts in *Notting Hill* declaring that she was "just a girl, standing in front of a boy, asking him to love her," I did forget how much I enjoyed writing the complex but simple genre. Creating *Seven Summer Weekends* brought me right back to my first love, the romantic comedy. And while the rom-com formula appears to be simple, it is surprisingly hard to do right.

In the beginning, two people meet cute. They may be instantly attracted to each other, or instantly at odds—either way, the reader or viewer can practically see Cupid hovering overhead with his bow. Just when the fated couple connect on a deeper level, they stumble on a misunderstanding or an obstacle that temporarily divides them. All of the zany side characters give their advice and opinions, until finally, one lover races by car, foot, train, plane, or horseback to the other, declaring that they cannot go on without them. They kiss in the rain, or on a bridge, or in a crowded airport, or under a rainbow, and they go on to live happily ever after.

And just like that, the rom-com has done its job providing literary comfort food.

While these days you are far more likely to find the romance genre on the shelves of a bookstore than a Blockbuster (as if), there are many amorous titles to choose from. I hope curling up with *Seven Summer Weekends*, in your favorite big comfy chair, with a cup of hot tea and a scone, brought you much joy and comfort. Just as long as said chair was not perched in a corner—because, you know, *"Nobody puts Baby in a corner."*

Discussion Questions

1. Addison's entire life changed in an instant. Can you think of something that occurred in your life that changed its direction?
2. In this new world of increased remote work, Zoom debacles seem to be happening more often. Have you experienced or heard about any? Care to share?
3. A family falling-out is common. Can you cite an example in your own family? Did this story make you want to encourage reconciliation?
4. If you could start over and follow your "I want to be an astronaut" childhood dream, would you? What would it be?
5. Would you have stayed in or sold Aunt Gicky's house? Why?
6. There are two women in the book who have been cheated on by their spouses: Addison's grandmother and Kizzy. Who handled it better, and why?
7. How much do you think your relationship with your parents (or grandparents) comes into play when choosing a partner?

8. Would you have let Rome into your house, as Addison did, or would you have slammed the door in his face? Why?

9. Did you have any idea of the subject of Shep's painting before he unveiled it?

10. Which summer weekend guest do you think had the biggest impact on Addison?

Jane's Rom-Com Booklist

Romantic Comedy by Curtis Sittenfeld
Beach Read by Emily Henry
Nora Goes Off Script by Annabel Monaghan
Every Summer After by Carley Fortune
Crazy Rich Asians by Kevin Kwan
One Day in December by Josie Silver
How Stella Got Her Groove Back by Terry McMillan
Bridget Jones's Diary by Helen Fielding
Goodbye, Columbus by Philip Roth
Pride and Prejudice by Jane Austen
As You Like It by William Shakespeare
The Light We Lost by Jill Santopolo
The Summer of Songbirds by Kristy Woodson Harvey
Best Men by Sidney Karger

Jane L. Rosen is the author of five novels: *Nine Women, One Dress*; *Eliza Starts a Rumor*; *A Shoe Story*; *On Fire Island*; and *Seven Summer Weekends*. She lives in New York City and on Fire Island with her husband and, on occasion, her three grown daughters.

VISIT THE AUTHOR ONLINE

JaneLRosen.com

JaneLRosen

JaneLRosenAuthor

JaneLRosen1

Ready to find
your next great read?

Let us help.

Visit prh.com/nextread

Penguin
Random
House